Honor's Pledge

KRISTEN HEITZMANN

◆◆◆◆◆◆◆◆◆◆◆◆◆◆◆◆◆◆◆◆◆◆◆◆

Honor's Pledge

BETHANY HOUSE PUBLISHERS
MINNEAPOLIS, MINNESOTA 55438

Published by Bethany House Publishers
A Ministry of Bethany Fellowship, Inc.
11300 Hampshire Avenue South
Minneapolis, Minnesota 55438

Printed in the United States of America.

Library of Congress Cataloging-in-Publication Data

Heitzmann, Kristen.
    Honor's pledge / by Kristen Heitzmann.
        p. cm. — (Rocky Mountain legacy ; 1)
    ISBN 0-7642-2031-4 (pbk.)
        I. Title. II. Series: Heitzmann, Kristen. Rocky Mountain legacy ; 1.
PS3558.E468H66   1997
813'.54—dc21   97-33846
                                                                            CIP

To my parents,
Richard and Jane Francis,
who instilled a love for storytelling
and the handling of the pen.

KRISTEN HEITZMANN was raised on five acres of ponderosa pines at the base of the Rocky Mountains in Colorado, where she still lives with her husband and four children. A music minister and artist, Kristen delights in sharing the traditions of our heritage, both through one-on-one interaction and now through her first novel, *Honor's Pledge*.

One

Abigail Martin jumped at the gunshots, dropped the bolt of blue calico, and hurried to the window. She caught her breath as Blake McConnel, red-faced, shouted threats to Mr. Montgomery Farrel, who stood cool and unresponsive. The gun discharged again, this time not at the sky, but at the feet of the tall gentleman, spewing a cloud of dirt into his face as he leaped backward. Farrel's cool demeanor ignited into fury. Blake took aim again and hollered, "Draw yer weapon and settle it!"

From her vantage behind the small-paned window of the dry goods mercantile, Abbie watched both men: Blake in his worn pants and tousled hair; Farrel in tan breeches, knee-high boots, shirt sleeves, and vest. A pearl-handled Colt hung at Farrel's hip, but he didn't reach for it, nor unclip the leather strap that held it in place. Thankfully he possessed greater self-control than Blake.

With her heart pounding, Abbie rushed for the door but was blocked by the corpulent Bailey sisters pressing their faces to the glass, oozing excitement.

"Will you look at that? It's the McConnel boy steaming like a kettle." Eleanor Bailey wiped the shine from her cheek and forehead with a limp white handkerchief.

Ruth giggled. "Maybe he'll injure Mr. Farrel so's he'll need doctoring."

"I'm afraid that job'll go to the doc, sister. Now that we have one."

Abbie's chest tightened as Blake raised his arm again and pulled the trigger, but the gun didn't fire, and she released her trapped breath. Blake hammered the gun with his hand, then threw it in the dirt and charged Montgomery Farrel, who stood poised to receive the onslaught.

Farrel had the benefit of a longer reach and more years, but Blake was huskier and out of his head with anger. Pressing herself between the two soft bodies, Abbie gained the door and pushed through. The townsmen hollered the fighters on with carnival shouts, but at Blake's next thrust, he was grabbed from behind by Deputy Clem Davis. He contained Blake's fury with arms as thick and powerful as a grizzly's.

Montgomery Farrel bent to pick up his hat from the dusty street. His dark hair no longer waved smoothly but bent into unruly curls down the back of his neck. He slapped the dust from his hat and followed the deputy into the jail, the lines of his face as hard as the rocky bluff for which the town was named.

"Five dollars gold says Marshal Haggerty'll dismiss it," Jonas Roberts hollered.

"Five says he don't," contended old Jake. "Now that the new deputy's got his hands on the young'un, he'll keep 'im awhile."

"All depends if Farrel's a mind to press a charge."

Jonas Roberts shoved back his hat and swiped his forehead with his shirt sleeve. "Anyone else an' they'd have let 'em fight it out. Guess we can't have no one lettin' loose on Montgomery Farrel, now, can we?"

Abbie bit her lip in frustration. *What on earth had Blake been thinking?*

"It's a shame Deputy Davis spoiled the fun." At her glare, Mag French tipped his hat to her with a yellow-toothed grin, then spat.

Abbie turned away. She wished she could throttle Blake herself, then wished he hadn't been hauled into the jail. All this for a few flattering words! True, Mr. Farrel's compliments had slid from his tongue as gold dust from a sluice box, but it was no more than any of the young men in town might have said, given the opportunity. And he had lingered as he bowed over her hand, held on perhaps longer than necessary. Blake had glowered like a ranch dog on a coon.

Even then, things might have been all right if Mr. Farrel hadn't remarked how very much he had enjoyed his visit the previous evening without mentioning at all that it was her father's company he'd shared . . . mainly. Blake had gone off like a cannon, but Abbie had figured that was the worst of it. When he had stormed away, she thought he'd lick his wounds and be done.

She watched the jail door for Blake to emerge, hangdogged but free. He was temperamental, but . . . gunplay! At least the fool boy was alive. Montgomery Farrel had never even drawn the gun that hung at his hip, though a man rarely invested in that fancy kind of hardware unless he could handle it. She shuddered to think if he had.

As the door opened, she clasped her hands together at her chest, but Mr. Farrel came out alone and prepared to mount. Her heart sank. He must have pressed charges after all.

Catching up her skirts, Abbie flew to his side. "Mr. Farrel."

He turned to her and tipped his hat with the slight bow that betrayed his southern breeding. It lost none of its elegance, even though his face was smudged, one sleeve askew, and dust up to his knees. "Miss Martin."

For a moment she faltered. "Blake's in jail?" That much was obvious. He opened his mouth to reply, but she rushed on. "Surely you know he intended you no real harm."

"I'm afraid I know no such thing." He spoke softly in the manner of the South, but his voice was deadly serious. "Had he not possessed an inferior weapon, I might have been forced to kill him. I don't consider gunplay a game."

Drawing herself up, Abbie tightened her mouth into a determined line. "He's just a boy, and I'm certain it won't happen again. If you would just drop the charges against him . . ."

Montgomery Farrel hooked his thumbs into his belt. "And what would lead me to think that it won't? That rascal has a hornet in his hide."

"It's all a misunderstanding. I'm awfully sorry for the trouble. I truly don't know what gave him the notion to behave in such a manner. . . ."

"Don't you?" The ghost of a smile played on his mouth.

She flushed. "Well . . . I . . . if I told him that my feelings are not what he . . . thinks they are . . ."

Montgomery Farrel ran a hand over the sleek sorrel neck of the stallion, loosening the reins from the hitch. "You believe his jealousy can be cured by a dose of truth?" Mr. Farrel smoothed back his hair and replaced his hat under the afternoon sun. His tone was cool but no longer angry.

"I'll speak to him. I'll speak to him right now." She flashed a smile and spun for the jail, her skirts swirling against her legs. Inside, she walked directly to the desk.

"Afternoon, Miss Martin," Marshal Haggerty said. Behind him, Deputy Davis removed his hat with a bearish grin. He dwarfed the marshal, and the tight space smelled of him, like an animal's den.

"Good afternoon. I've come to see Blake."

Marshal Haggerty motioned her by, and she moved to the single stone cell of the Rocky Bluffs jail. Blake sat on the thin cot, head hanging and hands limp on his thighs. He was too old to whip but looked like he deserved it anyway.

His head came up. "Abbie! What are you—"

"I need to talk to you, Blake."

He jumped up and encircled the bars with his hands. "This ain't a place for you."

"It's hardly a place for you, either. What have you gone and done?"

"I won't stand for that Montgomery Farrel comin' in here like he owns the whole darn town, makin' eyes at you with all that fancy talk. I warned him off, but he don't listen."

Exasperation choked her, and Abbie stamped her foot. "This is plain foolishness, and you've no right to be causing him trouble."

Blake's face fell. "You're not taken with him?"

"No, I'm not. But I'm not taken with you, either." She paused, softening. "Oh, Blake, I have great affection for you, but I haven't a notion what made you carry on so. You've been itching over Mr. Farrel since he came. Promise it'll stop now."

"Well, it won't exactly do me no good if you don't care for me anyway. Not that it much matters now."

"I believe Mr. Farrel will drop the charges."

"What charges?"

"What charges! Maybe attempted murder, and I'll wager he knows the law."

Blake cocked his head, shaking the hair from his eyes. "Are you bein' straight with me, or are you tellin' me all this to try to save my neck?"

"I've been completely honest with you."

He sagged. "I was afraid of that."

"Give me your word you'll not bother him again."

"You have it," he muttered.

"Say it, Blake, on your honor."

"I won't mess with Farrel no more . . . on my honor." He grinned, and Abbie squeezed the knuckles that protruded from the cell, relief washing over her.

"You'll find someone else to guard as ardently."

He slowly nodded. "Maybe I will. But it won't be the same."

He slumped down on the hard bunk against the wall.

That settled, Abbie rushed back out and searched for Montgomery Farrel. The narrow street cleaved the twin rows of single and two-story board buildings with false fronts feigning greater stature. Her eyes swept to McConnel's livery, where the smoke and noise of hot metal on an anvil rang into the air.

Only God had kept Wes McConnel from hearing the ruckus and thrashing Blake in the street himself. If Pa had been at work at the newspaper across the way, he might have done the same. She scanned the hardware store, sporting the name of the new owner on the sign: Peterson Hardware. Across the street she searched the General Mercantile and Dry Goods, then the grocer's, where the Bailey sisters were haggling over something.

The walkway by Mrs. Munson's clothier, the post office, and on down to Pa's news office was empty. Turning her head, Abbie gazed the other direction—town hall, lumberyard, bank, school, and the church, still closed up after the untimely loss of Reverend Peale. There were several horses tethered at the hitching posts, mostly before the saloon-hotel, where the men were no doubt drinking off their excitement in the afternoon heat. Mr. Farrel's unmistakable horse was nowhere to be found. With annoyance she realized he had gone, and with him her hopes of Blake's immediate release.

Two

Abbie raised her chin, climbed into her buggy, and started for the Farrel ranch. It was northeast of town, a good step farther than her own family's homestead, and over the prairie with hardly a shrub to shade her way. When the house came into sight, it was like an oasis in a grass desert. She pulled the horse to a stop beneath an arching cottonwood.

The house before her was impressive with a distinctive southern flair. She had not seen it up close before, though the town had buzzed over it for months. Montgomery Farrel had chosen the sight well, availing the shade of the trees already established by the creek that ran behind. Centered on the pink stone face of the lower story was a sweeping portico with white pillars and wide stone steps flanked by matching large-paned windows, and on the west side rose the narrow, arched windows of a room her eyes could only imagine.

Abbie raised her gaze to the white-painted second story, with its curved tower room at one end and five black-shuttered windows. So much glass dazzled her. Even the eaves and arches of the attic had small rounded panes. She was impressed in spite of herself. The house was generally considered extravagant, showy, and improvident, and every mother in town hoped her daughter would live there as the wife of the handsome, cultured Montgomery Farrel. Abbie's chin jutted. She had no such aspirations.

She mounted the stairs and applied the large brass knocker to the door. It resounded hollowly, and Abbie stepped back when it opened almost immediately. She stared into the grizzled black face of a man in a white coat and gray trousers.

"Yes, miss?"

She straightened. "I wish to see Mr. Farrel . . . please."

He stepped back for her to enter, closing the door silently behind. The entry was like a cathedral, all arches and carved wood. She followed him into a parlor that would have held the entire living space of her family's farmhouse.

"Who may I say's callin'?"

"Abbie . . . Miss Abigail Martin."

He actually bowed and backed out. Abbie eyed the low lacquered walnut table and a matching secretary with a marquetry of vines and leaves. She ran her hand over the settee, plush and velvety soft, tucked with buttons and edged with sloping wood, carved into an elegant floral fan at the center. She stroked the fabric again for the pure pleasure of its softness.

Across from the velvet-draped windows, the stone fireplace was crowned by a mantel that held a marble clock and two silver candelabras as well as a daguerreotype of a man in a gray Confederate uniform and a small portrait of a stunning woman in a lace-edged gown.

Abbie drew up close, studying the arching brows and delicate curve of the woman's mouth. In spite of her stiff pose, there was a sweetness in her smile, and she looked very young. Abbie jumped when Montgomery Farrel spoke behind her.

"My father and mother."

Abbie saw the likeness. "Your mother is beautiful."

"Yes, she was." His voice softened. "She died when I was seven."

"I'm very sorry." She turned to face him.

He bowed his head. "This is indeed an honor, Miss Martin." He was cleaned and groomed, as though the afternoon's altercation had never happened. She was certain he would never mention it again if she did not. But then, Blake was sitting in the jail. . . .

Abbie squared her shoulders. "I had expected—hoped—to be able to continue our conversation in town, but you'd already left when I finished at the jail."

The corners of Montgomery's mouth flickered. "I see. I'm sorry to have inconvenienced you. I didn't realize you had more you wished to say on the matter."

Abbie's temper flashed. "You might have considered that I would give you Blake's answer."

"Again I apologize. I failed to understand the immediacy of your concern." He motioned her to the settee. "I presume you told him the nature of your feelings?"

Abbie flushed. Why had Blake taken it into his head to embarrass her so? "Yes. And he's agreed not to bother you in any way. He gave his word and very much regrets his actions."

Mr. Farrel's smile broadened. "He said so?"

Abbie stammered for a reply, realizing he'd seen through her embellishment. They were interrupted by a woman carrying a tray with a pitcher of tea. The scent of the fresh mint leaves filled the room.

"Refreshment, Mastuh Monte." Her skin was like oiled mahogany, her hands large and thick.

"Thank you, Pearl. Set it there on the table."

She obliged and left the room.

"Are they your slaves?" Abbie bit her lip as Mr. Farrel frowned.

"Slavery was abolished with the war, Miss Martin. Although I don't expect you know much about it, do you?" He poured and handed her a glass.

Abbie wrapped her fingers around its chill. "I know what

I've read and what Pa has told me. It's all rather complicated."

"As is all war."

"Pa was sympathetic to both sides but believed we ought to remain a single nation, not divided into warring states."

Montgomery turned to the picture of his father on the mantel, his back straight and firm in his tailored coat. "I think my father believed that as well. But he fought for the Confederacy."

"Why?"

"Because honor demanded it. He knew we couldn't win. Unlike some, he saw that our resources would fall far short if the war prolonged, but our sovereignty and honor were being wrenched from us. For that, he fought."

He faced her, and Abbie saw a fire behind his words. Not only did he believe in what he was saying, he embraced it deep inside. His voice was low, but there was no masking the intensity.

"That is the honor I understand. The ability to do what one must, even when it is against one's heart." He softened. "Do you believe that's the honor with which your friend holds his word?"

At last she had a chance. "Yes, I do. Blake's impetuous, but he's honest through and through." And that was true. Blake would keep his word if it killed him.

Montgomery Farrel stood and leaned against the mantel, sipping his tea. "Where I come from, dueling, though not unheard of, is illegal. On occasion it may be handled privately by arrangement, but one does not accost another on a public street like two mongrels after the same scrap. Here, 'calling someone out' seems an acceptable means of settling quarrels."

Abbie sighed. "It's not so much acceptable as unstoppable. There are few enough who try to block a bullet aimed at another." Abbie could see that the afternoon's event had disturbed him more than she thought. Blake had insulted Montgomery Farrel's honor and made a spectacle of them both. "But truly Blake would never have shot you. And he won't repeat it."

"I'll accept your word for that."

"Then you'll drop the charges?" Abbie breathed hopefully.

His smile was warm and gracious. "I'll drop the charges."

"Oh, thank you!" She clasped her hands together at her chest.

Montgomery Farrel bowed again. "Would you do me the honor of remaining for supper?"

She was caught off guard. "Here?"

"Unless you have a preference."

Abbie glanced about her, absorbing the grandeur. *Clara will be green.* "All right. But I'll have to let Mama know not to expect me."

"I'll send the message to your mother."

"And to town for the marshal?"

He smiled crookedly. "And for the marshal." As he spoke he strode to the secretary, took out two sheets of thin vellum paper, and laid one out for Abbie with a pen and inkwell. She quickly sat and wrote the note explaining her whereabouts to her parents, then blotted and handed it to him. He folded it along with his own and called for James.

After dispensing instructions, he turned back to Abbie. "It's rather close in here. Would you care to walk outside until supper?"

"That's because of the heavy draperies. If you took the velvet off, left the lace, and opened the windows on either side, you'd get a cross breeze and cool it off nicely."

He raised an eyebrow and she added, "But yes, I'd like to walk."

"Well, then . . ." He motioned her toward the door. At the

foot of the stairs, Abbie gathered her skirts in a futile but required attempt to keep them from the dust. Montgomery Farrel clasped his hands behind his back and strolled beside her.

They walked in the shade of the cottonwoods, then turned onto a path that skirted the hill. Long shadows lined the pale, grassy fields. Abbie turned her face to the breeze, letting it scatter the damp tendrils clinging to her forehead. She glanced sideways at Mr. Farrel. The handsome, angular cut of his features, the dark brows and deep brown eyes, the firm, wide mouth all came together in a dashing blend that he muted with his nonchalance.

He didn't flaunt himself, and Abbie quickened to the thought that he had no need to. He was tall—taller than her father, who stood five eleven—and lean, but he moved with an elegance of motion that was as foreign as his slow, lilting speech, and she unconsciously matched her gait to it. Montgomery turned and she dropped her gaze. A sweat bee buzzed her head, then swung in dizzying loops up into the blue expanse.

As they dipped into a small valley, they came again under the shade of a line of cottonwoods and chokecherries spreading their dense branches over a clear stony stream. Hare bells and Queen Anne's lace flowered beneath. She couldn't help but exclaim, "How lovely!"

Montgomery Farrel smiled. "I'm glad you like it. This is my favorite spot on the ranch." He swept his arm forward. "To your right, bald Pikes Peak, and away east, the prairie. But within this little circle nothing seems as stretched and open."

Abbie followed his extended arm as he pointed, then turned back to him. "You're not used to the space yet. It'll grow on you. This place is solid as the rock beneath us. Beautiful, yes. Wild perhaps, but not as a jungle teeming with danger or an Arabian desert hiding its treasures beneath hot, blowing sands. Here you can grab hold of the land and feel its strength." She lifted a chunk of granite, pink and gray with sparkles of quartz and feldspar. "I think God started here and just spread out the rest of the world with what was left."

He was watching her curiously. "Is that spoken from experience, Miss Martin?"

Abbie smiled. "Limited, I guess."

He opened his mouth to respond, but the clanging of a bell broke the evening still. He raised an eyebrow conspiratorially. "That's the signal for supper, and if we value our necks we'll not delay."

As they started back, Abbie asked, "Mr. Farrel . . ."

"Please call me Monte."

"Monte . . ." She tested the name. Yes, it suited him. Outside with the breeze in his hair, it suited him well. "If your pa fought in the war, how is it that you didn't suffer the hardship that's upon the South?" She thought she must have offended him when he didn't answer. His gaze went far out before them.

"Long before the war, my father believed the future of the nation lay out west and filed this land on speculation as well as other pieces farther north. When the war ended, our southern holdings were decimated like everyone else's, but our western investments survived."

"How could he homestead the land without living on it?"

"He outfitted partners to homestead it the three years, and when they had full title, he purchased the plots from each outright. This particular ranch was the best of his stakes with free access to water and virtual control of the water source for miles on the open range. That far extends the original survey."

"Your pa was a man of foresight. Why didn't he come out here with you?" For a terrible moment she thought he might have been killed in the war when she saw Monte stiffen.

"He loved his home. So fiercely did he love South Carolina that he faced unspeakable horrors in her name. And when he returned from the war after being captured and imprisoned by the Yankees, he came back to a land he didn't know. There was no way for him to maintain his plantation without workers, his health was broken, and life as he knew it was changed. Yet he would not desert it."

Abbie tried to imagine how difficult it must have been. "Could he not have sold his holdings out here and rebuilt?"

"He could have, but he wanted this for me. When he died, his last wish was for me to make my life here instead of drudging through what was left of the 'glorious South.'"

"So your pa's gone, too?" Abbie stopped. "Have you no one else?"

"My sister, Frances, lives with her husband in Charleston."

Clasping her hands, Abbie drew in her breath. "I think it was very brave of you to come here alone and start a new life."

Monte smiled. "How old are you, Miss Martin?"

"If I must call you Monte, you may call me Abbie. I'm seventeen. Why?"

"I suspected as much."

"You're not so very much older?"

"Not so very much. But six years can be a great deal, and at times you seem substantially younger."

He was obviously amused, though she failed to see the joke. When he motioned, she preceded him up the stairs.

"Would you care to freshen up before we eat?"

"Yes, thank you."

Pearl showed her to a bedroom where a pitcher and bowl were prepared for her use. The cool water felt good on her skin as she wiped her hot face and neck. She unbuttoned her bodice front and swabbed the cloth down to the edge of her camisole, where it protruded softly before shrinking over narrow ribs.

Her hair was wild, so she picked up the brush from the washstand and ran it through the stubborn tangles, then tucked in the combs and tossed the spiraling curls out behind her shoulders. She reattached her bodice and went downstairs.

Monte ushered her into a real dining room as fine as the hotel, seated her at one end of the long cherrywood table, and took his place at the other. Pearl and James brought dish after dish to the table. Monte must have seen her surprise. "Pearl rarely has the opportunity to cook for company. She makes the most of each occasion." He muted his smile.

Pearl huffed. "I cooks what I wants."

"And in abundance."

"As any gen'leman would appreciate."

She bustled to the kitchen, but Abbie caught her look of satisfaction at having the last word. James offered each dish and served out the portions. Abbie felt four years old with all the attention.

Monte skewered a slice of chicken soaked in wine and cream and had it nearly between his teeth when Abbie said, "Hadn't we better offer a blessing?"

His mouth clamped shut with only a touch of sauce, which was quickly licked away. "I'm afraid living alone here has made me careless in more ways than one. Thank you for the reminder. Have you a special prayer that you prefer?"

"Oh no. Father Dominic at the mission says that it's always best to speak whatever thanks is on your heart."

Monte nodded and bowed his head. "Heavenly Father, I thank you for this food given from your bounty, and for my lovely guest with whom I share it, and for the hands of your servants who prepared it . . . in such abundance." He raised a single eyebrow at Pearl, who puffed out her cheeks and refused to acknowledge him. "Amen."

"Amen," Abbie answered. "Father Dominic teaches the small children the prayers to recite, but he says that when you know the Lord, you should speak to Him personally, with reverence, of course. But, after all, it makes sense. I mean, it's very nice to hear poetry and such recited, but it would be very trying to have someone speak to you that way all the time, don't you think? I mean it's—" She paused suddenly. "Don't you think it's rather difficult to converse all the way across the room like this?" She leaned to the side and gazed at him around the vase of larkspur and daisies.

Monte motioned to James, who immediately came to his side. "Move Miss Martin's place down here, please, James."

"Yessuh." He moved swiftly, carrying her plate and glass, down to the seat beside the head of the table where Monte sat. Abbie reached for her silverware and napkin, but Monte's eyes halted her, and James moved these also. Monte stood and seated her once again.

"I suppose this must be contrary to southern etiquette, but I've never had the misfortune of attending finishing school, so I'm afraid I say what I think and do what seems right."

Monte's mouth twitched. "Two admirable qualities that southern women disdain."

She savored the pork in raisin sauce and roasted potatoes, then dabbed her mouth. "It's strange to think that two areas in the same country would be so very different. I wonder what I would be like had I been raised in the South."

"Southern society would never be the same, I believe." Monte chuckled. "And I shudder to think what my competition would be."

"Why?"

"If there's one thing irresistible to a southern gentleman,

it's a belle who doesn't fit the mold." He skewered a buttered carrot. "Not that he would marry her, of course. He must be conscious of the future generations and choose a lady of impeccable character and lineage who will bear and raise his children according to the tradition and heritage of past generations." He bit the carrot, chewed, and swallowed. "It doesn't necessarily make for happiness, though, and the poor fool spends his life pining for the belle who might have brought him out of all that. It's much freer here."

"That's terrible!"

He startled. "What?"

"That a man would marry for those reasons and then continue longing for someone else."

"Ah, but we're a strange breed. And I suppose it's no worse than the customs of the West such as your bargain brides—women purchased by men they've never met. At least there's a noble cause behind it."

"A noble cause?" Abbie felt her ire rise.

"Preservation."

"Of what?"

"Of what matters."

Abbie laid down her fork. "Did your parents not love each other?"

He wiped the white cloth napkin over his mouth. "I can hardly say from experience, being so young when my mother died. But my father always spoke of her with tenderness and never chose to remarry. I would imagine he loved her very much."

"Then what you said is not always the way."

Monte laughed. "I didn't intend to distress you. Of course people marry for love, or at least affection. But sometimes there are strictures that make doing things you desire impossible."

"And you feel that if I were landed in southern society, I may be quite attractive but certainly not marriageable."

Monte sobered. "I see that my words have been careless. For that, I apologize. I never meant any such thing." He paused. "Although I must admit it's rather a different world, very closed and self-protecting. What's left of it, anyway." He sighed. "I suppose it will soon be like any other place, and none of the things we all thought inviolable will matter anymore."

"That's terribly sad. Has it changed so much since the war?"

"What was once idyllic and gracious is now tired and grasping, the unscrupulous trying to get their hands on whatever they can from the owners no longer able to sustain their family estates."

He gazed across the room. "I was fourteen when my father went to fight. I would have gone, too—I was desperate to go—but he'd have none of it. He insisted I stay and care for my sister, Frances. Aunt Bess and cousin Darcy came to stay with us, and at different times, I had households of women in my care. Father knew what he was about.

"It was not on the battlefront alone that the war was waged. I had my hands full hiding livestock and goods so that we and our neighbors didn't starve. Many a night I trenched the ground behind the houses so that silver and jewelry and heirlooms could be hidden away. Many times I rushed on horseback from plantation to plantation warning that the soldiers were coming.

"There were even times I hid the sisters and daughters of Confederate soldiers in holes in the swamp because if they were seen, the alternative was worse. Everywhere the soldiers came they brought ruin. If they couldn't beat us on the battlefield, for sure they would beat us at home, destroy our property, defile our women, starve, burn, pillage.

"I think it would have been easier to face the bayonets of the Yankee front line than watch my father's property ravaged and looted by marauding Union soldiers wantonly destroying what generations of Farrels had built."

Abbie tried to imagine strangers attacking her home and being helpless to protest. "How did you stand it?"

"What choice did I have? I was charged to protect those in my care. It was a sore trial for a young, able-bodied man to remain home, and there was more than one time I nearly slipped away in the night to find a company and join up. My spirit cried out to fight."

"What kept you?"

"Frances, mainly. She was . . . It was very hard for her. I recall one raid of the soldiers, very early on. She must have been eleven or twelve . . . twelve, I guess. She had a collection of glass horses, very dear to her."

He shook his head. "For sheer cruelty, a soldier smashed them. Not all at once, with an accidental blow, but one by one as we watched through the crack, holed up in the false back of the wardrobe. I think he knew we were there. My rumored presence made our home a favorite target for marauders, a game to tempt the coward southern boy to fight. He did it to bait me, and I had never before exercised such extremity of self-control." His eyes burned. "But I had Frances in my arms."

He sat silent a long moment. His temple pulsed. "For days she didn't speak. She gathered the pieces, sorted them out which piece to which horse, and fit them together, though there was no bond to hold them. It was a terrible sight. Had the soldier returned, I would have committed murder, no matter the consequence."

Abbie felt his raw pain.

"For what?" He shrugged. "If you think for one moment this war was fought over slavery alone, think again."

"Was your pa a slave owner?"

"He was born to it, and the economy required it. But our people were well cared for. Almost family. My father saw to

27

their needs as he did to his own children." He rested his fore-arms against the table edge. "On the day of the president's Emancipation Proclamation, he wrote to tell our people they were free, though many of our neighbors kept it hushed. Even so, not a half of them left us until his death, and James and Pearl chose to come out here with me. They are, however, compensated."

Abbie cringed. "I'm sorry. My remark was thoughtless. But Pearl did call you Master Monte."

"A title of habit and inflection." Monte motioned, and James served the coffee. "You've lived here long?"

"Since I was eight. Well, not actually here in Rocky Bluffs. Pa came out with Wes McConnel to prospect in Auraria, where building lots were free for the taking. Mama wasn't crazy about living in a mining camp, and Pa wasn't a miner, but I loved it.

"Sadie, she's my sister four years older, she cried and cried. I prayed every day that Pa wouldn't give up and take us back. My memories of Kansas City were the smell of slaughter-houses and too many people. He stuck it out until the twin camps merged into Denver City and grew fast enough to get a newspaper. Pa saw his chance. He signed on with the paper."

"Ah." Monte nodded.

"After two years Pa was feeling crowded. He filed for a homestead near the new town of Rocky Bluffs—more trading post than town—but he saw promise. He bought a press of his own and we moved. I was ten, though it seems I've been here forever."

Monte's smile was indulgent, and she felt suddenly provincial and backward. "But I've read about so many places. My grandfather works in book publishing, and he sends us books about everywhere. Ever since I was small I've imagined seeing Europe and Africa and China. Blake and I . . ." She stopped.

"Go on . . . Blake and you." His tone was smooth, but his eyes were again amused.

Well, she'd started it, so she might as well finish. "Blake's family has been our nearest neighbor from the start, and he and I, both being the youngest, spent much of our time together. I made up games, and we playacted. Of course, he expected me to play the helpless lady trapped in the jungle, and he the hero who came to my rescue." She laughed.

"Perhaps he didn't know it was playacting, and that's why he took it upon himself to rescue you from my attention."

Abbie dropped her eyes. "I suppose that's possible. I wish I'd known he felt that way."

Monte leaned back in his chair and studied her with a crooked smile. "How is it that you didn't?"

"I've always considered him one of the family. He's two months younger, and it was nice to think of him as a little brother. It gave me great license to bully him into giving me my way."

"I don't imagine it took much bullying."

"Maybe not lately, but at first it certainly did."

Monte laughed. "I don't think I'd like to try to withstand your bullying, myself."

"Well, lucky for you I've outgrown it."

"Now that you're all of seventeen."

Abbie's chin came up. "Actually I'm nearly eighteen." She dabbed her mouth with the napkin and pushed her plate away. It was instantly removed by James, whose presence Abbie had forgotten, and she blushed at having spoken so freely in front of a total stranger. Mama was right. She did need to learn to hold her tongue and be appropriate.

But after all, what was appropriate in this house? Monte didn't converse with the servants, except when something was required, and they didn't participate until called upon. Yet they shared a fondness, she could tell, and Pearl had positively glowed when he teased. It was confusing, and she wished she had not said some of the things she had, even to Monte. He seemed to draw her out and let down her guard—not that she had much of a guard, as Mama would point out. "It's getting late. I should go now."

Monte rose and pulled out her chair. "I'll get your carriage." He paused. "What amuses you?"

"The way you say carriage. It sounds like something for royalty to lark about in." Abbie could have bitten her tongue. Who was she to speak so to him?

He replied slowly, softly. "Perhaps I consider you royalty."

Her chest quickened suddenly at the look in his eyes. Then he turned, and she followed him to the door and out into the night. The sky was sugared with stars, and the air smelled sweet. Monte hitched her mare to the buggy and saddled his own horse.

"You needn't ride along. I know my way well enough."

"Although it stretches propriety to be out with you after dark, I intend to drive you back. This is wild country."

"It's really not necessary."

He tied his horse behind the buggy, placed his hands around her waist, and lifted her onto the seat. Sitting beside him in the dark, Abbie fell silent, the night noises creating a sleepy symphony of cricket song and wind in the grass. After the satisfying supper, the rocking of the buggy and the regular *thunk, thunk* of the horses' hooves lulled her. She fought the drowsiness spreading like a warm quilt, covering her senses. "It must be later than I thought," she murmured.

"We did rather linger over supper. I can't remember enjoying a conversation so much. Perhaps it was the table arrangement. I'll be sure to have it set that way the next time you come."

His words caused that unfamiliar jumping inside, and Abbie thought of Blake's remark. Perhaps she was not taken with Montgomery Farrel, but it was not out of the realm of possibility. His stiff shirt brushed against her cheek as her head drooped against his shoulder, and she pulled back.

"Rest if you like." He was perfectly at ease, and she wondered if others had slept on his shoulder.

The thought brought her up straight, and she pulled the shawl close. Even the midsummer nights were chilly. She curled her back into the corner of the seat but still felt him close. Her concern for Blake and the events of the afternoon faded into the darkness.

Three

Abbie threw the cloth into the dishwater when she saw Blake saunter into the yard. "Oh, Blake, you're free!" She ran through the open door to meet him. "You gave me a terrible fright!"

"Came straight over soon as they let me out."

"Didn't Marshal Haggerty get Mr. Farrel's message?"

"He said I may as well spend the night fer good measure." Blake jammed his hands into his pockets. "Come and walk with me."

"I have to finish the dishes."

"I'll wipe." He followed her in and picked up the cloth to dry as she plunged her arms back into the sudsy water, then dunked the dishes in the hot rinse tub. Blake made a cursory swipe and set them on the board.

"I hate to think of you spending the night in that cell on that terrible little bed. I hope it's taught you a thing or two." She handed over the heavy iron skillet.

He grunted. "Wasn't so bad."

Of course he'd say that. He was always in one scrape or another and never admitted the hardship. She doubted very much that any number of nights in the jail would change him, but he'd given his word, and that he'd keep. Abbie wiped her hands on her apron and pulled it off. "There now. We can run off for a bit anyway. Mama's gone to town, so she won't need me yet."

They headed down the path from the house toward the shelter of the craggy vale. The day was dry but hadn't yet worked up the heat of the one previous. No cloud marred the china blue sky. Suddenly, Blake grabbed her hand and took off at a run, rushing down the slope between the mounds of scrub oaks toward the rocky creek at the base. Abbie collided with his chest as he stopped short. Laughing, he did not release her but looked down and grinned. "Tell me the truth, Abbie. Are you my girl or ain't you?"

"Blake McConnel, unhand me immediately!"

"Not till I get my answer."

Abbie made a face. "I told you yesterday."

"But you didn't mean that, did you?"

"I wouldn't have said it if I didn't."

"Yes, you would. I know you would've helped me out any way you could."

Abbie softened. "Well, I guess so, but I really did tell you the truth."

"Are you so sure of that?" He tightened his arms and pressed his mouth to hers.

"Blake!" Abbie wrestled free and shoved at his chest.

He stumbled back, laughing. "Ah, Abbie. Didn't you like it a little bit?"

"I certainly did not. You might be able to get away with kissing Caroline Glazer, but not me."

"I was seven years old when I kissed Caroline Glazer!"

"Well, your manners haven't improved in ten years!"

His face sobered. "Abbie, I love you. I've loved you as long as I can remember."

"Blake, you can't mean that. You're like my brother!"

"Well, I ain't your brother. And soon, I'll be able to file for my own place and make a home for us. If you don't run off and marry someone else, that is."

Abbie tossed her head. "And who would I marry?" She pushed him aside. "Let's not talk about it. I'm going to wade." She sat and removed her high-topped shoes. Blake grinned. Sitting down beside her, he pulled off his own boots and stockings and rolled the legs of his pants. Abbie tucked up her skirts so that her legs were bare to just over her calf. "Don't you tell Mama, now," she ordered, seeing his eyes trail from knee to ankle.

"Aw no." He grabbed her hand and steadied her against the rush of the icy flow. The first minutes hurt as the water tugged at her ankles. She stretched to a flat rock farther out, avoiding its sharp edge and the myriad other stones. Blake leaped over behind her. "Numb yet?"

"Getting there." She lifted her reddened foot, then plunged it back in. A blue dragonfly rode the air on opalescent wings. She reached up to it, slipped, and Blake caught her.

"There, you see how much you need me?"

"Your strong arm is appreciated, but that doesn't mean anything." She watched a leaf spiral in an eddy, then shoot past. The hem of her skirt slipped down and dragged along her calves. She tugged it up again. "I should get back now. Mama and I are replacing the ticking today. She won't want to be held up."

Blake helped her back to the bank, and they held their bare feet up to dry in the sun and breeze. Abbie stretched her toes.

"You sure have purty feet."

She pulled them down immediately and rubbed them with the edge of her skirt, then tugged on her shoes and headed up the slope. Blake scrambled up and followed.

"I reckon I'd better get to the shop myself. Sure hate bein' sweat to death on a day like this, though."

"Your pa just wants you to learn smithing, Blake. You don't have to do it forever."

"That's right. First chance I get I'll be on to better things."

Abbie smiled. "You might find any work just as onerous." She let the word slide glibly from her lips to taunt him.

"Just as what?"

"Never mind."

When they reached the house, he tugged her arm. "You think on what I said, Abbie. It may seem too soon to you now, but I don't want no one gettin' a jump on me."

"And you think of what I said, Blake, and look elsewhere. If you're hankering for a wife, try Clara Simms. She's been gone on you for a year now."

He grinned. "You can't get rid of me that easy. I know you'll come around."

"Think what you like." Abbie turned up her nose.

Blake laughed. "One of these days you'll beg me to kiss you."

"Oh, go away!" she huffed. "You're simply impossible anymore!"

"You think on it," he called over his shoulder.

Abbie flounced into the house. Really, it was intolerable for him to have gone crazy all of a sudden. She had half a mind to ignore him altogether.

Mama was inside, and Abbie unpacked the bolts of ticking and heavy thread and spread them on the floor between them. She almost blurted that Blake was out of jail, but she was still praying Mama hadn't heard he was ever in.

"Was that Blake?"

"Yes. He's off to the smithy." She caught her wet hem under her ankles as she settled to the floor. "Mama? How'd you know you loved Pa?"

Mama took a good long look and removed the needle from between her lips. Then as she applied it to the material, she said, "Well, you remember that your pa worked at the newspaper in Kansas City."

Abbie nodded. She knew this part of the story.

"We'd just come to town and my pa planned to open a general mercantile, so he stopped at the newspaper to learn what was available for sale. He thought he'd get a more honest rundown there than the land office."

"And Pa saw you . . ."

"Do you want to tell the story or shall I?" Mama raised her brows. "Really, Abbie, you must curb your enthusiasm. Never interrupt, and never, never let on that you know something already."

"I'm sorry."

"Yes, Joshua saw me in the wagon and plumb forgot how to speak. My pa couldn't get a word out of him and thought him simpleminded."

Abbie laughed, imagining Pa without something to say. "I wish I could have seen his face!"

"Well, I had no idea he'd noticed me. But he told your grandpa that if he returned the following day, he'd have a list of properties. And he did indeed have a list that he had compiled the night before, naming only the opportunities close to the newspaper. My pa chose one and set up shop, and one day, as I was working the counter, your pa came in, introduced himself, and asked me to marry him."

"Oh, Mama, you must have been swept off your feet."

"I was appalled," she said flatly, not lifting her eyes from her work. "I'd never met this man who brazenly offered himself, and I told him I was sure I'd do no such thing."

"How did he change your mind?"

"He kept at me day after day, claiming he'd never realize his dream if I wouldn't go west with him. He said he'd be forced to keep working for his father, who was not an easy man, unless I consented. He brought me flowers and candies and tokens of his affection and refused to be daunted by my continued refusal, until one day I heard myself agree."

"Had you fallen in love with him?"

"It seemed more that I'd freed myself of a nagging gnat." She laughed, dropping her hands into her lap and tipping her head. "But I realized that little by little he'd worked himself into my heart, and I've never regretted it. Your pa is the finest, most high-minded man I've ever known."

"But . . . didn't you feel just a little crazy for him? I mean . . ."

Her mama grabbed up the fabric again. "I give myself credit for more sense than that. A love that starts from fluttering hearts and moony eyes is seldom one that lasts. I hope you'll find a husband who's intelligent and thoughtful rather than one who sweeps you off your feet."

Abbie tossed her head. "Blake has got the silly notion he'll be my husband."

"He said so?"

She nodded. "He believes he's in love with me."

Mama laid her hands together on the ticking in her lap. "I think that was inevitable, don't you? The way you two have run off together since you were small, and now that you've grown into such a lovely young lady . . . if only you acted like one more often."

"Mama!"

"Do you feel the same for Blake? He's a nice young man, and our families have been—"

Abbie threw up her hands. "You sound like a newspaper advertisement. I think it's a ridiculous notion. Blake is . . . well, he's . . . I thought you wanted me to find a cultured, educated man. Blake was too stubborn to learn more than the rudimentary skills in all his years at school."

"Nevertheless, he's an intelligent boy and well-mannered."

Would she say that if she knew he'd stolen a kiss and tried to shoot a man? And spent the night in jail?

"At any rate, you're young enough not to rush into anything. Perhaps you'll find he's the best choice, or perhaps someone else will come along. There's plenty of time."

Abbie worked her needle in and out. She kept her voice light. "Mr. Farrel's nice, isn't he?"

"Yes. Your pa enjoys talking with him. Lord knows he has few enough men with whom to talk literature. Did you enjoy your supper?"

"Yes."

"How exactly did you find yourself there at that hour?"

"I went to speak with him about a concern."

"Oh?"

"It was nothing really, and I didn't think you'd mind, as we'd been properly introduced and Pa was so fond of him. . . ."

"I'd prefer you not make calls on gentlemen in their homes uninvited, Abbie. You are, need I remind you, a young lady. I know things are not what they were back East, but some semblance . . ."

"Yes, Mama. But did you know he has colored servants?"

"I'd heard."

"They used to be slaves, but he pays them now. They came with him even though they were free not to."

"That speaks well for him. Obviously his family was not one that mistreated the poor slaves in their care."

"It's strange to be waited on like that."

"Many people have servants in other parts of the country." Mama sighed. "There's so much you don't know. If it was possible to scratch enough together, we could send you to one of the schools back East, or even in the South. The women there are taking girls into boarding schools and teaching them the arts of fine society in order to survive, poor things."

Abbie groaned. Finishing school! "Monte thinks I'm unacceptable for southern society."

Mama paled. "Don't tell me you've embarrassed yourself already! Did you forget your manners last night? And how is it you call him Monte?"

Abbie cringed. "He asked me to call him that, and I didn't forget my manners. We were merely discussing the differences between the stuffy old South and here."

Mama rocked back on her heels and pursed her lips together. Abbie knew that look. It was her all-knowing, ferret-out-any-unrevealed-detail look. She imagined God looked at her that way, too. She poked her needle through the fabric.

Her head came up, though, as the clop of hooves sounded outside. A boy knocked on the open door. The horse he rode was too fine to be his own, judging by his scruffy pants and shirt, and Abbie perked up as he told Mama he had a message for Miss Abigail Martin. She took the note, written on the same vellum paper she had used yesterday.

" 'Dear Miss Martin, would you honor me with your company for a ride this afternoon? I would call for you at one o'clock. I sincerely await your reply. Montgomery Farrel.' "

Abbie's eyes met her mother's and she giggled. "I told you I remembered my manners."

Mama glared, indicating with her eyes the presence of the messenger boy. "Would you like to go?"

"Can you spare me?" Abbie breathed hopefully.

"I can."

Abbie turned eagerly to the boy. "Tell Mr. Farrel that I accept his invitation."

He stuffed his hands into his pockets. "Don't you wanna write it down?"

"Gracious, can't you remember that little bit?"

He shrugged sullenly.

"Oh, all right. Hold on a minute." She rushed into the house. Their paper was not so fine as Monte's, but she wrote a pretty hand and scribed her acceptance with an extra flourish at the end of her name. She turned as the boy left. "It'll be two hours before he comes for me. If we hurry we can get these done and stuffed as well."

"You're a good girl, Abbie." Mama smiled. "Even if you are overly enthusiastic. But please try to maintain your poise this afternoon. Mr. Farrel is new here and not accustomed to a more relaxed social order."

"Oh, Mama, you worry unnecessarily. Mr. Farrel is perfectly relaxed himself and not at all concerned with the way things were for him." Abbie tossed her curls, and Mama sighed.

Four

Montgomery Farrel read over the note and smiled. "Thank you, Will." Then he strode into the hall, where he found Pearl swinging the feather duster. He coughed.

"I can't stop the dust comin'," Pearl huffed, "but I'll see it don' lay where it don' belong."

"Yes, quite. Pearl, I'll be out this afternoon. Can you locate the basket carrier from Versailles?"

"You havin' that young miss?"

"I am."

She puffed out her lips. "Then I don' know what you be needin' that fo'."

"Oh yes, you do. And don't bother scolding. I don't intend to intoxicate the young lady. Wine enjoyed alfresco is the regular practice in most of the world."

"Most o' the heathen world."

Monte headed to the cellar. He ran his hand over the bottles already collecting dust, chose one, and wiped it with the cloth that lay handy. He carried it up to the kitchen, where Pearl was stuffing the basket with bread and cheese.

"There are only two of us."

"I mean to fortify her against the devil's tool."

"Really, Pearl."

"Don' you gimme them eyes. I knows young men when liquor's involved."

Monte laughed. "I would no more compromise Miss Martin than rob a bank."

She shook her head. "Then, I don' know what you needs that wine fo'."

"Drink. Refreshes the palate."

"Water does the same."

"Much less satisfactorily." He slid the bottle into the side pocket and hung the basket over his shoulder. "I can't say when I'll be back. Don't trouble yourself over supper."

Climbing into the carriage, Monte took the reins in his hands and clicked his tongue to Chance. The horse tossed his mane and trotted forth. Unlike last night, Monte did not dawdle across the distance. Whereas having Abbie dozing beside him had given him cause to dally, her absence, and the anticipation of altering that, effected a snappier pace. He was as eager as Chance was fresh.

"Good afternoon," he called as Mrs. Martin stepped onto the porch. She was a handsome woman, but his eyes went directly behind her to Abbie. Was there ever a sweeter sight?

"It's a nice day for a ride," Mrs. Martin said.

"Yes, it is."

"Where were you planning to go?"

"I was hoping Abbie might show me about. I've not had the time to acquaint myself yet."

Abbie took his hand as he lifted her in. "I know lots of places. We'll be up in the hills."

Monte raised a brow, but Mrs. Martin waved them off. Apparently she was accustomed to Abbie's wandering.

As they rode, Abbie played her part as guide, pointing out the landmarks they passed and telling him whatever legend or lore was associated with the spot. Either her teachers had drilled her hard, or she had a head for history.

"At different times this was a meeting place for the Arapaho, Kiowa, Ute, and Cheyenne Indians. Great numbers of

them gathered here for their summer festivals or tribal meet-
ings. Don't you wish you could have seen it?" She didn't wait
for a reply. "What a thrill to be a part of that and see them
dancing to the big skin drums and ... what's so funny?"

"I'd like to see you dressed up in deerskin hides and dancing
to the drums."

"I didn't say be an Indian." She caught the side as the buggy
swayed. "But I can't help feeling I missed something. The
Sioux and Arapaho, Kiowa and Cheyenne have gone, and with
the government reservations ... well, now there are only the
Utes and an occasional band of Comanche."

"I don't think many consider it a loss."

"Well, I do. Can you smell the sage?" She jumped topics
with hardly a breath. "And see, that's sumac there and chokecherries. But you have chokecherries at your stream, haven't
you?"

"I have, and I'm flattered you remember." Monte edged the
buggy through a crevice and steeply up as she directed. He
should not have so blindly accepted her lead. "Are you certain
this is a trail?"

"I've never actually brought a buggy up, but I ride it horseback."

"It's a good distance from your father's homestead."

"It's no distance at all."

No, of course not. Not when all was distance out here. Cradled
by the base of the mountain, one forgot the emptiness of endless grass and sagebrush that made up his acreage. But though
this was pleasant, his grassland would prove more profitable.
Abbie bumped against him as the wheels took the rise.

"The scrub oaks make it hard to get through, but there's
the way ahead." She pointed.

He gauged the width askance, then proceeded on faith as
the gnarled, finger-leafed branches scratched against the sides.
"You do plan to get us out of here again...."

Abbie laughed. "I've never been lost yet."

"That's encouraging."

"Do you see how the ponderosas are joined by fir and juniper? If we went far enough up, we'd find lodgepoles and spruce and kinik-kinik."

"I see you're a botanist as well as a lore master."

"Not a master of either, but I like to know things."

"Ah, you see? A southern lady would never let on she was more clever than I."

She spun in the seat. "I never said that."

Monte laughed. "You needn't. And don't apologize. I highly value intelligence, even in women. Maybe especially so. Which way, scout?"

"Head over to the right. It levels there, and we can leave the buggy and walk if you like."

Monte unhitched Chance, tethering him to graze while they retrieved the quilt and basket and started up the hillside through the thick growth of scrub oak and mountain sumac.

"Watch for cactus." Abbie gathered her skirts and climbed. "Sometimes the needles go right through your boots, and the yuccas are worse. Spanish Bayonets. They'll slice your leg and give you a terrible itch." Her foot slid on the loose gravel. Like a mountain goat, she skipped onto a rock ledge, but not before he'd glimpsed a length of ankle and shin. If she realized, she made no sign, nor pretense at maidenly chagrin.

He followed. "How far up do you plan to go?"

"Far enough to see out to the pinery, over the bluffs, and all the way across the prairie. Maybe far enough to see the ocean."

"You'd need eagle eyes for that."

"Then I'll imagine it there. Tell me what it looks like." She stopped and turned out toward the east, where the brown and gold grasses stretched unbroken, except where the pinery lapped the hills blackly and the bluffs stood like massive, un-marked graves.

Monte pointed toward the horizon. "If you were standing now on the edge of the shore, as far out as you can see would be the deepest blue right up to the edge of the sky where the blues meet and almost merge. The sun glances off the peaks of the waves as off the facets of a sapphire, and overhead the white gulls swoop on their gray-tipped wings and call, dipping now and again to the water's surface, then winging up into the wind again. And down below, the white-frothed breakers roar in to throw themselves at the rocks encrusted with mussels and smelling of salt." He stopped suddenly, caught by the tears sparkling in her eyes, bluer than any ocean he had seen, with the lashes drooping down in long, graceful arcs.

"Hoh . . ." Her breath released. "You make it so beautiful. How I'd love to see it, really see it."

He felt speechless in the wake of her emotion and the vi-brancy she held within. "It's easy to describe what you know. Were you to tell what you see here from your mind's eye, you'd bring tears even to men." And he didn't doubt it. The way she had spoken of this land the previous day had moved him deeply. What would it be like to show her the places she imag-ined? It was exhilarating to consider.

He made for a cluster of ponderosas at the top of the ridge and spread the quilt in the shade beneath their branches. As he seated her, the breeze bent the pale, golden grasses and nod-ded the heads of the orange Indian paintbrush, yellow lupine, and blue Mertensias that dotted the hillside. Would he notice these if Abbie hadn't quickened his senses?

From the bushy mountain mahogany came the throaty call of a meadowlark. "That's a meadow—" She stopped.

"Yes?"

"I think you're tired of my lessons."

"I think I've never enjoyed lessons more."

"I talk too much."

"Then I'm guilty for listening." He opened the basket and laid out the crusty rye and the white ball of cheese. After their hike, he was glad Pearl had sent it.

"I teach at the mission, and it comes so naturally I forget myself."

"Ah." He took the wine bottle, twisted the coiled screw into the cork, and slowly slipped it free.

"I teach the little ones whenever I can so Father Dominic can drill the older children."

"Sounds like a good arrangement." The goblets were wrapped in cloth. Pearl did her part, no matter how reluctantly. And he couldn't fault her concern. At the end, drink had destroyed his father.

Abbie hesitated when he held a glass to her. "I don't know that I should have that."

"Come. It's a habit I acquired in France. But I promise the wine loses all ability to intoxicate when imbibed in the open air under the shade of a mighty pine."

She cocked her head. "Sounds like Indian lore to me. Some medicinal hocus-pocus."

Monte laughed. "I assure you I have no intention of endangering your senses. You're far too amusing in your right mind."

"Amusing?" She raised the glass to her lips. "Are you so gracious to all your guests?"

Monte laughed. "Of course."

"And I suppose you have plenty of opportunity."

"I've found no shortage of willing parties."

Her eyes flashed. "Are you so smug? Last night I could have sworn I dined with a gentleman. It seems I was mistaken."

"My most abject apologies." He took her hand, well shaped and strong, not soft and pale as others he'd held. He suddenly felt foolish toying with her. She had no coquettish airs. "Can you forgive me?"

She raised her face, surrounded by riotous brown curls only halfheartedly contained by the combs. "I'm not sure how to take you. If you're sincere . . ."

"I am always sincere." Monte had never been more so. He handed her an end of bread and a wedge of cheese. "Peace?"

Abbie smiled and accepted it.

"So." He raised his glass to hers, then drank. She took a swallow and puckered her face.

"Well?"

"Somewhat like . . . cider . . . that sat too long."

He laughed. "It'll grow on you." He drank his own. It was smooth and mellow. A wonderful Bordeaux. What a shame it was lost on her. "I presume your friend was released from jail?"

He surprised the color to her cheeks. "Yes. I appreciate your kindness."

"I'd no desire for revenge. I simply want to know that my person and property are safe from further incident."

She waved the bread in her hand. "Oh, Blake? Why, he's just headstrong and impulsive. He doesn't really have a wicked bone in his body. Though I guess we're a little alike in that we act before we think . . . sometimes."

"I would never have guessed that of you, Abbie. You seem so reserved." When she sighed, he chided himself for teasing.

"Mama wishes I were, that's for certain. And I do try to think before I speak, but sometimes the thoughts just come so fast I don't have time to check them over before they're out."

"That's what I find so refreshing. If there's subtlety in your nature, it's well disguised."

"Mama says I was left too long to my own devices and grew wild romping the hills with Blake. But truly I think the skills I learned will stand me in better stead than all the ladylike things I could have done."

Monte leaned against the rough-barked tree. "And what skills have you learned?"

"Oh . . . how to recognize and track the trail of seventeen different animals. I can whittle a stick and spear a fish and climb a tree even better than Blake."

"Let's see."

She turned to him, surprised. "See what?"

"See you climb a tree."

"I beg your pardon, Monte. I admit I'm lacking in social graces, but I do have a sense of decency. I can hardly climb a tree in this." She pinched up her skirt.

"And what did you wear to climb with Blake?" He watched the blush burn up her cheeks. What was he on to? This was too much fun to let go.

"I was a good deal younger then."

"And?"

"I'd rather not say."

"Oh, come now . . ."

"Really, Monte."

"All right then, I'll be forced to speculate."

Abbie tossed down the bread. "Well, if you must know, I tucked my skirts up. But I was hardly out of pigtails then, though I guess old enough to know better." She turned away.

"I'm sorry." He suppressed the laughter in his throat. "I assure you, your secret is safe with me."

Abbie wove a grass blade between her fingers and didn't respond. She was certainly slow to forgive. What was that intractable streak in his nature that took amusement at her discomfiture?

"I truly do apologize. And I don't think any less of you for it. In fact, I rather admire you. Who knows . . . one day you may need that very skill."

Abbie brushed the grass from her skirt. "I do actually have a number of appropriate skills as well."

"I'm sure you do. But I applaud your adventurous spirit."

"I'm just made that way, I guess. Some people are."

"That's true. I remember Duncan Williams had a similar bent. He was a constant thorn in his father's side because if he didn't find adventure, he created it. I recall the time he put gunpowder in the headmaster's stove. It was rather a more exciting opening to the lecture than we were accustomed to." Monte laughed at the memory. "Thankfully, no one was injured. Except for Duncan, of course, who couldn't sit on his horse for days." He drained his glass and filled it again, then held the bottle toward her.

She shook her head. "Was he your friend?"

"We were never close. The two I call friends are Chandler Bridges and Milton Rochester. Our families have been devoted for generations. There's nothing I wouldn't do for either of them."

Abbie murmured, " 'Thine own friend and thy father's friend forsake not.' "

Monte nodded. "Yes, exactly."

"That's how I feel about Clara Simms. We're nothing alike, but we understand each other, and she accepts my faults without complaint."

"And you hers, I presume."

"She hasn't any. She's perfectly well-spoken, gentle, and sweet."

"That's all well and good, Abbie. But life calls for variety. I'm far more interested in a girl who can track and fish and climb a tree."

"I wish I hadn't told you that."

"I promised to keep your secret. Now you can't think of it anymore." A sudden gust blew through her hair, and he followed her gaze to the sheet of gray looming over the mountain.

"It's going to storm."

"It's only clouds." He didn't want the time to end.

She ignored him and stood. "You don't know how suddenly

the thunderstorms come on." As if called upon, a flash and rumble echoed her words.

Before they had climbed down the slope to the buggy, the first raindrops slapped down, cold and hard, no gentle shower. By the time he hitched Chance, Monte was thoroughly wet. "You weren't joking." He climbed in beside her.

"I've spent enough time outside to know."

The rain was pelting and Chance strained against his hold, snorting as the first hailstones smote his back.

"There." Abbie pointed. "The hogback."

Monte veered toward the sloping ridge of stone and pulled under its shelter, soothing the horse with low tones. "I'll never doubt you again." He winced as lightning seared the sky.

"Mama will be worried. But we don't dare go until it's spent."

Water rushed past in the ravines, red and angry, as the white stones battered the ground and piled up like snow. Abbie shivered.

"Cold?"

"I forgot my shawl."

He retrieved the quilt and wrapped her shoulders. She snuggled into the thickness.

"Look at you, though. You're soaked through," Abbie said.

"It is a bit chilly."

"There's room for two." She held up the quilt edge.

Was she brazen or simply innocent? Nothing in her expression betrayed anything but concern for him. "Do you mind?"

"Sometimes circumstances call for concessions. Just don't tell Mama."

He settled into the folds. If ever there was a time for Pearl's suspicions, this was it. Abbie's thin shoulders almost asked to be wrapped in his arm, the scent of her soap was fresh and wild, and her eyes . . . No wonder Blake had taken a gun to him.

The poor kid was probably smitten senseless, and he could be, too, if the storm lingered.

If Abbie guessed his thoughts she made no sign, but then she was young. Too young. He shifted away, but her warmth stayed with him.

The hail thinned but still the rain drenched the land. Did anything happen gently here? At last the storm slackened. Reluctantly, he pulled down the quilt and tucked it against Abbie's side. "I believe we can make it now."

"It's better to wait."

Monte smiled. "Abbie, I have been driving for some years now."

Chance heaved and strained through the mud and flowing ruts. The flooding was worse than he expected, and their progress abysmally slow. Beneath the ragged fringe of gray, the westerly sun sent a fleeting glow, then slipped behind the ridge. The rear wheel bogged. Chance snorted, backed, and strove against its hold. The wheel stuck fast. Monte chafed, but he wouldn't force the animal. Tossing the reins, he jumped down and surveyed the wheel. "Can you drive?"

Of course she could drive. She could track and fish and read the weather. And he should have listened to her. He shouldered the buggy's side and pushed as she urged the horse. The wheel turned, climbed, and spun back down. Chance balked.

"Shall we both push?"

"Thank you, Abbie, I can manage." He sounded crosser than he should. "Again."

Once more the wheel spun. She jumped down, heedless of her dress in the mud. Monte straightened, but she didn't join him. Instead, she took Chance's head and pulled. The horse strained in the fading light, and Monte threw his weight against the carriage. The wheel caught, turned, and kept turning. As the horse leaped forward, Abbie stumbled but kept her feet, and Chance tossed his head, straining against her.

Monte strode forward and took hold of Chance. Abbie was breathing hard, her dress clung to her legs in muddy streaks, and her chin was smudged. But she smiled doggedly. She was an imp, and for one insane moment he felt like kissing her.

Five

B y the lantern light, Joshua Martin hailed them as Monte halted the carriage in the yard. Chance's head sagged, and Monte could only imagine the sorry sight they made, though Joshua's smile was forgiving.

"Looks like you two had a bit of a wet ride." Joshua handed Abbie down. "Come on in, Monte. I'll find you a dry shirt."

Mrs. Martin looked up from the stove. "Goodness!"

"We're fine." Abbie halted her mother's fuss. "The horse bogged down, is all."

"You're soaked to the skin. Get right out of those wet things." She dropped her voice. "And for heaven's sake, Abbie, there's mud up to your knees." She turned. "Mr. Farrel, you'll stay to supper?"

The kitchen smelled wonderful, and he was hungry. "I'd be honored."

"You'll get a taste of Selena's famous Irish stew." Joshua tossed him a shirt. "There's a basin in the back."

In the lean-to off the kitchen, Monte stripped off the wet shirt and washed, then wiped down his boots and toweled them dry. For all its lack of elegance, the Martin house was as clean as any, and he'd keep it that way. He hadn't missed Mrs. Martin's scolding to Abbie, though he rather thought it had more to do with him than her condition alone. He had brought her back in a sorry state, but that was her doing, and he guessed Mrs. Martin knew it.

Monte pulled on Joshua's dry shirt and rolled the sleeves, as the cuffs were too short for his arms. Then, after smoothing back his hair, he turned and went back to the kitchen.

Abbie looked as fresh as he felt. Her dress was changed and an apron tied over, her hair pulled back in a ribbon. Instead of having vapors and bemoaning their ordeal, she was briskly setting out the flatware and plates. A guest appearing now would never know she'd been out in a hailstorm, dragging a horse and buggy from a ditch. She was remarkable. Truly remarkable.

They sat down around the table in the small kitchen, and Joshua offered the blessing. Mrs. Martin dished the bowls of stew, then passed him the rolls, hot and crusty from the oven. In Joshua's shirt, with the heat of the stove at his back, Monte felt more at home than he could remember feeling for a long, long time. He took the cup of coffee Mrs. Martin offered.

"I'm pleased you could join us, Mr. Farrel."

"Monte, please."

She nodded. "It's a shame the weather was so inhospitable for your ride."

"There's no controlling that. I'm only glad we had shelter from the hail or Chance would have had a bad time of it." Monte sipped the coffee. It was rich and mellow, as good a blend as Pearl brewed, and he'd wager at half the cost of the beans he had shipped up from Louisiana.

Mrs. Martin laid her napkin in her lap. "Mr. Farrel ... Monte, I've been wondering, would you know a reasonable girls' school Abbie might attend?"

Abbie's spoon stopped halfway to her mouth.

Mrs. Martin must be more concerned than he thought. He clearly perceived Abbie's pique, but he hid his amusement and chose a formal tone. "I know of several, one in particular that is highly recommended. Mistress Bradley, the headmistress, is my late mother's second cousin."

"What's this?" Joshua tore his roll in two.

Mrs. Martin spoke softly. "I think we should consider a school of this type. There are areas where Abbie's education has been lacking."

"Lacking! She knows more—"

"I don't mean book learning. She's had more of that, no doubt, than she needs. I mean social graces."

Monte watched Abbie's jaw set. Her discomfiture was too tempting. "It never hurts to broaden your horizons. Develop new areas of proficiency."

Joshua shook his head. "You don't have to go halfway across the country to do it."

"There's nothing like that here, Joshua," Mrs. Martin replied.

"What she can't learn here, she doesn't need to know." Joshua spooned the stew but didn't take the bite. "Tell me, Monte, what did you think of Mr. Bridley's journal?"

Abbie's shoulders relaxed. It seemed Joshua had the final word.

"I agreed with a good many of his assessments. But on the Indian affairs, I think he's off the mark." He glanced at Abbie, but she refused to meet his eye.

"How so? Don't you think coexistence with the Indian is not only possible but desirable?"

"Coexistence between men is hardly possible. The War between the States has shown us that. You cannot blend the Indian's world with the white man's. You cannot further the gains of the one without diminishing the other. It'll end up all or nothing."

Joshua shook his head. "I hope you're wrong there."

"Mark my words, there are dark times ahead. The Indian, like the Negro, will find the arms of society do not embrace him. Look at your Sand Creek Massacre for proof. Women and children slaughtered inside the bounds of their reserved lands. And why? For simply being there." He took the slice of pie Mrs. Martin served and nodded his thanks.

"And that's the injustice. But that doesn't mean it has to continue."

"But it will continue. Do you think that because high-minded people raised a cry to free the Negro, they will open their homes and families to him? Do you think that any Indian bureau can erase the memory of scalped children, families brutally murdered in their sleep? I believe there'll be more bloodshed on both fronts before it's over."

Joshua cut his fork into the wedge of blackberry pie. "I'm afraid that's likely. But I can wish it weren't and do what I can to stand against it. I have a voice and it's a powerful tool. I can speak for what's right."

"That's all anyone can do." Monte scraped the last of the pie from the plate and pushed it away.

"Another piece of pie?" Mrs. Martin held the dish, but Monte shook his head and wiped his mouth.

"Thank you, Mrs. Martin, but I've been too indulged already. Joshua's praise of you is well deserved."

She smiled. "Thank you, Monte. And please, call me Selena."

Abbie stood to help her mother clear away.

"You'll want to get back," Joshua said, and Monte rose.

Abbie reached past him for the pitcher, still without a word or glance. Had he gone too far with his teasing? She was certainly quick to take offense, but it didn't sit well with him to leave it at that. He touched her elbow. "A word with you, Abbie?"

Selena nodded, and Abbie followed him outside. The night air smelled of the rain, but the clouds had torn open swaths of stars. Monte breathed deeply, leaning on the railing. "Why do I have the distinct impression you're displeased with me?"

"I'm sure I don't know." She didn't look his way.

"And I'm equally sure you do."

She spun. "You're a traitor!"

He feigned more dismay than he felt. "You have cut me to the quick! How have I betrayed you?"

"All that you told Mama. She'll never let it go now. And what of all that talk about preferring a girl who could track and fish and . . . was that just talk?"

"No, it was not. But I meant what I told your mother, too. There's a place for everything, all kinds of talents, and you ought not limit yourself to those you can't admit in public. Come, Abbie."

"Come nothing. How would you like to be trapped in some place where all you did was swoon and whine?"

He fought a laugh. Her description was more apt than he would admit. "Consider it an adventure, a jungle of sorts."

Her eyes deepened in the moonlight, the lashes casting delicate shadows on her cheek as she looked up. "And who would come to my rescue, I wonder?" Her brows raised . . . enticing him?

Monte leaned close, his breath suddenly tight in his chest. "Perhaps you would find you needed no rescuing. I believe you could conquer the entire jungle on your own."

Abbie tossed her head. "And establish myself as the belle men pined for but wouldn't dare marry?" She laughed. "That's all right. I wouldn't dream of marrying some fancified eastern gentleman with lily white hands, anyway."

That stung. Monte grasped his hands behind his back. "That's rather extreme, wouldn't you say? And whom would you dream of marrying?"

"Oh, someone who didn't care if I could embroider or simper over tea with the proper malaise in my tone."

"Like Blake, perhaps?" He twisted his mouth ironically.

"Perhaps."

"But you don't love him."

"Maybe someday I will."

She was indeed taunting him, the vixen. Monte laughed low. "Well, I wish him the best of luck, then—Blake or whom-ever you choose. He'll certainly need it."

Abbie's mouth fell open. "Hadn't you better see to your horse, Mr. Farrel?"

"Yes, I suppose I had."

"Good night, then."

"Good night, Miss Martin," he drawled, and she swept into the house without a backward glance.

At least he had evened the ground.

Six

As a funeral cloak on bony shoulders, the clouds hung ominously still over the mountains. Abbie felt the air. Yesterday's hail was nothing compared to what this storm promised, and she hurried with her chores, pulling the clean wash down from the line and tossing it into the large woven basket with less care than was her wont. The chickens were nervous and raced about wildly when she shooed them into their pen and tossed them their feed.

By the time she had the sheep herded into the large, airy barn, the wind, even in July, was chilling her. With one glance at the cow, horse, and hog safely contained, she grabbed her skirts and ran for the house. Abbie could smell the rain coming, and lightning split the sky as she closed the door against the wind behind her. "It's really going to hit us this time!" She found Mama in the front room darning socks. "The clouds are black with malice."

Mama looked up. "I wish you hadn't such a way of expressing things. You put a shiver right up to my neck. I surely hope your father has sense enough to stay in town and not try to make it home."

"Pa's sensible."

"Sometimes. Other times he doesn't think to look up or around him if he has a story in his head or a thought forming."

Abbie looked out. With sudden violence, the storm smote the house.

"Are the sheep in the barn?" Mama asked.

"Yes, and the other stock, as well."

Abbie put her hands to her ears at the growing cacophony of the rain becoming hail. She stared at the ice marbles bouncing on the ground outside that grew to the size of pullet eggs. Never had she seen hail of such destructive power.

Mama dropped the darning egg and came to stand beside her. "Lord, have mercy."

"I'm sorry, Mama. Perhaps it won't be so bad." But Abbie could see her words were false.

"Perhaps," Mama murmured.

✦✦✦✦✦✦✦

Monte dashed for the newspaper office in the wake of an earsplitting crack of thunder. He gained the door and burst through.

Joshua grinned. "You sure do take to this weather, Monte. Haven't you had your fill of the wet yet?" he hollered over the din.

"I have, but I don't seem to have the apparatus to predict it like you folks do," Monte shouted back, shaking himself like a dog. At least Chance was at the livery and would be cared for if he was delayed. He smoothed back his soaked hair. "I thought it was supposed to be dry out here."

"The only thing you can count on is that the weather will never be what you thought. Soon as you get set for dry, it floods, and when you're ready for rain, the ground plum shrivels up." Joshua watched through the window as the rain turned to hail. "Only the good Lord knows what we need better than we do."

"Looks like what we need is a good thrashing." Monte came up behind and followed his gaze.

Joshua shook his head. "Folks are going to suffer from this one."

As he spoke, a drop of water fell from the rough-board ceiling, followed by another, and then more. Grabbing a bucket, Joshua caught the flow. "Sure hope it's not hitting like this at home."

Monte pulled aside the shade on the west window. "I wouldn't count on that. Have a look at those clouds." He hoped Abbie hadn't been caught out again. This onslaught made yesterday's a lark.

As the night drew on, the rain continued, and the street became a young river. "I'm thinking it's foolhardy to try for home tonight," Monte concluded.

"I'm afraid you're right, though my belly has a complaint."

"What do you say I brave the street and fetch us something from the hotel?"

"I'd say you have a taker." Joshua reached into his pocket.

"Keep it." Monte pulled his coat up over his head and dashed out into the rain. Pearl would have something to say about him presenting her another pair of mud-stained trousers, but it appeared she might as well get used to it. The water rushed up to the top edge of his boots with enough force to threaten his footing as he leaped onto the far boardwalk and entered the hotel. He secured a couple of fried chicken dinners, then made his way back.

"You're a good man, Monte." Joshua grinned as he opened the box and viewed the meal.

They talked long into the night. Joshua Martin possessed a keen wit and good humor, but there was also a strength of character that reminded Monte of his own father before the war. He was challenged by Joshua's ideas and found himself wondering what the man was made of, and in turn, what he had passed on to his daughter. Though Abbie favored Selena in looks, he suspected it was Joshua's temperament she had inherited along with the startling blue eyes.

When they had burned the oil low, they set the chairs end to end, and Monte bent himself into the space while Joshua curled up on the bench. It was a comfortable companionship he shared with Joshua Martin, and more. He respected the man and suspected Joshua returned the esteem. He hadn't thought to find that here.

He cradled his head on his arm and shifted one leg under the other. The rain made hardly more than a murmur on the roof as he closed his eyes to sleep.

◆◆◆◆◆◆◆

Abbie's face drew into a long imitation of the sight that met her eyes when she stepped out into the bright morning sunshine. Unlike a morning following a gentle rain, in which everything is fresh and shining, the earth looked ragged and unkempt. Shredded greenery and mud covered everything. Each plant lay trampled and flattened, and the trees were nearly leafless, except for the hearty ponderosas. Even the indestructible yuccas were limp.

She and Mama made their way through to the garden and viewed the devastation. Mama lifted a tiny cucumber from beneath a matted wreck of leaves. She turned it slowly in her hand. There was not a mark on it, and she sighed. "Maybe you and your pa are right. Maybe a place like this doesn't want refinement. Maybe you just have to be able to survive."

Pa galloped through the gate and reined in beside them. Slipping from the horse, he surveyed the battered land, his expression grim. "Well, I guess we can be thankful it wasn't worse. How did the stock fare?"

"Abbie got them all in before the storm hit." Mama tucked the cucumber into her apron pocket.

"Good girl, Abbie." He caressed her cheek. "I know I can count on you to help your mama."

Selena bent and lifted the severed vine that held the remains of two more immature cucumbers. "This is going to set us back. There's not much to salvage, and with the grasshoppers last year . . ."

"We'll manage." Pa looked over the land. "We'll just have to buy our vegetables like the townsfolk do."

Mama didn't argue, though Abbie knew she wondered where the money would come from.

"I'll have a look at the damage." Pa made his way to the barn, and Abbie followed. She needed to milk Buttercup anyway.

The oozy floor showed the extent of damage to the barn roof. "The house is bad, too, Pa. We shored it up as best we could, but it'll need repair." The sheep pressed against her legs as she reached for the milking pail and slid the stool to the cow's side. "I wish Grant were here." She always missed her brother more than her sister, Sadie, but now when Pa needed him, she really felt his absence.

"Well, right now he's reading law at Harvard. You know that's always been his bent."

"I know, but there are times we sure could use him back here."

"We'll make do."

"I'll help any way I can."

"I know you will, and there'll be plenty to do for all of us." Joshua let the sheep out into the yard. "Go ahead and take them to the pasture, Abbie. I'll do the milking."

She kept to the high ground as she led the sheep, avoiding the pockets of wet earth. By afternoon the ground would be dry and in a week parched again, but for now it had slaked its thirst. She wondered if the storm had hit Denver, where Sadie lived with her husband, Joe. Then she thought of the mission in Rocky Bluffs and stopped short. Their roof had been needing repair long before this. If the hail had reached that far east . . .

She couldn't get away today. There was far too much to do here at home. But maybe tomorrow . . . what good would that do? Without materials . . . and the brothers took in no money. They fed the orphan children in their care with what they raised themselves, and clothed them with the castoffs Pastor Peale had provided. After the pastor's death, Father Dominic had said God would see to them. But how did God provide shingles?

Abbie opened the gate, and the sheep pressed through. First she would do what she could here, and then she'd learn how the mission fared. Mama would gladly spare her once she could.

Pa had ridden back to town to order in new shingles, though there was little chance the mill could keep up. Especially since the logs had to be hauled by wagon eighteen miles from the pinery. At least they might get their order in early.

Pa came back as angry as Abbie had ever seen him. "Hank Thorn's expecting payment in advance on the shingles. And he means to make a profit on folks' misfortune. He's raised the price to forty cents a bale."

Mama's mouth dropped open in dismay.

"I reckon I can cut my own shingles for that kind of money."

"How will you have time, Pa?" Abbie took his hat and hung it on the hook.

"I'll make time."

"But the paper . . ."

"The paper will wait. But I'll have a thing or two to say in my editorial when I do get back to it." He poured himself a cup of coffee from the stove. "It's worse for others than for us. Several of the homesteads were badly damaged, mostly those already in disrepair." He tossed down his saddlebag. "The Perkins homestead, for one. They'll be packing up within the week and heading back to Missouri."

"I'm sorry for them," Mama said.

"They hadn't the constitution to last out here. You saw the state of their place."

"Yes, but Blanche had her hands full with twelve children."

"Could have had plenty of help if they'd ever trained and disciplined them." Joshua shook his head. "I'm not passing judgment. Just seems like some folks ought to stay where things are easier."

"Sometimes it's hard to know how things can get." Mama laid a hand on his shoulder.

"I'm that sour today, aren't I?"

Mama smiled.

Abbie went out to the garden and made her way up and down the rows, gently mounding the dirt up around the potato and sweet potato plants that were hardly more than a few stems with straggling shredded leaves. The blossoms had already set, and possibly they would come back and produce the tubers, but it wasn't likely. The carrot greens were gone, but the roots were already strong and established. The lettuce, spinach, and chard were demolished, nor was there much she could do for the corn, pumpkins, squash, and cucumbers.

"Afternoon, Abbie."

She turned. "Hello, Blake. It's a dismal sight, isn't it?"

"I dunno. Seems like the purtiest thing I've seen."

"Don't go being crazy again," she snapped. "I'm talking about the garden, you fool boy."

"Is that any way to treat me when I come to offer my help to yer pa?"

"Did you, Blake?" She regretted her words immediately and slipped her arm through his. "Of course not. Forgive me?"

His cheeks were ruddy from the walk and the work he'd already done, no doubt. He flipped the hair from his forehead and grinned. "Maybe we oughta kiss and make up."

She pulled her arm away. "I declare, I don't know what's gotten into you!"

He was laughing, and she turned her back on him and continued down the row.

"Can I help?"

"I thought you were helping Pa."

"He don't need me till he reckons the damage."

"Surely your own garden needs as much work as ours."

"Ma and Mariah are seein' to it."

"Then you can gather the waste for the hog." Through the corner of her eye, she watched him obey and softened. He was as good-hearted as he was vexing. And with Grant away, his help would be a boon. "Thank you, Blake."

He looked up from where he bent and winked.

Seven

Abbie paced the mare, though Shiloh was fresh and eager to run. All around her were signs of the hail, but the prairie grasses were springing back better than the cultivated plants at home. As she approached the mission, she could see its adobe walls had withstood much damage, but she knew the beam and shingled roof could not have. The side building where the children slept looked especially battered.

She dismounted and tethered Shiloh. With a stroke to the mare's neck, she left her and went to the door. Brother José greeted her, beaming to the top of his brown tonsured skull. "*Buenos días.*"

"Good morning, Brother. *Cómo estás?*"

"One is always well in God's hands."

He led her in through the gathering hall where they took their meals and past the open kitchen. Brother Thomas rolled a great mound of dough over the floured board, nodding as she passed.

The children sat along the walls of the schoolroom with slates across their knees, and the empty space in the center showed Abbie what she had come to discover. Tarps and buckets kept the water from the wood plank floor. Father Dominic looked up from the book of Psalms he was reading aloud, and several of the small ones around him smiled at her. The room was impossibly still, though it contained fourteen children and the priest.

"Forgive my interrupting."

Father Dominic smiled. "Time is the Lord's."

"I can't stay today, but I wanted to see about your roof."

"It is as you see it."

Four-year-old Tucker squirmed, nudging the tarp edge with his toe. A rivulet started across the thickness, and Father Dominic caught his eye before the child could wiggle it again. Abbie wished she could gather the little ones out to the yard and work their letters, but she was needed at home. "Shingles may be hard to come by, but I'll see what I can do."

"Your gift is welcome. Labor we have, but few materials."

As she rode home, Abbie wondered how she could find shingles for them. If Mr. Thorne was charging so dearly, people wouldn't spare any from their own use, and Pa couldn't possibly cut more than they required. Maybe she and Blake . . . but that would be slowgoing for the two of them to cut so many. She shook her head. Somehow she'd think of a way.

◆◆◆◆◆◆◆

Four days later, Abbie perched on the ladder with a pail of water for Pa and Blake as they worked the old broken shingles off the roof of the house. She turned at the rumble of wheels on the drive. A pair of black horses pulled a wagon, and she recognized Chance and another black as like him as a twin. Monte drove them.

Shading her eyes, she made out his load. Fresh-hewn shingles. She caught her breath and hurried down the ladder.

"What's all this?" Pa followed close on her heels.

Monte tipped his hat to her, and she nodded stiffly back, remembering her grudge. He turned to Pa. "I took the liberty of sending to Denver for shingles, as the local mill was committing usury."

"I expect the freight ran you more dearly."

"I sent my own men after them and cut the price by ordering for two."

"Aha. You're a shrewd dealer. What's the cost to me?"

"Ten cents a bale."

Pa whistled. "That's music to my ears. I'd be weeks cutting this load by hand."

Monte jumped down. "And as it happens, my roof is under control, so I'm offering my hands as well."

Abbie hung in the shadow, still stinging from their last encounter. But this was a tremendous windfall, and it was good to see Pa so excited. It seemed Mr. Farrel was not afraid to work, and Pa could use all the help he could get.

"Now, there's a fine thing." Pa pulled off his hat and wiped his forehead. "Between you and Blake, I'll be set in no time."

Abbie bit her lip against a giggle as Monte glanced up to the roof. She wished she could see Blake's face right now. Monte's was inscrutable as he strode to the wagon bed and opened the back. Instead of fine trousers, pleated shirt, and vest, he wore a blue cotton shirt and denim pants, with a bandanna tied at his neck. Even so, he looked every inch the aristocrat. Blake would be fuming.

Abbie went inside. "Mama! Monte's brought shingles!"

"Oh my, what a blessing!" Mama cupped her cheeks. "I thought we'd be weeks without a proper roof!"

"There's a wagonful, enough for the barn as well, and . . . maybe there'll be some for the mission, too. I mean with all that Pa's cut already . . ."

"They're welcome to whatever we have. Oh, Monte's a good man. Did you ask him in?"

"He's on the roof with Pa . . . and Blake." Now she did giggle.

Mama frowned. "What happened between Monte and Blake

is not a lark. I certainly hope you'll not encourage any further trouble."

Abbie cringed. So Mama had heard. "I never encouraged any in the first place. Blake just lost his head. Lucky for him, I saved his neck." She collapsed, giggling, into the chair.

"Abbie, it's not a laughing matter."

But the idea of Blake and Monte together on the roof was altogether too funny to resist. She gave in to the laughter in spite of Mama's annoyance.

Monte wondered at the cause of Abbie's laughter filtering through the open doors. She had been stiff and aloof enough a moment ago. But it was a delicious sound, and he wished he'd been party to the source. He looked up to find Blake watching him. He'd obviously heard, also. Joshua paid no mind, but then he lived with the chance to hear Abbie laugh.

A pounding of hooves brought Joshua's head up. Sterling Jacobs reined up sharply in the yard. "Joshua!"

"What's the ruckus?"

"Paper's been ransacked. I think you'd better come see."

Joshua leaped to his feet but glanced at his companions.

Monte straightened. "Go on. Blake and I will handle this."

Joshua climbed down and ran for the barn.

Blake went to the edge. "Who done it, d'you suppose?"

"They're sayin' in town it was Hollister's gang."

"Why hit the newspaper?"

"Why does anyone do a senseless thing? Maybe they didn't like the column Joshua printed last week. He didn't mince any words describin' them."

Monte sat back on his heels. "Who's Hollister?"

"A two-bit thievin' scoundrel." Blake scowled. "He's been hittin' the stage and unsuspectin' folks for the past year. Has a ragtag bunch of no-goods tryin' to make a name for themselves."

Monte appraised Blake. "He's been at it for a year and not been caught yet?"

"It takes a bit of doin' to round up a gang like that. Too much open space, too much wild country."

Sterling and Joshua set their horses for town. As he watched them gallop away, Monte glanced at Blake. They were alone now, and the boy was clearly uncomfortable.

Blake hunkered down and worked his wedge under a shingle. "I reckon it's as good a time as any to beg pardon for losin' my head."

"No harm done." Monte busied himself with a patch of splintered shingles.

"I guess Abbie gets me a mite worked up."

"Perfectly understandable. She's an awfully pretty package."

"I figured you'd noticed."

"It would be difficult to miss." Monte heaved a handful of broken shingles over the side. "Hand me that hammer, will you?"

Blake passed it over.

"So what are your plans, Blake? Smithing like your father?"

"Not if I can help it. That's an awful hot an' dirty way to make a livin' in my book. I mean to go west . . . soon as I can talk Abbie into comin' along." He glanced up at that.

"Good luck. I don't get the impression Abbie's easily talked into anything."

Blake frowned. "No, she ain't." He yanked hard on a stubborn shingle.

Monte heard the door below, and in a moment Abbie joined them on the roof with the water bucket. Stopping on the flat portion above the porch, she gazed about her. "Sure can see a long way from up here."

Blake grinned. "Good as the old lightning pine, ain't it?" He made his way down to her from the ridge.

"Well, I wouldn't say quite—" She caught herself. "I wouldn't know."

"Sure you would. Remember how it . . ." Blake didn't catch her point until he took the cup of water and faced her glare.

Monte smiled crookedly.

"Lunch is almost ready." She dipped the cup again.

Monte took it, trying to gauge her mood. Was she still holding her grudge? Once the thrill of besting her wore off, he'd regretted it. She pushed a loose strand of hair back and tried to avoid his gaze, but with a will of their own her eyes met his, and he could see a throbbing pulse in her neck. She may be angry still, but she was having a difficult time keeping it. He drained the cup and handed it back.

"Thank you, Abbie."

She spun without answering.

Red-faced and sullen, Blake kicked a pile of old shingles over the side, then sat and yanked on the next row.

Abbie lowered herself onto the ladder. "Mama made your favorite apple dumplings, Blake. Get yourself good and hungry so you'll be sure to have room." She disappeared over the side.

Blake didn't speak again. When Selena called for them to come eat, Monte motioned Blake to precede him down the ladder, then followed. After washing at the pump, Monte went into the kitchen. He eyed the table overflowing with biscuits and corn bread, boiled potatoes with parsley and bacon, fried zucchini and onions, roast venison and cold chicken, and a big pot of Boston baked beans. "Selena, I have never seen a more welcome sight in all my life."

"Hard work builds an appetite." Selena set the milk pitcher on the table and they all sat down. "Monte, would you be so kind?"

"Ma'am." He bowed his head and folded his hands. "Our heavenly Father, we thank Thee for the bounty from Thy hand, and for all the good things that Thou dost bestow. Give us grateful hearts in all things and keep us ever in Thy sight. Amen." As he expected, Abbie peeked up at his formal prayer, and he winked.

She turned away, but not before he saw her amusement. She'd get over her irk. The work had built a hunger and Selena was a good cook, but his appetite died when Joshua stormed into the room in a fine temper. He tossed his hat at the hook on the wall and left it where it landed on the floor. Joshua's face was a mask of fury.

Monte knew before asking. "The press?"

"Destroyed! There's no repairing it." Joshua dropped into the chair and pounded his fist on the table. Abbie jumped. Clearly his temper rarely showed itself. But what man took this quietly?

Monte felt the affront himself. "What possible motivation could someone have for destroying the press?"

"What does it matter? What's done can't be undone." Joshua brushed away the cup Selena held out to him, his fury barely held in check.

This was not the time for guests. Once Joshua's head had cleared, Monte would talk with him, figure things out. But for now . . . "You'll want some time." Monte nudged Blake up and, with a hand on his shoulder, ushered him out. He had him to the porch when Abbie swept by and pressed a parcel into Blake's hand.

"Dumplings."

Blake grinned. "I'll be over tomorrow."

She nodded, and Monte waited silently while she watched him walk away. As she turned, he caught her elbow. "Walk with me."

"But—"

"Your parents need time. Alone." He directed her away from the house.

His jaw was set, his thoughts rushing. Memories of gun

stocks through leaded-glass cabinets ... china crunching underfoot ... ax gashes on banisters worn smooth as silk by the hands of generations of Farrels ... He drew in his breath and forced it to release slowly, evenly. "Tell me about your father's holdings." She jerked at his voice, and he realized her thoughts were as haggard as his.

"I don't know. I don't think we have anything but the homestead and the paper."

Her voice sounded small, and he responded instinctively, tucking her hand through the crook of his arm. God, where was the sense of it all? "Then there's no possibility of a new press?"

"Oh, Monte, I don't know. I can't see how. Things are tight ... very tight."

She didn't resist his comfort, and their feud was obviously forgotten. He could be thankful for that. "Well, this is the land of opportunity. There's always a way." He patted her fingers.

Clouds cluttered the sky, masking and unmasking the sun. She was unnaturally quiet as they walked, no chatter, no lessons from her today. He sensed her concern and searched for words. He'd played this role before, set Frances and cousin Darcy off from feeling the helplessness, the fear, the overwhelming loss. But never completely. "Blake's a good man."

She looked up. He had her attention at least. "A hard worker." He earned a faint smile.

"I was concerned for the two of you on the roof together."

"Did you think he might shove me off?"

"Perhaps."

"And would that trouble you?" He cupped her fingers, but she looked away.

They climbed the rise and came among the sheep. A brown-faced lamb bumped Abbie's skirt. Stooping, she stroked the soft head, burying her fingers in the new wool. The lamb nuzzled her face and grew so persistent he forced her to sit. Monte settled beside her and the lamb found his ear.

Abbie smiled as he pushed the animal away. "He likes you."

"He hasn't very good manners."

Losing interest, the lamb bounded away, and Monte stared out over the prairie. "Look at that empty space out there. With people moving west, this could be a great city."

"I hope not. I like it open as far as you can see and the sound of the wild things at night." Her voice caught. Wrapping her knees with her arms, she rested her chin. "I don't think I can bear it if we have to leave."

"Don't even talk that way. Of course you won't leave."

"I love this place. Can you understand that?"

"You asked why my father didn't leave the South, and yet you know his sentiment. Yes, I understand."

"Did you feel that way for your home?"

"I watched the South die. To stay would have been to live in a past that no longer exists. I have yet to find a love for this place, but I believe it holds my destiny."

Abbie lay back in the grass, her chest rising and falling. Monte wondered if she knew how alluring she was, lying there like that, and guessed not. If she even remembered he was there, it was far from her thoughts. And who could blame her? The loss of the press . . . he knew well enough the setback that would be, but until she spoke of leaving . . . Flashes of faces, hard and leering, blue, brass-buttoned chests, Frances's eyes wide with horror . . . Oh yes, he knew what it was to be forced from your home.

His chest burned as he lowered himself beside her and watched the darkening clouds. A single raindrop struck the side of his head and Monte glanced at her. "As much as I hate to say it . . ." He raised her to her feet.

She smiled. "Now it's you reading the weather. You're an apt pupil."

"I've never been dull, especially with an instructor so engaging. Perhaps one day you'll teach me to fish with a spear as well."

"Perhaps..." She tipped her head. "And what would you teach me?"

Monte reached out and raised her chin. "Were you not a child..." he drew her close, "there is much I could teach you." The skin of her cheek warmed to his fingers.

"I'll have to wait, then," she whispered.

"That's most unfortunate."

She stepped back. "Some things are worth waiting for."

Releasing her, Monte laughed. "Yes, indeed, some things are. Shall I wait, then?"

"That's entirely up to you."

Eight

Abbie eyed the half load of shingles left when the house and barn were repaired. Monte had not returned, but Blake had come each of the last four days and worked beside Pa. She toed a bundle beside the barn. "Have you a use for these shingles, Pa?"

He pulled a nail from between his teeth and placed it. "What are you thinking?"

"The mission was hit hard. They're in a bad way."

He hammered the new board to the barn siding. "Take them and welcome."

"Shall I have Blake drive them out?"

"He can manage the wagon."

Blake groaned when she dragged him back to the side of the barn to load the shingles, but he obliged and hitched Shiloh and Sandy. Abbie climbed up beside him.

"The way I figure it," Blake said as he drove over the rough track, "you owe me a bunch for this."

"God loveth a cheerful giver, Blake."

"Well, sure an' all, but . . ."

"Did you hear what Pa told your pa last night?"

"No. Did you?"

"I wouldn't be asking if I had. I don't like how he looked, all bleak and tired. Your pa was almost as bad, so it couldn't have been good news."

"Well . . ."

"I can't figure it. Pa's always one to discuss. He doesn't keep things to himself. Not like some men."

"That's—"

"But now it's like he's all bottled up. He'll answer if you ask, but then nothing. And today he's hardly said a word."

"Maybe he can't get one in."

Abbie shoved Blake's shoulder. "This is a serious matter. I can't stand not knowing what he's thinking."

"I'm sure he's got his reasons."

"And Mama, too. She hasn't scolded in days."

"Count yer blessings."

"You're impossible," Abbie huffed.

Blake shrugged. "Look, Abbie, if they wanted you to know, they'd tell you. If they ain't said nothin', maybe there's nothin' to say."

"But something has to be done. Pa can't make a living without a press. Our homestead is too rough and wooded to ranch for profit. We haven't the grazing for large herds and . . ."

"You're borrowin' trouble."

She sighed. "Maybe I am."

He reached over and patted her knee. "Ain't nothin' we can't figure out together."

He meant it kindly, so she didn't scold. But she had no confidence in his assurance. Things were being decided, and she was intentionally being excluded.

When they arrived, Father Dominic's face lit like Christmas at the bounty of shingles. "The Lord's miracle."

Abbie had never seen his smile so broad nor viewed his long ivory teeth. She almost believed God had multiplied the shingles, there were so many left over. But then, Monte had ordered an abundance.

The other brothers crowded close as Blake opened up the back. As they rolled the sleeves of their robes and helped him

carry the bundles to the wall, Abbie found the children working in the garden.

She groaned. Theirs was as decimated as her own, but they
had no funds to purchase vegetables so were salvaging even the
pieces. Little Tucker Finn lunged for her, and Abbie scooped
him into her arms, then reached for the others. Jeremy and
Emmy and Judith . . . even fourteen-year-old Silas stood close.

"We've brought shingles, Silas. They'll be needing you."

He grinned.

"Have you salvaged much out here?"

Felicity waved her arm. "Some. The wall kept the squash
and pumpkins safe."

"We got some peas." Tucker squeezed her legs.

Jeremy snorted. "They were beans, knucklehead."

Silas connected a knuckle with Jeremy's head. "How's that
for knucklehead?"

"Come now, none of that." Abbie pulled away. "What would
you say to hide-and-seek?" She feared their roar would bring
the brothers running and hushed them, laughing. "Who
should be 'it'?" She never doubted it would be she.

When Blake came for her nearly two hours later, she had
Tucker asleep in her lap and the others gathered together under the tree for her stories. She handed Tucker over to Felicity
and followed Blake back to the wagon. He lifted her in and
they started back. "Thank you, Blake."

"Yup."

"You were busy a long while."

"Yup."

She glanced at him sideways. "What—"

"I had a look at the roof."

Abbie slipped her arm through his. "And?"

"And I'll be out there tomorrow."

"Oh, Blake." She squeezed him.

He scowled. "Shoot, Abbie. It ain't nothin'."

She didn't embarrass him further. Blake had his own brand of devotion to God and to the meek brothers who served Him, though he'd never admit it. She knew it was so, but she would not let on, not to Blake anyway. She had come on him talking to the Lord in the woods one day, and he'd near died of embarrassment. Of course, he'd been thirteen and acting awkward anyway.

Besides, her thoughts were too preoccupied again. The children had provided a needed respite from her worry, but as they closed the distance home, all her trepidation returned. As soon as she went inside, Abbie knew Pa was ready to speak his mind. He sat her at the table and spoke softly, but she couldn't believe what she heard.

"No, Pa!" She gripped the table edge.

"Abbie, there's no other way. Grandpa has a position for me, and it's a good opportunity."

She pushed back her chair and jumped up. "There's opportunity here, Pa! That's what this is, the land of opportunity! That's why you came here in the first place. Can't you remember?"

Pa's hand was gentle on her. "I'm sorry. But we have to go. I'm not a cowboy, nor a man of commerce, nor a smith like Wes McConnel. I craft words, and I have to go where I can do it profitably."

"But what about Denver?"

"Yes, I could possibly get on with another paper there and scratch out a living working for someone else, but Grandpa's offered something better."

Abbie swallowed back the tears. She knew what this was costing him. The lump that had lodged in her throat grew hard. Pressing his hand, she forced a smile. "I know you'll do what's right. You always do."

He nodded, but his eyes were dull.

Abbie ran for the barn and saddled Shiloh. It wasn't fair to ride her hard after the work she'd already done, but she needed to release the ache in her chest before she could hope to tell Clara. She tethered Shiloh in front of the grocer's and rushed in.

Clara jumped up. "Abbie, what on earth—"

Abbie grabbed her hand and pulled her toward the stairs to their living quarters. "I have to talk to you."

Clara opened the door to her room. "I'm so sorry about your pa's press. Have they found who did it?"

Abbie shook her head. "They're sure it was Hollister. But that's not what matters. The worst is . . ." She forced the words out. "We have to go back to Kansas City."

Clara's hands flew to her face. "You can't! How will I ever get by without our chats and the way you make me laugh? What will I do?"

Abbie shook her. "It's not you, Clara. You'll marry Blake McConnel and raise up sons for your pa's business. I'm the one being uprooted. Kansas City! I'll suffocate for lack of mountains, open space, or a wild thing anywhere. I'll end up married to a bank clerk with a balding pate and spectacles and soft white hands." She dropped into the chair.

"Isn't there something you can do? Your pa could take out a loan at the bank and buy a new press."

"Pa won't take on a debt. He's never owed a man anything, and he won't start now."

Clara sat and folded her hands in her lap. Neat, honey-blond waves framed her dejected face. "How long do you suppose before you go?"

"I don't know. Pa will have to sell the homestead and whatever he can salvage from the paper. Maybe a few weeks. I don't know." The tears welled up, but she refused to let them fall.

"Does Blake know?" Clara's voice was hardly above a murmur.

"No." Abbie tossed her bonnet, covered her eyes, and cried.

Clara's arms circled her, and Abbie sniffed. "It's all right." She pushed away. "I just had to let it out. Now I'm done."

"Oh, Abbie." Clara pressed her hands. "We can write each other. You can tell me all the new things. You always wanted to see someplace new."

"Kansas City is not new." Abbie slumped. "I should be more careful what I wish for. I may not like it when it happens."

"Shall we have tea?"

"I couldn't swallow it."

"Oh, my dear. You will be here for your birthday, won't you?"

"August fourth is eight days away. I don't see how we can be gone that soon."

"Then I shall have the most sumptuous birthday party for you and invite all the girls. They'll want a chance to say good-bye, and you'll have presents to remember us by. I know exactly what I'll get you."

"No one can give me what I want. No one can give me this place."

"I wish I could, Abbie. I truly wish I could."

◆◆◆◆◆◆◆

Inside the rough cabin tucked against the overhanging cliff, Buck Hollister crossed his boots up on the table. "Second week with no *Chronicle* from Rocky Bluffs. Not bad fer two-bit black-guards."

"Word is he's gotta move back East now."

Briggs spoke low and Hollister eyed him. He looked more weasel than man, and maybe he was, the way he sniffed out news. He wondered how much Briggs kept to himself. "That'd be mighty fittin'." Hollister struck a match against the table and lit his cigar. "If he ain't got nothin' nice to say, he oughtn't say nothin' at all. Ain't that what you learnt in Sunday school, Conrad?"

"Amen." Conrad padded his soft, pink palms together piously.

"Shoot, Conrad . . ." Hollister laughed.

Briggs tugged out a chair and straddled it. "He's got hisself a right purty daughter."

Hollister sobered. Sometimes Briggs made even his blood run cold.

"Maybe he'd sell 'er and buy hisself a new press." This comment from the kid, Wilkins, tickled the men, and Hollister waited for the laughter to pass.

"Per'aps you oughta go an' ask 'im, Wilkins. Offer 'im a good price."

The kid colored like a girl himself and stammered. "I . . . I ain't offerin' nothin for no wench!"

Briggs bit a plug of tobacco and shoved it in his cheek. "Maybe we oughta have a look at the goods first."

"Aw, I ain't paid fer no goods in two years." Hollister dragged on the cigar. "If Wilkins wants the girl, jest take 'er."

"I ain't said I wanted 'er, so shut yer mouth!"

Hollister's gun flew from the holster to his hand. "Who's gonna make me, kid?"

Wilkins cowered, and Conrad sidled close. "The kid's just joshin', Buck."

Hollister kicked the chair aside and went to the door. Staring out into the night, he smelled the pines. "I'm thinkin' it's time to move on."

"Where to?" Briggs asked.

"Maybe down New Mexico."

"Nothin' but Mexicans there."

Hollister bristled. Briggs was the only one with brains enough to worry him. "You got a better place?"

"There's good pickin's up that Injun pass. Them gold digger's comin' through."

Hollister watched the darkness. Briggs had a point. "I'll think on it tonight."

Nine

The dun hide of Buttercup's flank was soft and warm against Abbie's cheek as she closed her eyes and worked her hands automatically on the udders. "Oh, Buttercup, we'll have to sell you and the sheep and everything...." The cow swung her head back, chewing with unconcern. The soft *fitt, fitt* of the milk in the pail marked off the seconds, each precious to Abbie now that her time here would end. As she urged the last bit of milk from the udder, a shadow filled the open doorway, and she turned to see Blake. His hair was slicked, and he wore clean pants and shirt.

"Mornin', Abbie."

Abbie smiled. "You going courting, Blake?"

"I am." He strode over and raised her to her feet. "I'm courtin' the purtiest girl in the whole territory."

"Now, Blake, I already told you . . ."

"But things are different now. You'll be eighteen tomorrow, and in two months I will, too. In four years I can file for land, and until then we could have the trapper's cabin at the edge of Pa's homestead."

"But, Blake . . ."

"If you marry me now, you won't have to leave. We can stay here or go west if you like. Whatever you want, Abbie."

She searched his face, tanned and freckled, pale blue eyes beneath brows that cut straight across, nose broken by a fall from his horse when he was eight. She knew him better than she knew herself.

Abbie hadn't considered marrying him, yet perhaps it could be as they'd played it in their childhood, she and Blake together. His arms came around her and she didn't resist but blushed as he brought his mouth to hers.

A horse in the yard interrupted them, and Abbie drew away, then peered out to see Monte astride a beautiful sorrel with black socks and mane. She lifted the milk pail. "I have to think about it, Blake. I'll give you my answer tomorrow."

Blake balled his fists at his sides. "That man is worse than a plague of grasshoppers!"

Abbie met Monte as he dismounted. "Monte, he's beautiful!" She ran a hand over the stallion's neck. It was arched and proud, and he held his tail like a plume.

"Good morning, Abbie. Is your father home?"

"No." She sagged. "He went to post a listing for the homestead."

"Ah. Then I'll try to meet him on the road."

"Won't you come in?"

"Not just yet, thank you." Monte pulled himself back into the saddle, tipped his hat, and whirled about. The stallion high-stepped, then dug in its hooves and broke into a canter. The yard felt empty as the dust settled behind him.

Abbie dragged inside and set the pail on the table. The skimming bowls were set out, and she poured the warm milk, then rinsed the pail at the pump. "Mama?"

Her mother came in from the lean-to.

"Blake asked me to marry him." Mama's cool fingers lifted her chin, and Abbie felt her scrutiny all the way inside her.

"Is that what you want?"

"I don't know. I want to stay, and Blake is . . . Blake. He's always been there, but . . ." Abbie searched for the words. "I don't know if I love him. I mean, of course I love him, but I don't know if it's the way he loves me. Wouldn't it be wrong to marry him if I don't know I love him?"

"Sometimes that comes later. Sometimes the feelings follow the promise. But you're both so young. . . . What did you tell him?"

"That I'd answer tomorrow."

"Then we'll pray today. When you give your answer tomorrow, there must be no second thoughts. If you tell Blake yes, it's a forever yes."

"I know that, Mama." Abbie's voice quavered. Unexpectedly she remembered Monte, close as he'd been that day on the hill, and her whole being trembled. But that was foolishness. She was nothing more than a child to him. He had said so himself.

She tied up her hair and pulled on her old skirt, then dropped to her knees on the kitchen floor and took up a brush. Sinking it deep into the sudsy water, she applied it vigorously to the floor. Her thoughts swept back and forth like the brush. Could she marry Blake? Marry Blake? Why not? Why? *Swoosh, swoosh, swoosh*, the brush whispered until her shoulders ached and her knees were soaked and weary.

◆◆◆◆◆◆◆

Halfway to town, Monte met Joshua on his way home and raised a hand in greeting. He swung about beside him and ordered his thoughts. Seeing Abbie so shortly before did not aid him in that. But nothing would be gained by jumping in too rashly. Joshua was a keen man and had not made his decision lightly.

"Fine day," Joshua said.

"Yes." Monte matched his horse's pace to Joshua's. "Aren't too many places you can find this kind of clemency with just enough weather to make it interesting."

"You're right there. I admit I'm going to miss it. Just about broke my heart telling Abbie. You know how she feels about this place. But you've got to be practical even in the realm of thought and journalism. Without a press, I can't be much of a newspaperman."

Monte surveyed him. Joshua appeared to have made peace with his decision. He would follow it through if Monte failed to sway him. "As a matter of fact, that's why I was looking for you, Joshua."

"Oh?"

"I've been thinking what a sore loss it'll be for this town without a newspaper. And a good newspaper needs a good editor. I can't think we'll find anyone to compare with you."

"Well, that's kind of you to say, but it can't be helped." Joshua fiddled with his reins, betraying his consternation more than his words had yet.

"I think maybe it can." Monte cocked his head. "I have in mind a business proposition."

"What sort of proposition?"

"A partnership. I'm taking a personal interest in seeing that Rocky Bluffs doesn't lose the best newspaperman west of the Mississippi, and I'm willing to make it worth your while."

"In what way?"

"I supply the equipment and you provide the expertise until such time as you can or desire to buy me out."

"That's a mighty attractive offer." Joshua veered down the gully and back up. "What makes you think it's worth your investment?"

"I told you, I appreciate your abilities. Where I come from, a man who can put into words what others want to think, or ought to think, is more highly respected than many others. You showed great courage in telling us what Hollister is made of and, in a way, cemented public opinion. Otherwise, it'd be too easy for a man like that to become a hero."

"Not if I can help it."

"We need that sort of conscience out here, and men of your wit and wisdom."

"That all?"

Monte raised an eyebrow. "I admit I take perhaps a slightly more personal interest in retaining you ... and your family."

"Aha! I imagine my journalism wouldn't be so sorely missed as my beautiful, blue-eyed daughter, eh?"

"Perhaps on a more equilateral basis."

Joshua laughed. "Well, Monte, you've given me food for thought. I sure would like to stay if it were possible."

"I've spent the last two weeks adjusting my accounts so that the purchase can be made immediately should you accept."

Suddenly, Joshua smacked his thigh. "By golly, of course I accept! I can't think of a partner I'd rather have." He reached across the gap between their horses, and Monte shook his hand. "What do you say we turn back to town and write us up a contract? I've a mind to cancel my sales notice!"

"Sounds first-rate to me." The satisfaction surprised him and went to his head. Monte wheeled his thoroughbred around and kicked in his heels. Joshua bolted after him, hooted a great 'yahoo,' and spanked the horse's rump with his hat.

◆◆◆◆◆◆◆

Abbie took the horses' reins as Pa and Monte dismounted. "I'll get them watered. Go ahead and wash for lunch." She was glad she had mentioned Monte's looking for Pa. Mama had counted on them returning together. She led Pa's Sandy and Monte's fine stallion to the water together and waited while they drank, then led them to the shade and tethered them.

When she went in, Monte held her chair for her to sit. His face was inscrutable, and whatever business had brought him seemed to have been inconsequential. She bowed her head. Pa offered the blessing with such enthusiasm that she glanced from him to Monte. When he had finished, Pa turned to her.

"You still hoping to stay here?"

Had Blake spoken with him? Was he giving his blessing here and now, feeling a load lifted from him? Her heart sank. "Of course I am, Pa."

"Then I guess we will."

Pa's eyes were laughing, and she turned to stare at Mama, who looked as surprised as she.

"I'd like to introduce my new partner in the newspaper business." Pa waved his hand toward Monte. "We'll be sending for a new press by the end of the week, and by fall we'll be printing our premier issue."

"Pa!" Abbie jumped to her feet and threw her arms about his neck, then turned to Monte and caught herself before doing likewise. "This is wonderful! This is ... I must go tell Clara!"

"We have a guest, Abbie," Mama scolded.

Monte smiled. "That's all right. Abbie would burst if she had to hold it in while we discuss details."

Grabbing her hat, she flew from the room. She heard her mother's sigh like a familiar farewell and covered the ground to the barn in a flash. She heaved the saddle over Shiloh's back, cinched and tightened it, slid the bridle between the mare's teeth, and tossed the reins over her head, then mounted. Throwing her skirts behind her, Abbie dug in her heels.

She didn't bother to smooth her hair before bursting into the store and grabbing Clara by the arms. "We're staying!"

Clara embraced her tightly, laughing and crying at once. "That's the best news! The girls will all be so glad!"

"Except Marcy Wilson." Abbie laughed. "Won't she be green when she hears it was Monte who made it possible for us to stay?"

"Monte? You must tell!"

"And I will." Abbie hooked her arm through Clara's. "Come

somewhere we can talk." They rushed up the stairs to Clara's room.

"Monte and Pa are partners."

"Partners how?"

Abbie opened her mouth and stopped. "I guess I didn't wait to hear that part. I just know that they're going to be partners at the paper, and because of that we're staying. And now I won't have to answer Blake, either."

"Answer Blake?"

Abbie choked. She hadn't meant to tell Clara about Blake's proposal unless she chose to accept it. When would she ever learn to hold her tongue? "Blake asked me to marry him." She took Clara's hands. "I'm sure it was that he knew how much I wanted to stay."

"That's all right, Abbie. I know Blake loves you."

"He doesn't really. He just hasn't looked at it practically. We'd be like two wolves at each other's throats. We're really too much alike."

"What will you tell him?"

Abbie shrugged. "That we've plenty of time."

Ten

Like a promise, the sun crested the ridge, igniting the blush of morning sky. Abbie could only remember one year it had stormed on her birthday. The sunshine was God's gift to her. She rose and dressed and went out. Dew jeweled the grass, and the chickadees chirped from Mama's apple tree. She headed for the pump with a towel and bayberry shampoo. Blake was there waiting.

"Can't a girl even wash before callers arrive?"

"I was up most o' the night. Took all my willpower to wait this long."

A lump formed in Abbie's throat. Why did he persist in these feelings for her? "Blake, I have some news for you."

"I know you do. And I surely hope it's the news I want to hear."

She hung the towel on the hook and set down the soap. "Pa's decided to stay."

"What?"

"Isn't it wonderful? We don't have to go! Monte and Pa are going to be partners, and they're getting a new press and starting over."

Blake frowned. "And what about us gettin' married an' all?"

"We don't have to rush into anything." She touched his arm. "It was gallant of you to ask, though."

"It wasn't gallant, and I ain't play actin'. I want to marry you. I love you somethin' awful, and whether yer pa leaves or stays makes no difference to me." His hands clenched at his sides.

She felt an ache in her chest. "I'm sorry, Blake."

"Hang that Montgomery Farrel anyway!" Blake kicked a clod as he stormed off.

Abbie closed her eyes. It was the right thing, but telling herself that didn't make it better. She hated to hurt him. Rubbing the soap into her palm, she hung her hair beneath the pump and lathered. When she finished washing, she went inside.

Mama caught her chin and raised her face. "Why so crestfallen? Surely a birthday girl must feel more cheerful than that."

"I talked to Blake. He's awfully upset."

"You told him no?"

Abbie nodded. "I'm not ready to be married, and now that we're not leaving..." Tears came to her eyes. "I surely never meant for him to care that way. I swear I never led him on."

"Sometimes it just happens."

"He blames Monte."

"Monte! Why on earth?"

Abbie shrugged. "I guess for making it possible for us to stay."

"I hope he shows better sense than he did the last time."

"He gave his word not to bother him again."

◆◆◆◆◆◆◆

The mirror reflected her glowing expression as Abbie viewed herself dressed and primped for her party. For once her riotous curls were contained, and her toilette satisfied even Mama's scrutiny. She pushed thoughts of Blake's disappointment out of her head. She would make it up to him somehow.

Pa lifted her into the buggy and drove her to the town hall, where she jumped down amid the girls who gathered around. "I'm so glad you're staying, Abbie." "Clara couldn't wait to tell us." "Happy birthday, Abbie!"

Ushered to the hall, Abbie gasped to see the room decorated with flowers and paper streamers. All the chairs were arranged against the walls. Clara clasped her arm. "So we have room for the games." She winked at Becky Linde. What was she up to? Abbie searched the excited faces as she was tugged in beside the two tables of dainties and finger foods.

"We all made them," MaryBeth Walker told her.

"You must be expecting an army."

"More like the cavalry . . ." Becky Linde giggled and Clara pinched her.

Abbie turned as Marcy Wilson came in the door. Leave it to her to arrive after the guest of honor. Fashionably late, she'd call it. "It's amazing she doesn't get a crick in her neck," Abbie whispered to Clara. "One day her nose'll stick up there, and she won't see where she's going."

"Shame, Abbie. Not on your birthday," Clara scolded. "Don't let a single thought ruin it for you."

"I'm sorry. That was uncharitable after all you've done. Of course you had to invite her, and I'll do my very best to appreciate even Marcy tonight."

Clara clapped her hands and announced Blind Man's Bluff, and Madeline Foley covered Abbie's eyes so she couldn't see. The girls spun her until she staggered and she heard them scatter, stifling their giggles. It seemed an awful lot of shuffling, and try as she could, she didn't touch a one of them. They must have spread to the very edges of the room, and there was a draft from the door. Were they leaving the room? Was this a practical joke? Clara wouldn't do that.

But what was that? It sounded . . . it was. The fiddle bow on the strings. Abbie pulled the blindfold from her eyes. "Surprise!" The crowd had swollen, not only with the girls, but the young men as well.

"Clara, what ..."

"Ma and Mrs. Munson are chaperones, and Mr. Peterson's here to keep the boys in line. Everyone wanted a chance to say good-bye, so it was the best I could do."

"I don't believe this," she said as the fiddle started to sing. "Most of these people don't even like me."

"Oh, Abbie." Clara laughed.

Marty Franklin and his brother Burt bowed to them, elbowing each other. With a smile, Clara took Marty's hand, and Burt swept Abbie onto the floor. He was clumsy, but he meant well. Over her shoulder, she saw Mack and Davy McConnel, but not Blake. She guessed he didn't feel like celebrating, but she hardly had time to think about it. Burt surrendered her to Phil Mayes for the next dance, and he in turn to Will Stoddard.

Laughing as Will spun her to the closing chord of the quadrille, she found Monte at her side. She had seen him enter, but as a moth to a flame, Marcy had fluttered to him ... then clung like a leech. He bowed. "May I have the honor before someone else commandeers you?"

Abbie laid her hand on his warm, firm palm. "It's that the girls are so outnumbered."

"I doubt very much that's it at all." He led her out to the center and placed a hand on her waist. "I took the liberty of providing the score for this dance."

"Oh?"

"It's a waltz that is quite fashionable abroad." He drawled "abroad" and smiled.

Around them the dancers paused as the fiddlers took up the three-four beat. Monte led her through the step until she was comfortable, while the others watched and then followed. "You have it?"

"I think so."

"Then follow me." He swept her in glorious circles, his motions smooth and graceful, but strong enough to guide her without error. "What do you think?"

She knew he could see her delight. "I hope it never ends."

"Would that were in my power."

"It feels wonderful to spin and step this way. Where did you learn it?"

"Vienna."

"Oh, Monte, you've seen the whole world!"

"Not quite." He smiled. "There's enough left to show you."

Abbie could not tell by his tone if he was teasing. She knew well enough how his tongue would slide as easily over a barb as a compliment, but he looked sincere.

"I'd be happy to see even a little piece now that you vouchsafed our staying. I'm so indebted to you."

"It was strictly selfish, I assure you. How else will I learn to track and fish and . . . climb trees," he whispered wickedly.

Abbie pulled back. "Don't you dare breathe a word of that!"

He laughed as they passed through the opposite couple, then joined hands again. "Surely you don't think I'd reveal your wild ways to all these fine ladies, do you?"

"That would be the end of me if Marcy Wilson got wind of it. Mama would send me off at the first opportunity."

"Then I'll guard your secret with my life."

His hand on the small of her back sent shivers up her spine. They faced a new couple, and he released her to be turned once by the alternate gentleman, then rested his hand beneath hers as they turned in a right-hand star, then a left. That part was familiar. She knew it from the Spanish waltz and others.

Then Monte's fingers were again on her back and clasping hers at her shoulder. He moved her with such skill she hardly felt the effort. The fiddlers stopped playing, and he bowed over her hand so closely that his breath and perhaps his lips warmed her skin. Abbie stood perfectly still as he surrendered her to Milton Fiske. She felt transformed.

Milton asked her something, but she didn't hear. She didn't even care that Marcy rolled her eyes and slandered her to Nora Thorne. Scarcely noticing, she curtsied to Milton and caught sight of Blake in the doorway, searching the crowd.

"Excuse me, Milton, I . . . excuse me." She pressed her way through. "Oh, Blake, I'm so glad you've come! I thought . . ."

Grabbing her hands, he pulled her outside the door. "I've come to say good-bye, Abbie."

Her chest convulsed. "Good-bye?"

"I'm leavin' with Mack in the mornin'. We're headin' to the mountains fer gold. Up Gilpin County. I know there's more to be found and I mean to find it."

Abbie fought for words. "You can't be serious!"

"I am serious, Abbie. And maybe I'll come back rich enough to buy you a fine, fancy house and all the things Montgomery Farrel would give you."

Abbie's hands fell to her sides as a hard knot gripped her stomach. "You think that's what I want?" Tears stung her eyes.

Blake faltered. "I know what you're tellin' me, Abbie. I just don't know what to do with it. Maybe when I come back you'll feel different, an' that's my hope. But either way I gotta go."

The tears slid over her lids. She felt as if a part of her were being torn away, and Blake wrapped her in his arms.

"Don't cry, Abbie."

"Oh, Blake . . ." She couldn't tell him to stay because she could promise him nothing. Why did things have to change for them? Why couldn't they still be friends? Pressing her face to his chest, she cried, and Blake held her without speaking. At last she looked up, and he kissed her tenderly.

"Good-bye, Abbie. I sure do love you."

Through the tears she watched him walk away. The wild thought of running after him and accepting his proposal filled her, and her feet almost obeyed, but it wasn't right. Maybe one day it would be different, but for now her love was not what he wanted it to be.

She heard a step behind her and knew without turning that it was Monte.

"What is it, Abbie?"

"Blake's going prospecting. He's leaving because I wouldn't marry him."

Monte turned her. "If you don't want him to go, why don't you tell him to stay?"

"Because I can't promise what I don't have to give him. I can't marry him if I don't love him." She turned away. "But I feel so wretchedly awful."

"Blake's his own man. You're not responsible for his decisions. Maybe you just helped him with his timing."

She closed her eyes.

"Abbie." He raised her chin and made her look at him. "You're eighteen years old tonight, and there's a whole roomful of people here to honor you. Come in and dance."

"I can't."

"Yes, you can. In a small way it's doing what you must, even if your heart's not in it. It's honor, Abbie."

Drawing a deep breath, she wiped the tears from her eyes.

"That's better. And since I found you, I'll claim this dance. Then you'll be all over your sniffles with no one the wiser."

"I'm not as good at conquering jungles as you thought."

"Perhaps I don't mind playing the hero on occasion."

He led her in on his arm. Marcy was hovering near, probably waiting for him to reappear, and her expression soured. Abbie wondered what she had overheard, but Monte winked and led her to the floor. By the time their dance ended, she had contained her tears, though the ache in her heart remained. A quick search showed her that Mack McConnel had gone as well, and she sighed.

"Chin up, now," Monte breathed in her ear, then left her to Clara. The chaperones were clearing the floor, and Mrs. Simms had the girls cleaning up the tables.

"Let's slip away," Clara said, taking her hand. They crossed the street to the store and hurried up the stairs. Inside her room, Clara closed the door behind them and went to her wardrobe. She pulled a small box tied in ribbon from the drawer.

Abbie took it and sat on the edge of the bed. Pulling the ribbon free, she opened the box and lifted out a necklace of small blue beads. Clara dropped down before her. "It's made by Indians, Abbie."

Abbie stared at her. "How did you get it?"

"You remember Mag French and his awful son Travis? Last time they were through, Travis had a whole string of these, and I remembered that he sold several to Mrs. Linde. She wanted to send them to her nieces in Boston. She had only this one left, and I convinced her to sell it to me for you." Clara smiled triumphantly.

Abbie looked at the beads and tried to imagine the Indian woman stringing them. Perhaps she had a papoose on her back and feathers woven through her hair. "You don't know how much this means to me. Thank you."

"Now let's get changed for bed."

They undressed and climbed into the covers side by side. Clara turned down the wick of the lamp and rolled to her side. "All right, out with it," she whispered.

"Out with what?"

"Whatever it is that made you cry tonight. I know you too well to be fooled by that smile you pasted on when you came back in with Monte. What happened? Did he—"

"It's not Monte." Abbie bit her lip. "Blake's leaving."

"Leaving?"

"He's going to the mountains to hunt for gold with Mack."

Clara was silent.

"I'm so sorry, Clara."

The words seemed flimsy. As she slipped into the cusp of sleep, Abbie felt Clara's shoulders shake and heard the quiet tears. She couldn't remember feeling so empty.

Eleven

Monte sat his horse as well as any man out there, but he was less sure what to do with a herd of cattle, especially these bony-looking, long-horned brutes that moved sprightlier than any cattle he'd ever seen. He'd opted for the Texas breed after learning their suitability to the Colorado pasture, but these looked more like something fit for the wild.

Well, he had hired the men to deliver the four hundred head of cows and heifers, and this they'd done and were well paid for the job. Now it was up to him. He watched the cowboys circle the herd, whistling and shouting, keeping them moving, keeping them contained. He would need more men than he currently had.

Riding up beside him, Cole Jasper tipped his hat. "Well, Mr. Farrel, here's yer herd and they're a fine bunch. You'll want to get them branded right away, 'fore any rustler gits an eyeful."

"They look a little rangy."

"If you mean they're long-horned and long-legged, you're right. That's the Texas cow. But you'll find they're good feeders. They're quick and produce a hardy calf. You get yerself a couple Durham bulls and give 'em run o' the ladies a few years, you'll develop a superior breed in no time."

"Thank you, Cole. Your men have done a good job."

"Guess we'll be movin' on then."

"Before you go, you wouldn't know any good hands looking for a position, would you?"

"Who's yer foreman?" Cole cocked his hat back and wiped the grime from his face with the back of his arm.

"Well, it seems I am."

"Nope. Don't know any cowboy worth his salt's gonna work for a tenderfoot who ain't got a foreman. No offense."

Monte considered the man's insight. He'd watched the way Cole handled the men, obviously well respected yet not taking any guff when it came time to work. Sizing up the man, he guessed him to be early or mid-thirties, though the sun and air had leathered his skin. Ruggedly handsome, tough and wiry, he looked as though he'd been born on a horse at the backside of a herd, and Monte liked his honesty. "How would you like the job of foreman yourself?"

"I ain't lookin' fer a change."

"What are you paid now?"

"Well, I ain't a foreman, just a trail boss. I git eight dollars a week."

"I'll make it sixteen. I have a good bunkhouse, a handful of men, and you can hire as many more as you need. The only condition is you teach me what you know."

Now it was Cole Jasper who scrutinized him. "You won't git in the way?"

"Not until I know as much as you do." Monte smiled.

Cole grinned back. "That'll be the day. All right, Mr. Farrel, I'll take it." Monte held out his hand, and Cole shook it firmly. He wheeled his horse around. "Hey, you lame-dog, good-fer-nothin' scoundrels! Anyone wanna stay and work for Tenderfoot here? You'll be answerin' to me."

Several of the men looked at each other and there were a few unsavory comments, but, surprisingly, not a one rejected the offer. Cole was indeed the man he needed. Monte turned Sirocco back to the house.

The branding proved his shrewdness in acquiring Cole Jasper. Monte watched the men rope the new cattle from horseback, then leap down, yank the animal to its back, and immobilize the thrashing legs. The acrid reek of burnt hair merged with the smell of the herd as the hot iron was applied. Then the steer or heifer was released, sporting the half moon bar over the star that showed the animal belonged to his Lucky Star Ranch. With jovial if disrespectful amusement, Cole showed Monte how to use the rope and how to throw it, but he wouldn't allow him near the herd while the men were working. "We got a job to do, Mr. Farrel."

Monte suspected Cole was testing the waters, keeping him to his pledge of noninterference. He held his tongue and returned to the house. After sliding the rope from the saddle, he weighed it out in his hand, opened the loop, then gripped and spun it over his head. Shooting his arm forward, he aimed for the fence post. The rope fell useless at his feet, snagged by his shoulder. He kicked it and left it lying.

Cole could work the ranch and report to him at the end of the day. He strode forward, worked the pump lever, and splashed in the cold water, colder still in the chilly air, then smoothed back his hair and straightened. Maybe he'd go see Abbie. Nothing would cheer him more, nor so effectively take his mind off the cattle business. He looked in the direction of her homestead.

He hadn't seen her since her birthday three weeks ago when they'd danced. That had been a night of revelation. She was no longer Joshua Martin's pretty daughter. She was important to him in her own right. He shook the water from his hands. Two things about that concerned him greatly.

One, Abbie seemed set on delaying her maturity and was not the least interested in being romantically courted, and two, her tears at Blake McConnel's departure had revealed a far deeper attachment than he had believed present. If she cared so deeply for Blake, it wasn't prudent to pursue a relationship. She needed time to sort out her feelings. Practically, it was easy enough to meet with Joshua at the newspaper office. Personally, it took all his strength of will not to ride over to see her.

He entered the house and went to his study. The ledger lay open on his desk, and he looked over the start-up expenses. Four hundred cows and heifers at ten dollars each. That was an outlay of four thousand dollars already. But he'd taken Cole's advice and sent for a pair of prime Durham bulls, five hundred dollars each, and on his own initiative scouted a herd of Shorthorn. He'd buy fifty Shorthorn cows next year and put some beef on his breed. He might not be able to rope a steer yet, but when it came to business, he knew how to turn a profit.

◆◆◆◆◆◆◆

Abbie walked the mare up through the scrub oak turning from green to multihued reds and oranges, clothing the feet of the mountains in color. Above, bright flashes of yellow displayed the aspens' glory, sharply contrasting with the rich dark hue of the evergreens. Of all the seasons, she loved autumn best and breathed deeply the cool September air.

These last weeks had been solitary. Clara was hurt and angry about Blake's leaving, and Abbie had spoken truly that most of the girls from town were not close acquaintances. She and Blake had schooled at the mission, and she was never one for many friends if she had one or two dear. Without Blake, she was left to herself. This, too, she wouldn't have minded, except that she didn't know herself anymore. Too many feelings conflicted.

Again Blake's absence ached inside her as she turned the mare's head up the mountain. Did the land miss him as she did? No. It was nothing but stone, and yet there was an echo of all the times they'd spent here. Only God knew where he was now. She wondered for the hundredth time if she'd done the right thing. She tried to imagine herself setting up a home for Blake. Maybe it would be in a tent in a mining camp somewhere far away. She saw him coming in the flap, taking her in his arms . . .

She shook her head and kicked in her heels, and the horse bounded up the steep incline over the trackless ground. The trees thickened, oak and pine and spruce, and she strained to see the summit of this first ridge. Arching her head back, she murmured, " 'I will lift up mine eyes unto the hills, from whence cometh my help.' "

The woods were silent but for the soft thud of a cone striking the brown, brittle carpet of needles. Had even God tired of her?

Monte and Pa had printed the first edition of the new expanded *Chronicle*, adding a literary column reviewing the best and newest works, a fashion column written by Marcy's mother, Judge Wilson's wife, and a weekly contest. Pa and Monte were pleased with the enterprise, at least according to Pa. She hadn't seen Monte since her birthday. Abbie frowned, skirting a towering moss-covered boulder.

In the pocket of her skirt, the pistol banged her thigh. Since the fires south of them had driven hunting parties of Comanche and Jicarilla Apache into the area—two historically antagonistic tribes—Pa insisted she carry it. She knew how to shoot. He'd taught her when she was twelve. She touched the weapon concealed in her skirt but was not concerned. The Indians had been peaceful and kept their distance. Sightings, but no incidents, were reported.

Abbie had seen none. As though in answer to her thought, from around the rocky projection through the trees came a Comanche brave astride a paint mustang, followed by four more.

Abbie pulled up her mare and sat perfectly still. The stern, black-haired men scrutinized her, and she in turn, them; their buckskin leggings and bare chests, their hair braided with fur strips and feathers, and on their backs the long slender bows and quivers. They looked magnificent. There was something so wild yet indescribably noble in their bearing.

She wondered if she should be frightened, but wasn't. Perhaps her admiration showed, because after a long moment the leader lifted his arm in salute to her, and she smiled in return. Just as swiftly, they turned and vanished back into the shadows, and Abbie released a thrilled breath.

She wished they had spoken. Not that they would have understood each other's words, but she longed to have communicated something. Perhaps she had. Like her, they were part of this place, and perhaps the love of the land had connected them. The look in the brave's eyes as he saluted her had been one of respect. She descended the slope cautiously until she was free of the trees, then gave Shiloh her head and cantered toward town.

She burst into the store. "I have to talk to you, Clara."

Clara hurried behind. "What is it? You look like you've seen a ghost."

"Do I?" Abbie laughed. "No, but I did see a hunting party of Comanche as close as that door."

Clara's eyes widened. "Tell me!"

"I was riding in the hills and had just gotten to the edge of the trees when they came out of the shadows, not making a sound. Five of them, all dressed in feathers and buckskin, and we all stopped and looked at each other—"

"You mean they saw you, too!"

"Yes, and then the leader raised his arm like this and saluted me, and then they were gone. It's the most exciting thing that's ever happened to me!"

"Abbie!" Clara dropped to the chair. "You could have been

killed or worse—captured and carried off!"

"Nonsense! They were no more interested in harming me than I was them."

Clara shook her head, then turned away.

"Are you angry with me, Clara?"

"Why would I be angry?"

"Because of Blake."

Her shoulders sagged. "It's just . . . we're so different. It's no wonder Blake could never see me. You're . . . it's like being a very dim star next to the moon."

"No, Clara . . ."

"I know it's not your fault. It just hurts so much that he thought there was no one else worth staying for."

"Maybe it'll be different when he comes back."

"If he comes back."

"He will. I know he will. Blake is as much a part of this place as I am. He just needs to work out the trouble, and then he'll be back."

"I don't know."

"Oh, Clara, I've questioned myself over and over. What could I have done differently? How could I have kept him from leaving? But in the end, Monte was right. Blake alone is responsible for his decision."

Clara walked to the window. "Have you seen him lately?"

"Who?"

"Monte."

"No. Pa says he got in a herd."

"Judge Wilson's had him out to supper twice this last month. I know it's Marcy's doing. I saw them out on the porch together last evening, and she fairly hung on his arm."

Abbie was surprised how that rankled. "If Monte's foolish enough to fall for her, he deserves her."

"Her father is a judge."

"So what. Monte's hardly a fortune hunter. Not that

Marcy's any great treasure. Oh, that was unkind. You would never have said that."

"I might have thought it." Clara suddenly laughed. "Oh, Abbie, I've missed you. I'm terribly glad those Indians didn't steal you away."

Abbie hugged her. "I have to run. Mama will be looking for me."

"Come again soon."

"I will." Rushing outside, she nearly collided with Monte.

"Why, Abbie, what a pleasant surprise." He removed his hat.

"Is it?"

"Indeed."

"I suppose you've been busy."

"I've been converting my ranch into the real thing and trying to learn how to run it. There's more to being a gentleman rancher than at first appears."

"I imagine there is. Lucky for you Marcy Wilson can provide a distraction from your labor."

Monte's eyebrow raised. "Why, Abbie, I believe you're jealous."

"What a ridiculous notion." She pushed past him and loosened the reins from the post.

"Won't you stay and have supper with me? At the hotel?"

"I'm sorry, Monte, but I prefer my invitations premeditated."

He stared. "Are you turning me down?"

Abbie sweetened her smile. "I need to get home. Mama will worry, and it'll be well nigh dark before I return as it is."

"And you shouldn't be out alone at all. There are reports of Comanche in the area."

"Yes, I met them earlier." Abbie tucked her foot in the stirrup.

"Met them?"

"I saw them in the woods when I was riding. That's what I came to tell Clara."

Monte frowned. "Well, thank God they didn't see you."

"Oh, but they did. Actually they saluted me. I think we understood each other." She pulled herself up.

He grasped the reins. "You wait for me, Abbie. I'm going to escort you home."

Abbie laughed. "What's the matter? Do you think I'm going to run off and live in a tepee?"

"I think you have far less sense than I suspected."

"Well, thank you anyway, but I'm perfectly capable of seeing myself home. Doubtless the Comanche would not have saluted me at all if he'd seen your sour face beside me."

She tugged, but he refused to release the reins. "I'm asking you to wait for me to get my horse."

"Oh, all right."

Monte let go and returned in a moment on the black-socked sorrel.

"You'll miss your supper in town, but maybe Mama will ask you to stay."

"Acquiring supper's not my purpose."

"Then what is your purpose?" Abbie clicked her tongue, and Shiloh stepped out.

"To inform your father of your experience and suggest he not allow you to ride alone until these Indians have left the area."

Abbie pulled up sharply. "You wouldn't!"

"Oh yes, I would. You have no idea of the danger you placed yourself in."

"I was in no danger at all! And I had my pistol if there had been trouble. But they were as noble and honorable as you." She urged Shiloh ahead. "Monte, if you tell Pa not to let me out, I'll never forgive you."

"If I don't say anything, will you promise not to go up into the woods until we know they're gone?"

She considered his offer. "Well, I won't go into the woods."

"Abbie, I mean stay away from any place the Comanche might be. A successful hunt just might include you, too, and you might not think them so wonderful if you have to share a tent with one. I'm sorry if that offends your sensibilities, but you have no idea what that salute meant. It could just as easily have been marking you. Is it possible you don't know what the Comanche do to female captives? How they are tortured and disfigured?"

"I've heard. I'm not a child you need to scold."

"No doubt they noticed that, too. And when they'd made sure you'd never be fit for white society again, they'd no doubt have their way with you."

The idea of being wife to one of those men was not as exciting as simply seeing them in the woods. But Abbie was sure that had not been their intent. Something unspoken but true had passed between them, something Monte didn't understand.

"I think you're wrong, but I'll stay away from the hunting ground. Only don't tell Mama or she'll never let me out again." Digging in her heels, she called, "I'll race you to the bluffs!"

Monte overtook and passed her, the long, smooth strides of his thoroughbred cutting through the prairie. Abbie lay down close to Shiloh's neck and urged her to more speed, shortening the gap but not catching him. Drawing near the bluff, he slowed and brought the horse around. "Better luck next time." Monte smiled. "But you should choose your races more wisely."

Shiloh choked and dropped her head. Abbie knew how she felt. The stallion held his neck arched and back-stepped in Monte's hold, submitting to his master, but only just. She thrilled at the sight and wondered if Monte would ever consent to her riding him.

"I've never seen such a horse! If you raced him he'd be unbeatable!"

Monte dismounted and rubbed the stallion's neck. "He is unbeatable. His sire, Rahjim, was one of the finest."

Abbie slipped down beside him. "What's this one called?"

"Sirocco. He comes from the desert where the siroccos blow hot across the sand."

She stroked the bony head and muzzle. The horse seemed barely contained, as though wild dreams of hot desert nights burned in him still. Solid, sweet-tempered Shiloh had no chance against him. Abbie looked past his head to Monte. "Why haven't you been out to see us?"

"Have I been missed?"

"Of course. Pa enjoys your company, as he has so few well-read friends, and Mama, too."

"And?" The corners of his mouth twitched.

"Well, the chickens haven't really made your acquaintance, nor Buttercup, either, but the little lamb you met on the hill has been bleating dreadfully." Abbie swiped a spiral of hair from her face.

Monte stopped and grabbed her hands. "Are you ever going to grow up, Abbie?"

She smiled impishly. "I suppose it'll happen one day."

His voice grew husky. "Did you miss me?"

"Yes," she whispered.

Monte straightened. "Dusk is drawing on. We'd better go."

Twelve

It felt like the walls were closing in, and the silence, usually welcome, only made her want the breeze and birdsong of the mountainside. Abbie chafed. Why had she promised not to ride? Monte did not understand. He didn't see the Indian affairs as she and Pa did. He was mistaken about her danger; she knew he was. But she had given her word.

She went outside and headed for the line where the clean sheets puffed like roosters' breasts. They smelled of sage and wood smoke. Working quickly, she folded them into the basket, then, while she was near, she gathered the chickens into the pen and locked the door.

Back inside, she peeked into the oven at the sweet rolls, her peace offering for worrying Mama last night. Even Pa was on edge when she'd returned late, though he appreciated Monte's escort. And Monte hadn't breathed a word. In a few days she would be out again, with Mama none the wiser.

The rolls were rising nicely but hadn't begun to brown. She grabbed a shawl and made her way to the slope where the sheep carelessly uprooted the grasses, an irritation to the cattlemen whose herds had the sense to bite the grass off and leave the roots. But she liked the gentle animals even if they were dull-witted, and she called to them as she climbed through the fence for the shortcut. The sheep recognized her voice and pressed against her legs. She pulled open the gate and led them through. Ever since their old dog Rip had died, they'd had to lock them up in the barn for the night or the coyotes would have their way.

They pressed together in the enclosure, and she secured the gate. Pa had the team, so she filled Buttercup's box with fodder and went out. She froze at the door. Five Comanche braves stood directly before her on their mustangs. Monte's words flashed to her mind. Had they marked her for capture? Across the backs of the spare horses were deer and antelope, as well as braces of rabbits, some skinned and some not. They seemed out of place here in her yard, and not at all as they had appeared in the woods, somehow larger, more menacing.

They were nearly motionless, but suddenly the paint tossed its head. Without thinking, she reached up and stroked it, and a curious expression passed over the face of the leader. After a moment, he reached down, untied a brace of skinned rabbits, and handed them to her. Abbie received them. "Thank you." And then with a sudden thought, she added, "Wait," and hurried into the house.

Pulling the hot rolls from the oven, she wrapped a good portion of them in paper, then went back out and handed them up to the brave. He smelled the paper, then nodded and handed the package to the other braves to smell also. The last slipped it into a pouch. They never spoke but wheeled their horses and rode away. Why had they come? Had they been looking for her? Had they felt that same oneness she had experienced yesterday?

In the kitchen she washed the rabbits and prepared them to roast. Mama would have convulsions when she learned she had received them from an Indian right here on the homestead, but Abbie would not disdain his gift. She seasoned them with thyme from the garden and basted them with a little melted butter, then tucked them into the oven to bake. Mixing up a corn bread batter, she poured it into a heavy iron skillet smeared with bacon fat and placed it beside the rabbits. That finished, she wiped the counter and washed out the cloth, then dried her hands on her apron and untied it.

She curled up in the window seat with a book, and soon the aroma from the oven filled the house. What did their gift mean? Had they counted her as one of their own, not a stranger or a threat, nor a usurper? She wanted to believe that. She hoped Monte was wrong and that the government reservations would soon be unnecessary. But she'd heard talk and knew that in one thing he was right. People did not forget the horrors, of which there had been plenty, and as long as fear drove their decisions, there would be no joining of worlds. She jumped up when Pa pulled open the door.

"Why, Abbie," Mama said. "What's that cooking?"

"Come and see."

"Rabbit? Where did you get rabbit?"

"They were a gift." Abbie turned to Pa and explained. Mama's face paled.

Pa patted her shoulder. "It's all right, Selena. We'll likely never see them again, and Abbie was right to treat them with respect. Not only was it the safest thing for her to do, but they're God's children, too, even if their ways are different from ours."

"But think what could have happened!"

"Whatever could have, didn't, so we'll enjoy this meal. Give me a hand in the barn, will you, Abbie?"

As soon as the door was shut behind them, he turned to her. "Did you have your gun?"

Abbie shook her head. "No, Pa. I was right here. I only take it when I go away from the house."

"Abbie, I have great respect for the Indian Nations. But your mama's fears are justified. I don't want you to take this lightly."

"I don't. But I know they wouldn't hurt me."

Pa laid a hand on her shoulder. "Don't let respect replace caution."

Abbie enjoyed the meal more than many she'd had, and as she knelt beside her bed that night, she thanked God for the braves and the people they would feed from their hunt. "I don't expect they know you, Lord, as we do, but somehow I think You know them."

As she lay in her bed to sleep, she saw in her mind the Indian brave and felt again the excitement of what had passed between them. She couldn't wait to tell Monte she had been right.

◆◆◆◆◆◆◆

"But you should have seen his face! Even Pa understood and said I did right. I tell you, Monte, it doesn't matter what people say about the Indians being savages. These men were honorable, and they paid their respects as nicely as any southern gentleman." Abbie set her chin stubbornly, and Monte frowned.

"I don't know that I appreciate the comparison."

"Well, you ought to."

Monte shook his head. "I don't suppose I have a chance of convincing you otherwise, so I won't try. I'm just glad they got their game and left the area."

Abbie brushed the hair out of her eyes as she strolled along beside him. His reaction was far less satisfying than she had anticipated. "How is it coming with your cattle?"

"I understand why your father has sheep."

Abbie laughed. "Not going so well?"

"I made the best investment ever in hiring a foreman. I admit I'd be lost without him and not continue the enterprise."

"What would you do instead?"

"I don't know. There's mining opportunity. But that's a

rough lot, and I've never been a gambler. What I'd really like is to raise thoroughbreds. Arabians."

"Why don't you?"

"I don't think there's a market for that sort of horse out here."

"Well, you could send them back East."

"Not until the railroad comes through."

Abbie frowned. "Do you think it will?"

"Of course it will. It's only a matter of time, and I wouldn't think much time."

"Oh, Monte, it'll spoil everything!"

"Honestly, Abbie. I think you're an Indian at heart. Having the railroad will bring commerce and culture. Freight will no longer be carried tediously by wagon and oxen. It'll enable people to come and go great distances with ease."

Abbie plucked a reddened leaf from the gray knobby branch of a scrub oak. "I suppose there is a positive side."

"Indeed there is. Why, you could easily travel to all sorts of places just to see them."

She smiled. "I'd like that."

"Yes, you would. There's a whole world out there that you haven't begun to experience."

"Only in my imagination." She laughed.

They arrived back at the yard as Pa pulled up in the wagon. "Ah, Monte. Come and help me unload this meat."

Abbie looked into the bed at the slabs of meat from the hogs that Pa and the McConnels had butchered together. She hated the idea of raising the animals just to slaughter them, but the hogs would provide meat all winter and through the spring until they acquired another weaner and began the process again.

Monte pulled himself into the wagon. "If you're interested, Joshua, I could show you how to build a true southern smokehouse and you'd have the best mouth-watering hams and chops you've ever tasted."

"That just might be worth the trouble." Pa took the slab Monte handed down and carried it to the shed.

Two days later they finished the smokehouse back behind the barn. Abbie watched them hang the slabs of meat inside and start the slow wood-smoking. They laughed, coming out grimy and hot, and splashed in the water from the pump. Pa clapped Monte on the shoulder as though he were family. She wondered if it helped fill Monte's void.

The October evening was cold, and the soaking at the pump had the men pressing close to the stove to warm themselves. Abbie smiled as she reached around Monte to gather the dishes.

"Well, Selena," Pa said, crowding into the kitchen as he buttoned his cuffs. "You'll have yourself some fine meat this year."

"Are you sure the coyotes can't get at it? I'd hate to give them more of an invitation than before."

"It's safe as can be. Unless they can figure that catch Monte rigged better than I can." He leaned over the pot of corn chowder simmering on the stove. Mama shooed him from the trout browning in the skillet.

"A feast fit for a king tonight," he declared. "Abbie, if you learn to cook half as well as your mama, you'll make some lucky man mighty happy."

She squeezed past and laid the checkered cloth napkins around the table. "Oh, Pa, most men'll eat anything."

"Now, there's a fine attitude."

Mama pulled the johnnycake from the oven. "She already cooks well, as evidenced by the job she did on those rabbits."

Monte frowned. "Well, if it's rabbits Abbie's needing, I hope we can find a better way to provide them. I'll hunt them myself if need be."

Abbie opened her mouth to protest, then relented. How could she explain? Monte was honestly concerned for her welfare, and that gave her a warm satisfaction that rivaled any emotion evoked by the braves.

Thirteen

The first frost dusted the ground as Abbie hurried beside Mama down the boardwalk to Pa's office, but he burst out to meet them with Sterling Jacobs behind him. "How bad is it?"

"They're coming in just now," Mama said. They made their way back through the crowd as the marshal rode to meet the crippled stage. Gus held the team of four with one arm while the other lay bloody in his lap. Riding alongside, then cutting off in front, Marshal Haggerty brought the horses to a stop.

Pa pushed forward. "Where's Crocker?"

"Inside," Haggerty said. "He wasn't as lucky as Gus."

"God have mercy." Pa pulled open the door. Abbie was pressed into the crush as people pushed forward to see. The body lay across one seat, and the two faces across from it were nearly as pale.

"All right, everyone back off!" Marshal Haggerty spread his arms and nudged them back so Gus could climb down from the seat.

Abbie stepped away as Pa escorted a heavy woman with a handkerchief to her nose. Red streaks ran down each cheek and her eyes were puffed. Abbie could hardly blame her.

"Oh, my dear!" Ruth Bailey squeezed through. "Who would have thought . . ."

"Aunt Ida! Thank the dear Lord!" Eleanor pressed her aunt's hand between her palms as Ruth led her off. The other man in the stage stepped down, straightened his vest, and looked around him.

Abbie watched the muscle in his jaw tense. He was probably as frightened as the Baileys' aunt, but he wouldn't show it. Poor man. He was thin and balding, with the hands of a clerk.

She turned as Pa asked, "Any guesses who did this?"

"Don't need to guess." Gus staggered and leaned against the stage. "It was Hollister."

"So he's added murder to infamy." Pa's tone was as cold as the air.

"And we'll hang him now." Marshal Haggerty led Gus through as Doc Barrow took his other arm.

Deputy Davis galloped in, sliding to a stop before them. "Trail's cold, but there's somethin' to start with." He leaped down and rifled under the driver's seat. "They got the deposits and the post dispatch."

"Actually, we regathered the post dispatch," the passenger spoke. "It's inside, somewhat the worse for wear."

The deputy eyed the loose pile of letters scattered on the floor of the stage, then shook his head. "Someone give me a hand with Crocker."

Wes McConnel shouldered through, his face as ruddy as the thick red muttonchop sideburns. They hauled the body out.

"Someone get them letters."

Abbie stepped forward. With a deep breath, she climbed into the stage and gathered the mail. On one letter she recognized Blake's handwriting and tucked it into her pocket, then hurried the rest to the Post Office.

Back outside, she tore open the envelope.

Dear Abbie,

We're doin' fine. Found some gold but ain't much of it. Mack had a fever, but he's better now. Some of the men get drunk a lot, but we're keepin' our money in our pockets and bringin' it home. Hope you miss me, cuz I sure miss you. Hope you ain't married to Farrel yet.

Love forever,
Blake

Abbie clutched it to her chest and breathed a prayer of thanksgiving. Running directly to the grocer's, she burst in on Clara. "Blake's safe!" She waved the letter and crushed Clara in her arms. "They've even found some gold. And they're keeping their heads. That'll be Mack's doing."

Clara slipped free. "Could I . . . would you mind if I . . . saw the letter? I know it's written to you. . . ."

Abbie handed it to her. Clara read, then looked up. "Married to Farrel? Montgomery?"

Abbie waved her hand. "Blake has gotten that fool notion into his head from the start. Remember when he tried to shoot him?"

"Is Montgomery Farrel courting you, Abbie?"

"Of course not. We've had a picnic or two, and he comes to the house mainly to see Pa. We do walk on occasion, but there's nothing more than that." Abbie felt her cheeks burn.

"Why, Abbie Martin, I declare you're sweet on him!"

"I'm not, either. Monte's nice, and I enjoy his company, but I'm in no rush for romance, I assure you. I've had enough of the whole business for a long while."

Clara handed the letter back. "I have to remember you're younger. I'll be nineteen next week and . . . I'm beginning to want a home of my own and . . . Marty Franklin's been calling on me."

Abbie's mouth dropped open. "Are you saying you're not going to wait for Blake?"

"Oh, Abbie, you read it yourself. Blake loves you. He always has, and even if you never marry him, he'll still love you. I want someone who sees me first, not as a replacement. And Marty is sweet and funny and kind."

"But this is so sudden."

"It doesn't matter. He . . . asked me to marry him last night and . . . I accepted."

"You accepted?"

"Yes. And we're going to be married next month, and as soon as the house is ready, I'll have you to my own home for tea."

"I guess that means you won't slide down the banister anymore."

Clara grabbed her arm, laughing. "Hush! You want Ma to hear?" Then she squeezed her hand. "Besides, Marty's building a loft."

Abbie smiled. "I am happy for you, dear Clara."

But as Abbie rode home in the buggy beside her mother, she felt more dismay than pleasure for Clara. How could Clara marry Marty when she had loved Blake so long? Did she just put away her feelings like linens in a drawer? She helped Mama carry the flour and beans inside, then stood at the window, her wrap over her arm. Mama bustled around her, then took hold of her shoulders.

"Abbie, go have a walk. You're in too much of a fog to help me here."

"Yes, Mama." Abbie pulled her wrap from the hook. As soon as she was out of sight of the house, she broke into a run and rushed across the grassy slopes, the crisp air making her lungs ache until she at last collapsed on the ground and lay back. Her bonnet had flown off, and her hair lay loose, snagged on the dry grasses. She closed her eyes and tried to imagine Clara as Mrs. Marty Franklin. There was nothing wrong with Marty. He was nice as Clara said. But she couldn't believe that Clara loved him, and marrying for any other reason was unthinkable. The cold air carried the scent of woodsmoke, and Abbie felt the changing of the season deep within her. Suddenly a twig snapped and her eyes flew open.

"I'm sorry I startled you." Monte stood over her. "Please don't get up. You're absolutely enchanting lying there in the grass as though you've taken root."

Abbie sat up and pulled the grass from her hair.

"I called at the house, but your mother said I'd find you out here."

"And you have." Abbie smiled. "In total disarray." She untied the strings to the bonnet hanging down her back and lifted it.

"Don't put it on, Abbie. I like it just the way you are right now." He settled to the ground beside her. Abbie dropped the bonnet.

"So tell me, what were you thinking so hard about?"

"Clara's getting married."

"That bothers you?"

"How can she marry someone else when she's loved Blake so long?"

"It happens more often than you know."

Abbie frowned. "Next thing, you'll be telling me you're marrying Marcy Wilson."

His eyebrow raised in humorous surprise. "I will never tell you that. I give you my word of honor."

"It just doesn't seem right."

"You have a fairy-tale notion of marriage, Abbie." He pulled a grass blade from the hair behind her ear. "It's not always the way you want it to be . . . true love ending in lifelong marital bliss. I've no doubt Clara will make a good wife for her husband and be happy in the process. Familiarity breeds affection, and affection can become love."

She shook her head. "Then why does God give us the capacity to fall in love in the first place? It doesn't make sense."

Monte chuckled. "Are you questioning the good sense of the Almighty?"

"No. Just your interpretation of it. I don't believe God plays some divine game of heartbreak. I think He intends us to love with our whole being."

His voice thickened. "I wish that were always so, Abbie," he said, his eyes traveling to her face. "But then, who could ever be joined, short of finding that perfection?"

"I don't know. Maybe people settle for less before they find the one they were meant for."

"You would never settle for less, would you." It was a statement, not a question.

His finger traced the line of her jaw, and Abbie raised her eyes to him. "I hope not."

He turned away. "I came to tell you I'll be going home for a while."

"Why?"

"My sister's husband has been working with our solicitor to sell the plantation, and I'm required to conclude the transaction. I don't know how long it will take and . . ." He smiled. "I didn't want you to think I was avoiding you."

Abbie sniffed. "Why would I think that?"

"You did the last time when you were jealous of Miss Marcy."

"I was never jealous! With whom you choose to spend your time is of no concern to me."

"None at all?" His mouth still smiled, but his eyes deepened.

"I told you I missed you."

"You might miss an old dog or a favorite book as well. Tell me truly, Abbie, will you think of me while I'm gone?"

"Yes, I suppose I will."

"You suppose?"

"I will," she whispered.

He leaned close, and her heart crescendoed. "You'll never be far from my thoughts, Abbie Martin. Nor have you been from the first time I met you."

A strand of hair blew across her face and he reached up to brush it back. The touch of his fingers on her skin awakened her senses, and she caught her breath sharply.

"Perhaps when I return, I'll find a young lady ready to be courted in earnest, instead of a tomboy girl more interested in Indian braves than a gentleman who seeks her affection."

Abbie forced her voice to steady. "But you've no idea how long you'll be gone. Perchance another gentleman will make the discovery first."

Monte grasped her arms and pulled her against him. "Then remember your own words, Abbie, and don't settle for less until you know what I would give you."

She trembled as his hands slipped from her arms to encircle her. "Monte, I . . ."

His lips found hers with passionate determination, and Abbie surrendered. His hands on the small of her back pressed her close, and she felt the firm muscles of his chest. Her fingers slid over his shoulders and caught in the waves of hair on the back of his neck. Gently, he kissed her again, then released her.

"Think of me while I'm gone, and know that every waking moment and every dream I dream will be consumed with you, my darling. Nothing will keep me a moment longer than must be, and when I return . . ." His finger traced her eager lips. "Well, we'll see when I return."

Abbie sat still, her chest rising and falling with ragged breaths. The thought of his leaving now was terrible. Tears burned her eyes, and he gathered her in a soft embrace.

"Now see what I've done?" he whispered. "I should have left

you in childish oblivion, but selfishly I drew forth your womanly response. Forgive me?"

She nodded, laying her head against his chest, and he held her again.

"I'll miss you dreadfully, Abbie."

"I'll miss you, too . . . far more than an old dog."

He threw back his head and laughed, pulled her up, and spun her. Planting his hand on her waist, he waltzed her on the hillside to the music of the wind, then kissed her hand. "Good-bye, Abbie."

The lump in her throat made it impossible to answer, but as she watched him go, she knew that she loved him as perfectly as she had ever dreamed.

Fourteen

Blake looked up as Mack dropped the small bag of gold dust onto the rough table and sank into the chair. "We're barely payin' our way." Mack fondled the measly bag, then tossed it aside. "We'd make better use of our time smithing or workin' any other job than this. Face it, Blake. Whatever gold there was to be found has done been found, and it ain't been us that done it."

"I ain't goin' back broke."

"I should've never brung you in the first place." Mack sounded more regretful than bitter. "And I ain't goin' back without you. But, Blake, you gotta realize when we're whooped. We ain't gonna make it big. We prob'ly ain't gonna make it at all."

Blake ran a finger over the jagged edge of the table. "If you wanna quit, then go on back. I ain't leavin' without gettin' what I came for."

Mack shook his head. "Can't you see it's a lost cause?"

"Ain't no such thing if you work hard enough. I mean to find gold."

Sighing, Mack jabbed his fingers through his hair. "You're just past yer eighteenth birthday and as stubborn as an old mule! We got enough for one more month's provisions. If we ain't no better off when that's done, we're goin' home . . . both of us . . . if I have to tie you to my horse an' drag you."

133

"One more month." Blake grinned. He already had two inches on Mack. It'd be a sight for Mack to haul him anywhere.

Blake was up almost before the sun the following morning. The one thought that got him out of bed, that made him keep on when his back was burning with the effort and his hands were raw, that drove him to continue searching, was already consuming his mind. Abbie. He would find what he needed to be able to provide her with everything she desired. He pictured her in his mind, imagined her waiting for him, anticipating his return. Her tears when he left had been all too real. He knew she cared for him even if she didn't know it yet herself, and nothing would stop him from returning, triumphant, to claim her.

Mack stumbled out of the shanty that kept off most of the rain—if very little of the wind—when they slept, then groaned. "You at it already?"

"Yup. It's fixin' to rain, and I intend to use whatever time we got left."

"Want some coffee?"

"Sure." Blake kept sifting the sluice waters. "Bring it out here, okay?

"Yup."

When Mack went in, Blake stood, leaning back to stretch his tired muscles. The air was cold and the sky dark and threatening. It might be more than rain this time. Could easily snow, being October. He caught his wrists behind his back and rotated his neck. As he did so, his eye skimmed the mountainside above him and snagged on a dark recess he hadn't noticed before.

The rains that caused last week's flash flood must have opened it up. He squinted. It looked to be a sort of narrow crevice. Grabbing the lantern from the porch, he started up the mountain and scaled the ridge. When he estimated he was over the crack, he let himself down and landed close to the opening.

Inside yawned black, and he stooped to light the lantern. It burned with a poor grade coal oil that smoked badly but served its purpose.

Pressing himself sideways into a crack scarcely wider than his chest, he held the lantern before him and squeezed through, ducking to avoid a low projection. After some twenty steps, the passage broadened considerably to the span of three men, and his torch sent flickering shadows across the walls before shining on the prettiest vein he'd ever laid eyes on.

He closed his eyes and prayed. "Thank you, God. I know you gave me Abbie now. I mean to do right by her an' You, all the days of my life." Then quietly and carefully he climbed out and made his way down the mountainside. God had directed them to this claim that contained this cave and led him up here this morning. He would continue to provide.

Mack was standing, annoyed, beside the sluice box holding his coffee when he returned. "You gotta go halfway up the mountain to relieve yourself?" he asked.

"That ain't what I was goin' for." Blake took the steaming cup and swigged the bitter brew. "Mack, I found us a gold mine."

✦✦✦✦✦✦✦

Abbie sat with Tucker leaning on one side and Jeremy the other. At her knees, Emmy and Pauline held the reader as Pauline sounded out the words, her finger inching over the page syllable by syllable. "Long 'I,'" Abbie said.

"'Find . . . a . . . h—ome.'" She looked up. "Like us. The pup ain't got a family."

"Doesn't have. The pup doesn't have a family. But you do. You have one another and Father Dominic and Brother Thomas and Brother José."

"It ain't the same." Emmy lisped her "s" through the gap in her teeth.

Abbie folded her hands in her lap. "It's not exactly the same, but it's a home with people who love you."

Tucker stroked her hand with his fingers. "We ain't got a ma."

Abbie's chest constricted, and she closed the little fingers inside hers. "Well, you have me." As he pressed in closer, she wrapped him in her arm. "And you have Jesus. Remember He told his friends, 'Suffer the little children to come unto me, and forbid them not; for of such is the kingdom of heaven.' Emmy, you have a turn now."

Emmy slid the reader closer. " 'All night the storm … raged. …' "

Abbie looked at the faces around her, so young, so trusting. She hated to think what these children might be like were it not for the brothers' care. How the mission came to be there was still a miracle as far as she was concerned. It was there before the town, an outpost of Christianity for the Indian tribes. Father Dominic had come after his predecessor was lashed to a tree and burned by the Indians he came to serve. Now they served the children.

Emmy stammered, "Vor … vor … a …"

"Voracity. It means greed, gluttony. Because of the other dogs' greed, the pup went hungry."

She went on, her lisping voice even. " 'He found a … place away from the pack and lay his head on his paws.' "

"Thank you, Emmy. And now I have to go." Abbie stood. "But I'll see you all tomorrow."

She pulled on her cape and found Shiloh ready in the stable. Brother José had given her mash, then saddled and bridled her. Abbie led her out. Starting back across the brown prairie, she remembered the one time Reverend Peale had suggested the town families adopt the children. Though no one had openly reproached him, he was bad-mouthed behind his back. Not only were the children foundlings, but they had been raised thus far by Roman Catholic priests, which was not actually true, as only Father Dominic was ordained to the priesthood.

That hadn't mattered so much until one faction headed by Mildred Beatty set up an outcry of contamination, as though the children were tainted by smallpox or worse. It was the first time Rocky Bluffs had been torn by divisions. Previously people took religion as they could get it, from one denomination or another, and mostly considered themselves lucky to have both the brothers and Reverend Peale. It shook Abbie to see people choosing up sides, when all Reverend Peale had intended was to give homes to children in need.

That was the year Mama suffered pneumonia, and so even in the Martins' Irish Catholic family, no orphan came to stay. Reverend Peale never repeated his call, but he spent a good deal of time and strength seeing to their needs and providing the brothers with medical supplies and clothing. And on Sundays he called the townsfolk to charity and faith in the Savior who provides even for the sparrows.

Abbie wondered if the children weren't better off where they were, in the direct hand of God. When her family attended mass at the Mission on Sundays, she would come to tears at the sweetness of the children's voices raised in song and repeating the Latin mass parts, lisps and all. Surely God wasn't divided as they were. She had seen His hand on Reverend Peale as surely as it guided Father Dominic. It was their own limitations that fenced in God, even in a place where people needed one another to survive.

She tightened her grip on the reins. Her hands were cold, her nose and cheeks nipped as she set her face into the wind. With the days so short, she'd be hard pressed to make it home before dark.

Fifteen

Smoke spewed from the stack as hissing steam shrouded the wheels grinding to a stop. The station was amass with people as Monte stepped off the train, stiff and sore from inactivity. The smell of salt air hit him immediately even through the drizzle. He sought and found his sister, Frances, coifed and elegant beside Kendal Stevens. Her husband looked as dandy as ever. How Kendal managed to keep them in their finery, he didn't know.

Frances leaned her cheek forward to receive his kiss, and Kendal pumped his hand, saying, "It's good to see you again ... great to see you again, although the Wild West seems to agree with you."

"That it does." Monte looked around him at the crowd. They were a queer assortment. Worn-out gentry, gauche new arrivals flaunting ill-gained riches, white trash who had allied with the Federals suddenly raised in status, carpetbaggers come to take their pound of flesh, Negroes with frightened, angry, or sullen eyes thrust into a world they didn't know.

Monte shook his head, forcing a bright tone. "I don't recall seeing so many people in the same place at once. We're rather more spread out in the Colorado Territory. Decidedly sparse, you might say."

"And you must tell us all about it." Frances slipped her arm through his. "But let's hear it someplace warmer."

The cold drizzle soaked his coat as he grabbed his bags and climbed into the carriage that looked as though it had seen much use. It creaked forward as Kendal giddapped the horse, an animal Monte would not have looked at twice. Still, they were riding, which was more than many of the old guard.

"We've found a new place," Kendal told him. "More suitable for a family."

"Is that an announcement?"

Kendal laughed, puffing his chest. "As a matter of fact, yes."

"When?"

"Next April." Frances smiled, but not with the enthusiasm he might expect.

"That's wonderful news. Congratulations!"

"You might experience the same if you ever settled on one woman." Kendal fingered the waxed end of his mustache with a crooked grin.

"Monte's head is too much in his business." Frances brushed the moisture from her skirt. "He hasn't time for romance."

Monte smiled. He needn't verify nor discount either statement. The carriage rolled through the muddy ruts toward a black-shuttered, white brick townhouse, tall and narrow, but more than sufficient.

"Here we are, then." Kendal reined in.

Monte leaned out. "Very nice, Kendal. You keep my sister well."

"It isn't the plantation house. . . ."

"It's better this way." Monte felt the stirring of resentment. How slowly those feelings die. "The place was falling to ruin. You'd have had a time maintaining it. A new start is best."

"Perhaps."

Monte followed Kendal up the front stairs and into the hall. "Very nice indeed. I see Frances's hand everywhere I look."

"Oh yes, I insisted she decorate exactly as she wanted."

Monte nodded. "A wise choice. Not only as my dear sister has impeccable taste, but as you'd never hear the end of it." He winked at Kendal and Frances huffed.

"You'll never change, will you, Monte? Always the tease."

"Would you have me otherwise?"

"I might." She raised her chin. "Now let me show you the rest of the place." She led him upstairs.

Kendal followed with his bags, and Monte asked, "Where's Rawley?"

"Passed on," Kendal said. "Hard to replace a darky like him these days. They're a shiftless lot and expect more than they're worth."

Monte didn't reply. Kendal's flaw was his disparagement of the Negro. Probably better that he have no manservant. Not that he mistreated them; Frances would never condone that, but he didn't consider them as people at all. Monte had seen their humanity very young, and though the reshuffling of the societal order had brought the demise of all he had treasured, he could not dispute the justice. So one built new dreams. His father had been right to send him west.

"I expect you'll want to retire early after your travel." Frances opened the bedroom door and waved him in.

"It was tedious."

"Shall I have your supper sent up?"

"No, no." He took the bags from Kendal. "I'd rather catch up on your affairs."

"Then I'll have supper served, and we'll all make it an early night."

"Frances . . ." Monte caught her arm as she turned to follow Kendal out. "Are you feeling all right? You look pale."

"I'm fine, Monte." She stroked his fingers on her arm. "Always the concerned big brother."

"I don't want my stay to tax you . . . in your condition."

"I've been longing for your return."

Monte paused. Her eyes were shadowed, not so as to raise concern, yet . . . there was something. "Well, an early night will do us all good."

◆◆◆◆◆◆◆

Monte stepped out with Kendal from the solicitor's office the following day. Kendal closed the door behind. "Mr. Bernhart is handling this as a personal favor. His fees—"

"Will be paid from the proceeds." Monte started down the walk. "Clarence Bernhart was Father's solicitor. He does not work for the Farrels pro bono."

"Yes, but . . ."

"Come, Kendal, let's have an end of it. We'll turn some profit, and that's more than others have done."

"Well, of course. Anyway, we've several weeks before the money clears and everything is completed."

"Yes, I expected as much." His breath fogged in the frigid air as he stepped down into the street, crossed, and remounted the walk.

Kendal kept step beside him. "Frances will be pleased. She was afraid you'd slip in like a shadow and be gone the next day without a chance for her to show you off to her friends, old and new."

"I'll admit I'm eager to return. But as long as I'm here, I'll see everyone I can."

"And satisfy Frances. Thank heaven for that. You've no idea what I had to endure once she learned you were indeed coming. But then it's no secret between us who comes first in Frances's heart."

Monte shifted uncomfortably. "Come, Kendal. Don't speak foolishness. Frances feels she must order my life, as she does yours and anyone else who will let her. Motherhood, I'm afraid, will only accentuate that trait." He was gratified to see Kendal puff again with the shift in conversation. The last thing he wanted to face was Kendal's old envy.

They only had time to wash and dress before supper. As Monte lathered himself in the bath, he fumed again at Kendal's presumption upon Mr. Bernhart. To expect a man to work for nothing when you had even a penny to pay was despicable. No one with integrity would consider it, but Kendal . . .

He sighed, pouring the pitcher of hot water down his back. Well, Kendal was different. He rubbed himself dry and dressed in his black long coat and tan breeches, wiped his boots up to the knee, and tied on his cravat. He checked himself in the mirror, straightened the gray quilted vest, and went downstairs.

Kendal's other guests, two business associates, were already in the study, and Kendal held out a hand to him. "Ah, gentlemen. Here he is, Frances's illustrious brother and western entrepreneur."

Was the glint in his eye the touch of brandy or something else?

"Montgomery Farrel; Elias McDonald and Frederick Glenn."

Monte didn't recognize either name. He shook their hands in turn and bowed. "I'm honored."

"Certainly the honor is ours," McDonald said. "We've heard nothing but praise of your accomplishments."

Monte waved a hand. "I've merely seen to what was at hand."

"Ho. Methinks he doth protest too much." Glenn laughed and sipped his brandy.

Kendal handed a snifter to Monte and offered the candle to warm it. Monte shook his head and instead held it cupped in his palm, slowly swirling. "Tell me, Kendal . . . brandy *before* supper?"

"Things are changing, Monte."

"Ah. And what has my sister to say for that?"

Kendal stroked his mustache, smiling. "Your sister has much to say about everything."

Monte sipped. "He that has ears to hear, let him hear."

McDonald and Glenn laughed rather too raucously, and Monte studied them. Something nagged. They were too smooth . . . too elegant. But then, didn't Kendal look the same? He sipped again. His purpose here was not to monitor his brother-in-law. Probably chasing ghosts anyway.

They were served at supper by a Negro house girl and an older woman . . . ah yes, Dilcey. Monte nodded to her as she filled his glass and she smiled. He turned to find Kendal watching with an ill-disguised smirk. Let him. Monte had thrashed him once on the subject; he'd do it again.

Glenn and McDonald were decidedly vague about their business. Once again Monte bit his tongue. Kendal was having a hard enough time of it with the horrors of reconstruction all around him. He was entitled to run his affairs his way, and Frances seemed none the worse for it. She sat at the end like a beautiful sculpture, ordering everything impeccably. No sign of weariness tonight. She glittered with jewels.

Monte imagined Abbie in just such a sapphire necklace. His chest constricted. No, better he not think of her yet. The ache of longing quenched his appetite, though the fare was superb.

After the meal he declined Kendal's offered cigar but accepted another brandy. The men were growing tedious with their constant questions about his western concerns. Monte drained the last of his brandy and smiled. "Forgive me, gentlemen. But it's been a long day and I have engagements tomorrow."

Sitting at the escritoire in his room, he slid out a sheet of paper and the pen. *My dearest Abbie* . . . His eyes came up to the wall, and he held the pen poised. He could almost smell the scent of her still. What insanity had induced him to behave as he had with her on the hillside? Such insanity he would never do without again. He had almost thought to claim her, but honor refused. His heart rushed. As soon as he returned he would speak for her. The thought alone was ambrosia. His pen returned to the paper and the steady *scritch, scritch* transferred his thoughts to words. Soon he would return. Soon.

Sixteen

Chandler Bridges crowed when Monte strode into the stable. He was a creature of habit, so Monte had expected to see him right where he was and had the element of surprise in his favor.

"Monte, you look incredibly good considering you've been so long from polite society. You've even kept your scalp."

Monte laughed. "I have indeed, though I notice yours is rather diminished."

Chandler stroked his fair hair, then sparred good-naturedly with him. "I heard it rumored you were back. Shame on you for taking two weeks to show up."

"Frances has commandeered my every moment with friends whom I was obliged to entertain with tales of the West."

"Any worth telling?"

"Only the ones I fabricated." Monte chuckled. "I fear my sister will never visit me."

"Then, shame again. You've not grown out of your roguish ways."

"Ah, but I have. I'm a man of commerce and a gentleman rancher."

Chandler shook his head, grinning. "Care to join me on my rounds?" He tightened the cinch under the horse's belly.

"Certainly. I haven't seen the old place in ages. But you

must give me a fresh horse. Kendal's nag is near death from the journey here."

"Good horseflesh is dear if you can come by it at all."

"So it appears."

As they rode, Monte noticed the careful patchwork that replaced true maintenance, the fields left fallow. "How do you manage it?"

"It's a bit of a balancing act, but the soldiers never hit us like they did you. Too out of the way, I suppose. Father has had to place himself in a bit of jeopardy with a loan this last year. Rather a sizable one I'm afraid."

"I'm sorry to hear that. But the land is still profitable?"

They rode into the dim November daylight. "It is if we can figure out the labor problems and file all the necessary forms to use our workers . . . and barring any natural or man-made disasters."

"I admire you, Chandler. You and your father are the fighters. You won't allow the Yankees to master you."

"We're all changed, though. Even those who didn't fight the war have been scarred and even maimed, though not physically. It's as though the North is not content with tactical victory but must rip out our soul as well."

"I'm sorry." Monte clapped a hand on his shoulder. "Being removed from it all these months, I almost forgot how it is here." He let his gaze settle on the hazy horizon beyond the gray fringe of barren trees. This place had been as much a home to him as his father's plantation, the families as thick as true relations, and closer now with the debt of honor that lay between them.

Monte never forgot that Chandler's father had saved the life of his own in the battle of Seven Pines when the Confederate forces were driven back. Nathan Bridges had stood between Monte's father and enemy fire as he dragged him, injured, from the field. Monte sighed. "I must say it is a different life in the Colorado Territory, new and exciting to be so free and prosperous."

"I'm glad for that. But don't get me wrong, there's plenty to celebrate still, and we never miss an opportunity if we can help it. As a matter of fact, we're having a bit of gaiety tomorrow night in honor of my sister's engagement."

"Which sister would that be?"

"Aileen."

"And who has the honor of her hand?"

Chandler sent him a sidelong glance. "Whom would you guess?"

"Surely not Duncan?"

"The very same." Chandler laughed.

Monte whistled with surprise. "I thought your father swore never to give the hand of his daughter to that prankster."

"She'll have none other, and Father hasn't the fight left in him. Besides, for all his faults, Duncan is of the old guard and a far superior choice to any of the new rabble who would seek her hand." He frowned. "Aileen is the least of our worries. It's Sharlyn who's really causing concern."

Monte reined in. "Not meek, sweet-tempered Sharlyn, who wouldn't say boo to a horsefly?"

"I'm afraid she's too gullible for her own good."

"How so?"

"It's rather an involved situation that goes back to Father needing the loan. There's a certain blackguard who would get his hands on our land by any means. He first tried to buy it outright for an insulting price, and when Father sent him packing, he began to make trouble with our people—the workers, I mean.

"Learning of the loan, he then tried to purchase the note, no doubt intending to call it immediately and force the sale. Thankfully, Mr. Rochester at the bank would never stab an old friend and refused to turn over the note for any profit."

Monte's anger flamed.

"Failing to achieve his ends, this scoundrel began to pay court to Sharlyn."

"Your father received him?"

"No, indeed. But, Monte, things are different now. Let's face it, if a girl wants to see a man, she'll find a way whether or not it's approved by her family."

"I can't believe that of Sharlyn."

"She's bewitched."

"She must be. How can she go against her father in this?"

"She doesn't realize the intricacies, and Father cannot bear to break her heart by revealing the mercenary nature of his attention. We're hoping the fool will betray himself before we must lay her heart open to the reality. As it is, she'll hear nothing against him. Perhaps your coming will prove a great boon."

"How so?"

"Sharlyn was always inordinately fond of you."

"Fond? More afraid than fond, I think."

"That was not fear, Monte; it was awe."

"Well, whatever it was, I rarely got a word out of her. But then she was young."

"Not so very. She's twenty, you know. Just seems younger, being so petite and shy." Chandler nickered to the horse and it stepped forward and Monte's followed. "As a matter of fact, I thought I'd have a brother of you by now."

Monte quirked an eyebrow. "How so?"

"Your pledge, man."

"What pledge?"

"To marry Sharlyn."

Monte threw back his head and laughed. "Good heavens. I'd forgotten all about that." He shook his head, sobering. "It comes back clearly enough, though. I recall the expressions on our fathers' faces. I'd never seen them so long, so filled with angst, yet trying with all that was in them to hide it. I tell you,

Chandler, I'd have signed anything. I wonder what happened to that note."

Chandler shrugged. "I'll wager Father holds it still."

"Well, at fifteen, and with the war starting, marriage to anyone was the farthest thing from my mind."

"What about now? Twenty-four is none too young to consider it."

"And I may yet. But we both know Sharlyn would faint dead away if I ever approached her with it."

Chandler chuckled. "She's grown up a bit, you'll see." His smile faded. "Too much, maybe."

Monte was quiet. "Well, I'll be glad to talk to her if you think it'll help."

"Do that, Monte. If she'll listen to anyone, it would be you."

"You far overestimate me."

"Not where it comes to the ladies. And don't bother contesting that. I've known you too long . . . and heard you claim hearts with words alone. The worst of it is, you did it without trying."

Monte laughed, glad that Abbie was not there to hear. The thought of her sweetness put away all previous ventures. He was closer to matrimony than Chandler knew, but until he spoke for Abbie, he'd keep that to himself. He turned the horse's head. "Well, I may surprise you yet."

◆◆◆◆◆◆

Abbie stirred and gazed out the window. The snow lay deep on the fields and another storm threatened. It seemed this would be a wet year. Sometimes they went a full month or more between blizzards, but already this month it had stormed three times. She hated being confined to the house and hadn't been able to get to the mission for over a week.

Closing the book that lay across her knees, she sighed. If only Monte would write again. The letter he sent just after arriving in South Carolina had been filled with details of all that he was seeing, things he knew she would love to hear, as well as veiled references to his affection. Already, it was limp and ragged from being opened again and again each night and clutched to her heart. She missed him so much! Would he be home for Christmas? Oh, gracious! How would she survive the time until he came back?

When Pa came home, he winked and pulled an envelope from his coat pocket. "A little something from Montgomery Farrel, I'd wager."

"Thank you, Pa." She reached for it with studied nonchalance.

"What does he have to say?"

Mama poked him. "Don't tease, Joshua. Abbie can fill you in after she's read her mail in privacy."

Abbie went to her room and carefully worked open the envelope.

My dearest Abbie,

I spoke more truly than I knew in saying I would miss you dreadfully. Not a day goes by that I don't wish I was at your side, there or here it matters not. How I miss our chats and all the quaint ideas you share so candidly. More painfully, I miss feasting my eyes upon your sweet and glowing face, and the feel of your delicate fingers tucked into my arm. I cannot close my eyes without seeing you lying in the grass, your hair in wayward disarray. If I continue like this, I'll go mad; therefore, I shall now describe to you how I occupy my days.

There are suppers and parties at which I see as many of my old friends as possible. It is strange how time does not separate friends, don't you think? I have not seen Milton Rochester for three years, since he went to medical school and I moved west, but when we were reunited last night, it was as though no time had passed. And, of course, Chandler Bridges is like a brother to me still.

The sale is nearly completed, and I have only a handful of other

*concerns before I'm free to return, but I feel honor bound to spend
some time at least with my mother's relations and various others
who have been kind over the years. Still you must know that each
moment away is bittersweet. Had I the courage I would have taken
you with me in spite of propriety, but then I would not damage
your reputation, which has remained intact in spite of the interesting array of skills you have acquired.*

Abbie could almost see the crooked grin and the teasing
glint in his eyes as he wrote that, and she caught her breath as
the longing rose fiercely within her.

*I must close now, and as I will be traveling from place to place
the next few weeks, I will reluctantly not ask you to write back,
but will anticipate instead the response you will prepare for my
return.*

> *My greatest affection,*
> *Monte*

Tears stung her eyes as Abbie clutched the letter to her
chest. What a remarkable ability he had to make her heart sing
and ache in the same moment. If only he would come home!

Seventeen

Aileen Bridges' gala was well attended, Monte noted, and he nodded to those he knew. It had been some time since he was surrounded by such grace and class as assembled there. And he was not unaware of the figure he cut and the eyes upon him. It recalled him back to the days before the war. Even then he'd been aware of his stature and attractiveness, but in the years that followed . . . the growing into manhood through the madness . . . he'd set aside less serious thoughts than those of commerce and survival.

Now, with his love for Abbie awake in his breast, he felt everything more acutely. The beauty of the women, the music of the orchestra . . .

"Ah, here you are, Monte." Chandler pumped his hand and lowered his voice. "Come, let me present you to Sharlyn. She's in a state since Father refused to allow Denman to escort her tonight."

Monte followed him to where Sharlyn sat on the plush settee. She had changed very little from the delicate girl he remembered. Her eyes lit with surprise and delight as he bowed over her hand. She trembled. Poor, shy girl. "How very nice to see you, dear Sharlyn, and how lovely you look tonight."

She blushed but surprisingly answered quite calmly, "Thank you, Monte. This is a tremendous surprise."

"I'll leave you two to get reacquainted." Chandler bowed.

Sharlyn flipped open her fan, for the storm outside and the fires at either end made the crowded room stuffy. "I didn't know you were back."

"Only temporarily. I had business to attend."

"It matters not the reasons that bring back an old friend," she murmured.

He stared. "Forgive me for asking, Sharlyn, but when did you learn to speak?"

Her sweet laugh tantalized him. "Oh, I suppose it came on me gradually."

"May I?" He took the seat beside her, recalling Chandler's words. She wasn't despondent now. Perhaps he could distract her after all. "How is it that I find such a delightful creature unescorted tonight?"

Her cheeks flamed. "The gentleman who would have done so was not admitted."

"Not admitted? Why?"

"Father wouldn't have him."

Monte handed her a glass cup of punch from the tray offered him by the servant. "That seems unlike Nathan Bridges to deny you anything." He waved the man away.

"I can't understand it. From the start, Father has taken a dislike to Robert Denman." Her eyes were like cool green pools as she glanced at him and then quickly away. Monte wondered if he'd ever seen them directed to him before.

"Surely he must have his reasons. But whatever the case, Robert Denman's misfortune is my advantage. Would you do me the honor of a dance?"

He led her out to the floor among the other dancers. All the gentility of this place settled upon him as he danced. He found her a far more sanguine companion than ever before. What had been crippling bashfulness was now demure reserve. She was pleasant company, and he commandeered her for the next dance as well. If his thoughts were really a thousand miles away, and his heart as well, he didn't let on.

"Tell me about Colorado." Sharlyn arranged her skirts as he returned her to the settee in the alcove by the window.

"It's wide open, rough and broken and dry, mainly gold and brown until you come near the mountains, which seem to erupt from the prairie like a mighty wave, causing the land all about to ripple into scrubby wooded hills. There are very few trees outside of the mountains, mainly one variety of pine, but there is a rugged beauty that is incomparable, unless it is to South Carolina you compare it."

"And the town in which you live?"

"Rocky Bluffs is a busy place for the area, but you'd laugh to see what distance there is between the homesteads, some an hour apart, others even more. The cultural activities are some-what limited, though there is talk of an opera house. Only talk I imagine. Unlike the mining camps that sport cheap imita-tions of theatrical arts, Rocky Bluffs maintains a surprising discrimination. Because of that they have no theater at all." He laughed. "But the businesses are multiplying as more people seek the opportunity of the West."

"And what is your business, Monte?"

"I have pokers in several fires. But the newest is cattle ranch-ing."

Her eyes widened. "Is it really the way they portray it with the cowboys and the cattle?"

Monte smiled. "I don't know how you've seen it portrayed, but the cowboys are a singular breed. I have over a dozen work-ing for me, and there is no end to the distraction they provide."

Sharlyn folded her hands in her lap. "And the ladies?"

"Western ladies are a hardy lot, yet surprisingly genteel as well." He thought of Abbie's graceful bearing contrasted with the image of her lying in the grass the day he had kissed her. "They're like thoroughbred horses, delicate to behold yet strong enough to ride the wind."

Her eyes were shining.

"I know one who can track seventeen different animals, which by the way is more than I know, and catch a fish with a spear she whittles herself."

"Please tell me more. What's her name?"

"Abigail Martin. But she's known as Abbie. She met a whole band of Comanche warriors in the woods one time and was not in the least afraid, but thought it a great adventure. And that, even though she's two years younger than you."

"How fine that sounds. You must be very happy there. I hear it in your voice."

"I admit it agrees with me."

"You'll return soon?"

"I'm not sure when I'll have things wrapped up here, and I intend to visit as many friends as possible. I would imagine I'll see out the end of the month, but I want to be home by the holidays at least." He imagined a Christmas proposal to Abbie.

"Katherine Devereaux will be holding her annual Christmas Eve gala. It's a pity you'll miss it."

"Perhaps by then you'll be allowed to spend it in the company of your Mr. Denman." Monte watched her reaction.

Blushing fiercely, she whispered, "Yes, I hope so." But her eyes flicked up to him again and retreated.

"Tell me about this lucky young man. What's his business?"

Sharlyn hesitated. "I . . . I don't really know. It all seems quite mysterious, but I believe he doesn't want to tire me with unromantic details."

"More likely the poor devil finds he can't think straight when caught in the gaze of your lovely eyes."

Those very eyes stared up at him in surprise, too astonished to look away. "Well, I . . . I don't know about that. . . ."

"Oh, come now. Surely he's mentioned the spell he must find himself under whenever you turn his way?"

"Monte . . . I declare I don't know what to say."

"My apologies. I didn't intend to make you uncomfortable. Whatever sweet words of his have captured your affection, it's none of my affair. Please forgive my impertinence."

Her gaze fell demurely to her hands still folded in her lap. "There's no need at all to apologize, I assure you," she whispered. He bowed over her hand and felt her tremble once again.

◆◆◆◆◆◆◆

The message was vague, but its urgency unmistakable, and Monte hurried down the stairs to find Frances. "There's some trouble at the Bridgeses'. I don't know if I'll return by the supper hour, so please don't wait on me."

Frances glanced up from her sewing, some lace thing for the baby, no doubt. "It's not even noon. What possible trouble could keep you from supper? I've planned tonight's company for two weeks. If you're not here to escort Mary Saunders..."

"Frances, I don't know what's happened. I only know I'm urgently requested."

"Well, you're urgently requested here, too."

Her pout reminded him not to push. For all her twenty-one years, she seemed not a day over eight. That was partly his fault. Father hadn't the heart to chastise her after the war. In fact, he'd hardly noticed her. It was to Monte she had turned for everything, wheedling and simpering, then fuming and pouting until he gave in, as he inevitably had.

Once again, he buckled. He kissed her cheek. "Set my place, dear. I'll do my best." He hired a cab to take him out to Willowdale. He was admitted and shown to the study, where Chandler paced. "What's happened?"

Chandler gripped him by the arm and pulled him in, closing the door behind them. His face was haggard as he took a note from his pocket. "We intercepted this on its way to Sharlyn from Denman."

Monte took the note and read.

My Darling,

The time has come for us. I cannot stand another day away from you and will no longer be put off by your impossible hopes of convincing your father to let us be wed. He will and must accept it when the deed is done. You have promised to trust me in this, and I tell you that we must steal away this very night. I shall await you at the normal hour.

Yours passionately,
Robert

"Good heavens. The man's determined."

"The man's dead."

"What?" Monte searched his friend's face.

Chandler took back the note. "When Father found this, he flew into a rage such as I've never seen."

Monte had witnessed the rages of Nathan Bridges. He could well imagine this one.

Chandler crumpled the note. "Monte, Denman didn't stand a chance."

"You're not telling me Nathan . . ."

"Denman was skulking in the barn, waiting to see that his missive was delivered. I saw none of it myself, but Isaiah reported it all. He swears Father gave him time to prepare. . . ."

"Then that will stand at the inquiry."

"There won't be one."

"What are you saying?"

"I ran when I heard the shots. Besides Isaiah, I was the first one to them. I thought Denman's bullet had also found its mark, but . . . Father was struck down by a hemorrhage in the brain. Doctor Brown can't say he'll recover."

Monte stood incredulous.

"He's barely able to speak, and his strength is dwindling. He asked me to send for you."

"Why?"

160

Chandler shook his head. "I don't know. Will you come up?"

"Of course."

The room was dim, but even so, Monte was shocked by the sight of Nathan Bridges, always imposing and proud, now lying limp and pale. He was a man of fiery temper, and Monte had often wondered how he could have produced such mild-mannered offspring. Nathan raised a trembling hand, and the doctor nodded.

Monte sat in the chair beside the bed. He tried not to notice the drool from Nathan's sagging mouth.

Almost inaudibly, Nathan Bridges spoke. "Your father was my best friend."

Was the man wandering? Monte nodded. "He felt the same for you, sir."

Swallowing, Nathan worked his mouth. "I have little time left. Listen now."

Monte drew up closer to hear him.

"Sharlyn must never know what's happened this day. She could not live with it. . . ." He drew a ragged breath. "Your father and I spoke of a match between you and my daughter. You recall the pledge?" His eyes probed.

Monte began to sweat. "It was a wartime oath . . . in the event you didn't return. . . ."

"It was a pledge. I am asking you now to honor it. Marry Sharlyn."

Monte's throat turned to sand.

"Take her away from here. She's loved you since she was a child. She'll accept your proposal." He closed his eyes, and at first Monte thought he had no more to say, but then the man gathered his strength. "It is God himself who brought you back here in time." The breath left his chest in a low wheeze, and he raised his hand faintly again. "It must be today . . . now . . . before she learns . . ."

Again Monte wondered if Nathan was delirious, hoped it were so, but the eyes suddenly cleared and burned into him.

"Will you do this for all that our families have been to one another, by your honor as a gentleman and your father's son?"

Oh, God! Nathan called upon his honor. What of Abbie? What of the life they would have together, the love that even now burned so fiercely in his chest? *Oh, God! How can I turn my back on that?* He recalled his own words to her. *"The ability to do what one must, even against one's heart; that is the honor I understand."* Monte shuddered. He had never meant the words prophetically.

But he suddenly understood what was being asked of him. He was bound by honor, by the debt his family owed this man, and by his own pledge. A noble cause, he had called it. Preservation of what mattered. He closed his eyes.

What would Sharlyn do if she knew her father had killed the man coming for her and himself in the effort? How would she live with it, she who could bear to hurt no one, who could scarcely face praise, let alone this shame. There was desperation in this house that for reasons known only to the Almighty, he alone could ease. All that Nathan Bridges had stood for, fought for, all that Monte's own father had believed in, was wrapped up in the honor that required him to accept.

"I will." His voice was blank, but it was done. His pledge given once again, and Abbie lost to him.

Nathan Bridges sank into the pillows and smiled thinly. "Go now and find your bride."

Monte held himself straight as he walked out.

"Monte, I had no idea. . . ." Chandler faltered outside the door. "Sharlyn is a wonderful girl . . . I think she'll make you a fine wife. . . ."

Monte nodded. He had to get his mind cleared in order to accomplish what he must. "Do you know where she is?"

"In the garden. She knows nothing. Father insisted he speak with you first."

Monte wished Chandler would not look so closely. He knew him too well.

"We'll hold the ceremony immediately in Father's room, as he desires."

Again Monte nodded. That was good. Get it accomplished before he had time to think of what it meant.

"Give me a moment, will you?" Monte slipped into the office before going to the garden. There was one thing he must do before he saw Sharlyn. He would not fulfill his pledge without first bringing an end to whatever expectations he had put in motion before coming, lest he prove faithless and false to both Abbie and Sharlyn.

With a hand he barely kept steady, he took paper and pen. He had intended to write Abbie tonight, but, God help him, not like this. Just seeing her name in ink on the paper made him want to crush and throw it away, to run upstairs and refuse. Nathan would understand. He would have to. Sharlyn . . .

Monte closed his eyes, and the pain in his heart seared like a branding iron. Yet he had known Sharlyn too long to deny the wreckage this would make of her spirit. It was not in her to bear guilt. He gripped the pen with grim resolve. *Dear Abbie, Do you recall our first discussion, when we spoke of honor and its purpose? You know*—He refrained from adding "my dearest"—*that I must follow that honor wherever it leads. Therefore, for reasons which I cannot disclose, I am married to another. Please know that I remain ever your faithful servant, and my heart will think of you always. Most sincerely, Monte.*

It was inadequate. Wholly so. He concealed the paper in the envelope and recorded the address. Then he took another sheet and hastily penned: *My dear sister and Kendal, Events have transpired that have changed my*—He almost wrote "life"—*plans. You will rejoice to know that I have taken Sharlyn Bridges as my wife and plan to leave immediately for a European excursion. I will send for my bags. Please see that the letter included is posted to Rocky Bluffs, Colorado Territory, at your earliest opportunity. This is important. Wish me well, Monte.*

There. He would not need to face Frances or withstand her scrutiny. His secret was safe. He scrawled the number and street and stepped into the hall. "Here, lad."

"Yessuh?" The young Negro boy came close.

"Take the letter to this number and see that it is delivered directly into the hands of Mrs. Stevens."

"Yessuh."

Monte pressed a coin into the boy's palm, then setting his face, he strode toward the garden. There he found Sharlyn with her white blond hair and lashes, green eyes, and flawless rose-petal complexion seated like a beautiful fairy amid the leafless trees. He slowly drew in his breath. Sharlyn must never know that his request was insincere. Forcing a smile, he approached.

"Monte!" Her smile was instantaneous. "How nice of you to come."

He bowed over her hand, beginning the role he would play from then on. "You are the fairest rose in the entire garden."

The color went clear to the roots of her hair. "There are at present no roses in the garden."

"The season matters not. Were it summertime with every bush in full bloom, still you would be fairer." He sat beside her on the cold stone bench and heard her indrawn breath. Forcing himself not to think of the consequences, he spoke gently. "I have two things to tell you. One, I fear, will bring you grief, and one, I pray, great joy."

Her smile faded. "Why, Monte, what is it?"

"I'm afraid your father has suffered a hemorrhage and will perhaps not have long to live."

Her hands flew to her face.

"Therefore the decision that's upon you must, and I apologize, be made in haste."

"What decision?" Her voice was tremulous.

He lifted her tiny hand in his, noting how soft and fragile it appeared. The hand of a child. "It's your father's wish that . . . you and I be wed. I would consider it a tremendous honor if you would consent to be my wife." Monte was satisfied that his tone was sincere, and he hoped Sharlyn could not detect the agony those words had caused him. How many times he had dreamed of saying them to Abbie! How would he ever make Abbie understand? Could she ever understand?

Sharlyn stared.

Bringing her hand to his lips, Monte kissed her fingers. "I know it's someone else you hold in your heart . . . but I'll try to be all that you hoped for. . . ."

"Oh, Monte, you're wrong. It's not that way at all! I just never dreamed that you would ask me!" Tears started in her eyes as she whispered, "I have loved you forever."

The irony clawed at his heart, and he felt compassion for her as he gazed on her tearstreaked face. "And you accept?"

"Oh yes!"

It was done. Part of him had hoped, had dared to believe that she would refuse him, but she had not. He stood and raised her to her feet. "I must prepare you; your father is not as he was. But his desire is that we be wed immediately in his room. Are you able to face that?"

"I can face anything now," she murmured, allowing Monte to lead her upstairs to her father's bedchamber. She ran at once to his side, bending low, the tears streaming down her cheeks.

Nathan smiled weakly. His color was gray, and it was clear he was fading fast. When her weeping persisted, he mumbled, "Not supposed to be sad. You'll marry Monte?"

"Yes, Father. Gladly."

"And you'll leave tonight."

"No. I couldn't leave you."

"You'll leave tonight." He addressed himself to Monte. "Take her abroad. Be frivolous."

Monte barely had time to nod before the minister arrived and was ushered into the dim, still room. It was a brief ceremony and subdued, and when instructed to do so, Monte leaned down and kissed Sharlyn gently, seeing at once the radiant joy in her eyes. Nothing would ever be the same for him again, and he prayed God would give him the strength to accomplish what honor had demanded.

◆◆◆◆◆◆◆

Frances threw the letter to the floor. How could he! Monte married? And to Sharlyn Bridges? Why, she was no more fit for Monte than . . . than . . . Oh! She clenched her fists at her sides. And to go off secretly without so much as including her in the ceremony. How like Monte to shun the pomp his wedding should have held. But to exclude her altogether . . . And the dinner guests would be arriving any moment. She kicked the envelope, and it slid to Dilcey's frightened feet.

"Take care of that trash. And here . . ." Frances scooped up Monte's note and crushed it without reading further. She didn't care what apologies he made. She now saw very clearly what place she had in her brother's life.

Kendal came in the front door and nearly stumbled over Dilcey. "Good heavens." He glanced at Frances. "What on earth are you . . ."

"Mizz Frances, there's a letter in he'ah. . . ."

"Burn it! Take it to the stove right now and burn it!"

"Frances." Kendal took hold of her shoulders.

"Burn it!"

Dilcey rushed for the kitchen.

Frances worked her mouth to voice her hurt and outrage to Kendal as he gripped her shoulders in alarm, but her thoughts grew fuzzy, and she collapsed into his arms.

Eighteen

When Christmas had long passed and all of January as well with still no word from Monte, Abbie fretted. Where could he be? He had said he would be visiting relatives, but this was too long! Taking her cape, she wrapped it about her. "I'm going out, Mama. I won't be long."

"It gets dark early, Abbie."

"I'll be careful."

She hurried Shiloh over the brown, frozen ground to Monte's house. She had not been here since the first time they dined together. Instead, Monte had become a regular in their home. She dismounted and approached the door. James answered her knock as he had before. "Yes, miss?"

"Can you tell me please when Mr. Farrel is expected to return?"

"I couldn' say, miss. But maybe Mr. Jazzper, he knows."

"Where can I find him?"

"He'd be in the barn or the bunkhouse."

"Thank you." Abbie found Mr. Jasper as he strode from the barn almost into her arms.

Startled, he steadied her and apologized. "Pardon me, miss. I'm not lookin' where I'm goin'."

"That's all right." Abbie smiled. "Mr. Jasper I hope?"

"That's right." He pulled off his hat.

"Could you tell me when you expect Mr. Farrel to return?"

169

"'Fraid not. Haven't heard from him in some while."

Abbie sighed.

"Is there anything I can do for you? I'm handlin' things while he's gone."

"No, thank you. It can wait."

"Would you care to leave yer name?"

"Abbie. Abbie Martin."

"I'll tell him you called, Miss Martin."

"Thank you."

She felt Cole Jasper watch her mount and when she turned, his eyes were still on her. He replaced his hat as she kicked in her heels.

••••••••

After dickering with Clara's father over the eggs she had brought him, Abbie made her way to Pa's office. February had passed without Monte's return, and still no letter had come. No matter how hard she tried to put him from her mind, she couldn't. She felt dull and empty without him.

As she pushed open the office, warmth enveloped her. Pa looked up from the press, his fingertips black and a smear on his cheek. "Aha. Just the sunshine we were needing."

She handed him the basket. "Mama says for you to share and not make Mr. Jacobs beg."

Sterling Jacobs looked up from the table where he was sorting letters into the type boxes, assisting Pa and learning the business. Pa peeked in at the muffins and breathed deeply. "Tell your mama she's lucky I'm a Christian man, or he'd not have a crumb." He winked at her.

Back outside, she stopped short and gripped the post as the stage pulled up in a cloud of dust. Her heart nearly pounded her ribs when Monte climbed down, resplendent and even more handsome than ever. With her breath catching in her throat, she refrained from rushing forward and throwing herself into his arms, but before he saw her, he turned and helped someone out of the coach behind him.

Abbie stared at the delicate creature with emerald eyes and hair so pale it was almost colorless. She was dressed in a green velvet cape with a fur-trimmed hood. Could this be Frances? She didn't resemble Monte at all.

As he tucked the dainty girl's hand into his arm, Monte looked up. His face revealed for an instant an inexpressible emotion, but it was swiftly veiled and he smiled. It was not the smile she had dreamed of all these months. It was indescribably vacant and mirthless.

He turned to receive the bags and trunks being handed down to him, then called to a boy and paid him to load the baggage into a wagon. His companion's gaze found her, and Abbie felt herself recognized. They approached.

"Monte," Abbie breathed.

"Hello, Abbie." He took her hand and bowed over it stiffly. "May I present my wife, Mrs. Sharlyn Farrel."

For a terrible moment, Abbie thought she might faint as the blood rushed from her face. Lungs that had never failed her before suddenly refused to breathe, and she stood like a statue, inanimate and stone cold.

She forced a greeting, not sure what she said to the tiny person who was Monte's wife, and then she left them behind, moving one foot in front of the other until she reached the mare, mounted, and dug in her heels. Clinging by sheer reflex, she flew across the plain, the angry sobs exploding from her like a torrent bursting a dike. "How could he! Oh, God, how could he?"

Abbie swiped the tears from her eyes, but they filled again. She kicked her heels in, and Shiloh lunged and panted, nostrils flared. The frozen air hung in droplets from her muzzle as her sides began to heave. Abbie paid no heed to where she was, the tears blinding her. Suddenly a windbreak loomed, and the mare veered. Abbie landed hard. Pain shot through her head, then a welcome stupor covered everything as the first dry pellets of snow began to fall.

At first the places being probed seemed disconnected from her body, but then she recognized the pressure on an arm, a leg. When the hands reached behind her neck, she forced her eyes open. The man smelled of leather and tobacco. His breath fogged over her face as he leaned close to examine the swelling at the back of her head. She tried to speak but only managed a moan.

"Don't be movin', now, till I see nothin's broke." His fingers moved across her collarbone to the shoulder on each side. "I reckon I can lift you."

Abbie tried to place him. She had been close to him before; the eyes, the weathered skin . . . Cole Jasper. Monte's foreman. She panicked. Where was she? She struggled to see past his shoulder as he lifted her, but her eyes would not focus. "Please . . ." Why wouldn't the words come?

"Don't fret. I'll git you home."

She relaxed. As he thrust her onto the horse, the pain in her head surged and waves of sickness rolled over her.

Cole pulled himself up and held on firmly. "All right?"

She tried to nod, then lay against his chest. He shielded her from the snow all the way to the homestead and carried her to the door. Mama thrust it open.

"Took a fall from the horse, ma'am. Don't seem to have nothin' broke, but she's mighty cold. I'm thankful I was lookin' fer strays, or no one mighta been out that way fer a long while."

"Oh, dear Lord . . ."

Cole laid Abbie on the sofa. "I'll fetch the doc. I don't reckon you want to leave 'er."

"You're so kind, Mr. . . . ."

"Cole, ma'am. Cole Jasper." He tipped his hat, then swung back into the saddle.

Abbie felt like a rag doll as her mama removed the wet clothing and dressed her warmly. Rather than clarifying, everything seemed to be dimming, a confusing hodgepodge of motion and shadow. Of course it was a dream. A terrible, impossible dream. She slept and woke. Men's voices. Mama's cool hand on her cheek. Then sleep again.

◆◆◆◆◆◆◆

Monte turned as Cole was shown into the library. "Where have you been?"

"Mr. Farrel, if you wanted a welcoming party, you shoulda said when you'd be comin'."

"The other men checked in hours ago."

Cole fingered the brim of the hat he held. "I've been doin' a bit o' rescuin'."

Something in Cole's manner caught Monte short. "Oh?"

"That young Miss Martin that come lookin' fer you the other day took a fall out round Templeton Gap."

Monte stood as though Cole had struck him.

"Got a good knock and purty near froze. I fetched the doc."

"What is it, Monte?" Sharlyn's skirts rustled as she entered.

Monte's mouth felt like chalk. "Cole, this is my wife, Mrs. Sharlyn Farrel."

His eyes widened. "A pleasure, ma'am."

"And for me, Mr. Jasper. Monte's told me wonderful things about you."

"That right?" Cole cocked his head.

Ordinarily, Monte would have come back with something cutting, but his temple was throbbing and he gripped the brandy decanter.

"Monte?"

He turned to Sharlyn. "You remember the girl you met in

173

town this morning? Cole found her unconscious in the snow."

"Is she all right?" Sharlyn faced Cole.

"I reckon so. But it's lucky I wandered up that way or she'd be a goner by now, I guess."

Monte winced. "Well, thank God you were there. We'll discuss business tomorrow."

"Yes, sir." Cole tipped his hat to Sharlyn on his way out.

Monte recoiled at Sharlyn's touch on his arm, then caught himself. "I'm sorry."

"Poor Monte. You're so fond of her."

He swirled the glass cupped in his palm. "Abbie's father is my partner, as you know. He's a fine man." Sharlyn's eyes rested on him. He could not avoid this, but how could he speak of Abbie? "They were the first to welcome me here, and Abbie ... she's like this place. Fresh and strong and uncorrupted. She ..." The brandy burned in his throat.

Sharlyn was perceptive. Not too perceptive, he prayed. Even these few words conjured memories and desires he must restrain. What he had expected to feel at his return was nothing near the terrible reality. Not to saunter over to the Martin homestead and sit at their table, sharing a meal and lively banter, nor to stroll the hillsides with Abbie, nor to see the look of anticipation in her eyes when he arrived. . . .

Instead, he would endure the memory of her shock and condemnation. He had expected disdain, though part of him had hoped she would understand and accept the message in the letter he had sent through Frances. But the wild look of incredulous pain ... Had she refused to believe his words? Had she hoped the letter would prove some cruel trick?

And now she lay injured, as much as by his hand. He wanted to tell her everything, to explain what had happened and why, but that would betray Sharlyn. The depth of his loss left him hollow.

Sharlyn waited.

"I am concerned for her," he said simply.

She nodded. "I pray she'll recover soon. She must be very special to earn such respect from you."

Monte's jaw tightened, and he reached for her hand. "You're special, Sharlyn."

Her color rose up. "You make me so happy."

◆◆◆◆◆◆◆

Cold, darkness, sweat, and shivers. Abbie's head was thick. The darkness lessened, and faces appeared. One face, pale and smiling, so delicate . . . eyes like mossy pools . . . Sharlyn, Sharlyn Farrel. She jolted awake. The room was dark, but she could make out the shape of a man slumped in a chair in the corner. Monte! No, too thick to be Monte or Pa. A medicinal odor accompanied him. Doctor Barrow. Her eyes closed again.

◆◆◆◆◆◆◆

"I believe she's past the worst of it now." Doctor Barrow's voice filtered to Abbie. "Pneumonia is a threat with a chill like this, but her constitution is strong. I'll check back day after tomorrow."

Through the thickness she saw him gather his things. What day was it? Why must there be a tomorrow? A pain worse than her head gripped her inside. She had been foolish to ride so carelessly, but she was worse than a fool to have trusted Monte with her heart.

Mama saw Doctor Barrow to the door, then returned to her side. Abbie recalled waking at odd times, the lantern in her eyes, the smell of Doctor Barrow's fingers. She must have hit her head hard, but things were clearing now. She wished they weren't.

Mama made no small talk. "I'm sorry about Monte. I know

it doesn't seem possible, but it will pass. 'To everything there is a season, and a time to every purpose under heaven.'"

Closing her eyes, Abbie nodded. Did Mama know how it hurt to think God had allowed this, after all?

Nineteen

Abbie took her shawl and stepped outside, breathing in the smell of spring, even though it would still be some time before the green returned in earnest. Though in other places March meant spring, here it was a crazy back-and-forth affair between the wet, heavy snows and warm, dry days.

A magpie called as Abbie headed for the hills through the scrub oaks, bare with the buds still encased in bark. She was amazed how shaky her legs were, but then it had been so long since she was up and about. The magpie launched into the air, its white breast and shimmery blue-black wings rising high above her. That would be something to experience. If she could fly, she would go far, far away, away from the memories, the places that called out Monte's name to her, the sights that brought his face to her mind. She looked from the bird into the wide open sky and wondered how she had failed.

A cottontail darted out of hiding and scampered across her path. She remembered telling Monte how she could track and fish and climb trees. No wonder he hadn't wanted to marry her. He wanted a proper lady for his wife, but the cruelty of his empty promises was not diminished. *Please God*, she prayed. *Please help it not to hurt so. . . .*

She bent and parted the stubby winter grass to reveal a wild crocus just opening its petals to the sun. She ran her finger over the fuzzy bloom. It looked as fragile as she felt—she who had prided herself on her hearty constitution, on her ability to take whatever came. Well, face it she would.

Two weeks in bed with a concussion and pneumonia had sapped her strength, but she could feel it returning. She breathed the scent of smoke and sheep dung and sage, then turned her steps homeward. An unfamiliar horse was tethered to the post, and at the table with a cup of coffee sat Cole Jasper. Abbie smiled as he stood.

"Abbie, this is Cole Jasper, who found you in the storm," Mama said.

"Yes, I recall. I hoped I'd have the chance to thank you." She could not have sought him out at Monte's ranch. Not even the debt of her life would bring her there.

"That ain't needed, Miss Martin. I just came to see that you're on the mend. Mr. Farrel was askin', as well."

Abbie raised her chin. "You may let Mr. Farrel know that I'm completely recovered. I haven't been thrown since I was very small. I'm lucky you happened by when you did." Cole looked too restless and windblown for the kitchen to contain him. His green eyes and riotous blond hair belonged on the range.

"Well, I'll just be on my way. Thank you fer the coffee, ma'am." He nodded to Mrs. Martin.

Abbie walked him to the door. "Thank you for everything, Mr. Jasper. I owe you my life."

Cole pulled the hat down on his brow. "I'd be obliged if you'd call me Cole."

"Very well, Cole. Give my regards to Mr. and Mrs. Farrel." Abbie said the proper words with the proper tone.

"I will, miss."

"Abbie," she corrected.

"Miss Abbie." Tipping his hat, he left.

"That was kind of him to come, wasn't it?" Abbie knew her voice was flat. Even she didn't recognize it.

"Yes," Mama replied, looking long at her.

♦♦♦♦♦♦♦

The thawed ground was soft beneath the buggy wheels, and the baby leaves of the scrub oak, sumac, and mountain mahogany were unfurled as Abbie passed through on the way to town. Stopping before the grocer's, she nodded to Clara's pa, then went inside. "Why, Clara! What are you doing here?"

"Now there's a greeting."

Abbie laughed. "I'm sorry, but here you are behind the counter . . . and in your condition."

"I'm filling in for Ma today, who's poorly, and it's I who should be surprised to see you. It's been ages since you've come to town!" Clara tipped her head. "How are you, Abbie? But for this baby I'd have come . . ."

"I'm strong as a horse. You know that." She handed Clara her list.

"Have a licorice." Clara pulled the flour sack from the shelves behind her.

As Abbie took a licorice drop from the jar, the door opened, and Sharlyn Farrel came in. Abbie's chest lurched.

Sharlyn's face glowed, her hair a pale halo, her smile angelic. "Miss Martin! I'm so glad to see you've recovered. I've wanted to visit, but Monte said it was too far for me to go alone."

Abbie heard Clara's breath catch. Sharlyn's words stung, but she made no sign. Of course Monte would not escort her over, though it was little farther to her homestead from his than the trip Sharlyn had made to town. At least he had the decency to keep his distance. "Yes, I suppose it is far when you're not familiar with it."

"So this is fortuitous. Could you . . . would you come to tea this afternoon?"

Sharlyn's cheeks flushed, and her face was so hopeful that Abbie bit back the instant rejection that had risen. She was aware of Clara behind her, who knew her so well she would read her expression, hear the falseness of her lie. She hesitated.

"Monte's with the men for roundup, and I'm longing for company." Sharlyn seemed to shrink into herself with this admission.

"Thank you. I'd be delighted." Abbie gripped the box that held her order. "I'll wait outside." She couldn't bear to have Clara watching her another minute. The bell on the door jingled as she pressed through and slid the box into the buggy. Her eyes glanced toward the church with the notice on the door. *Pastor wanted.* As though some reverend wandering by might see it and stay.

She sighed. She felt very much like a lost sheep. She had begged off the Sunday morning trips to the mission, claiming the distance too much for her yet. But it wasn't the distance across the land. It was the gap between her heart and God that kept her home. She tried, but she felt parched like the cracked stream beds awaiting the spring runoff.

Shaking her head, Abbie drew herself up. *What's done is done. I'll not be pitied.*

Mr. Niehman, the postmaster, stuck his head out the door of his tiny office. "I've a letter for you, Miss Martin. Came on the stage today."

"Blake," Abbie breathed. She dropped the box and ran to fetch the letter. "Thank you." She worked it open and slipped out the paper within.

Dear Abbie,

We did it! We found gold and we're comin' back. Now I can give you everything you want. Mack an' me sold the mine and we'll be packin' up soon, so you wait for me. I love you, Abbie, and I shore hope you feel the same now.

Blake

Abbie stuffed the letter into her pocket. Picking up her

skirts, she burst back into the store. "Blake's coming back! He and Mack found gold, and they're coming back!"

Clara clapped her hands. "Oh, Abbie, I'm so glad!"

"Blake?" Sharlyn asked.

Abbie had forgotten her. "A friend. A dear friend."

She wished she could go somewhere alone and sort out her thoughts, but she had accepted an invitation. James drove Sharlyn's buggy and Abbie followed with her own. It was wonderful news that Blake was returning. Surely it was wonderful. Then why did it fade and leave her so empty?

It was more painful than she imagined to walk into Monte's house, and Abbie wished she hadn't come. She had never coveted his wealth, nor did she envy Sharlyn her grand home. Only Monte had mattered. But if they were all to live in the same town, she would have to get past the hurt, and she prayed silently to be able to start now.

Sharlyn was at ease with the servants, and bitterly Abbie realized that she had been born to that. Monte had chosen a woman bred in his heritage and traditions who would raise up his children properly. The ache gripped her. It had turned out exactly as he had said. She wondered if he pined for her. Well, she would not. She would get past this pain if it took all her strength to do it. She replaced her humble prayer with hard resolve.

They sat together in the parlor, and Pearl brought them the tea tray. Lifting the pot, Sharlyn poured out the steaming liquid into the fine china cups and handed one on its saucer to Abbie. "I'm so glad you could come. From the start I've wanted to meet you. You were the first person from Colorado Monte told me about."

"I guess he'd have to start somewhere." Sharlyn's eyes flicked to her, and Abbie changed her tone. "I imagine you're used to many more people."

"Yes . . . I miss my friends and family, though I've never been one for crowds. I think if I were more like you . . ." She blushed.

Abbie forced a smile. "And what am I like?"

"I shouldn't speak of what I don't know. Of course I . . . I can't say. . . ."

Abbie softened. "You don't have to worry. I'm the worst for saying inappropriate things."

"I don't believe that."

"Well, you don't know me."

Sharlyn twisted her hands. "I would like us to be friends. When I was younger I was painfully shy."

Abbie felt Sharlyn's discomfort and wondered what had changed.

"You're all the things I wish I could be. Brave and strong and adventurous."

There was a cold sinking in Abbie's stomach.

"Monte spoke with such enthusiasm. I couldn't hear enough. I was as excited to meet you as to see my new home."

The girl's southern accent, so like Monte's, gave her voice a soft lilt that sweetened her words. Sharlyn couldn't be mocking or baiting her. She was almost childlike in her honesty. Was it possible she had no idea what had been in Monte's heart? But then, what had? Lies and dishonor—nothing he would reveal to his wife.

"That's very kind." It sounded false and patronizing. "Had I known Monte was bringing you, I . . ." Abbie's throat constricted. She couldn't lie to the guileless woman. "It's a surprise, of course."

"It was sudden. I keep pinching myself." Sharlyn pressed the skin of her arm between her fingers, leaving a rush of pink on white. "But please, tell me about Blake. Is he your beau?"

Abbie paused. "I don't know what he is. Just Blake, I guess. He taught me woodcraft and hunting and . . . things I don't suppose a lady needs to know."

"Why not? When Monte told me the things you could do, track and carve a spear . . ."

Abbie's anger flared, incensed that Monte had told Sharlyn all the personal things she had shared with him. What right did he have to reveal her soul to this stranger, this usurper? She wanted to run and scream and tell Sharlyn that it was she whom Monte had held in his arms, her lips he had kissed!

A sudden flush burned Sharlyn's face clear up to the hairline. Her voice quavered. "I've offended you."

Forcing down the resentment, Abbie willed herself to remain seated. "Not at all. Did Monte tell you about Blake?"

"Not a word."

"Well, when Monte first came to town, Blake tried to shoot him."

"What?"

"He was a bit overprotective." There, let that sink in. But to her surprise, Sharlyn laughed, and Abbie found herself laughing, too, the sudden release like sun after a storm. The parlor door opened and Monte stood there. Abbie's laugh died in her throat.

Sharlyn turned. "See who I have here, Monte?"

"Yes." His eyes were on Abbie alone.

"I was just leaving." Abbie stood up stiffly. "Thank you for tea."

"Must you go?" Sharlyn wilted.

"I'm afraid so."

Abbie had brushed by Monte and made it down the porch stairs before he could reach the front door. "Abbie, wait!" he called, but she threw herself onto the wagon seat and took up the reins.

"Ha!" Shiloh jumped and Abbie did not look back.

◆◆◆◆◆◆◆

Monte lay in the dark. How would he survive this? He

closed his eyes, and her face appeared behind his lids. Silky brown hair springing from her soft skin, eyes that made him weak when the lashes drooped just so, and the soft mouth that had responded so richly to his ardor. He flung his body onto his side, and Sharlyn stirred.

He looked at her lying like an angel in her white gown. He could almost imagine wings sprouting from the thin shoulder blades beneath the fabric. What man would not be thrilled to have so exquisite a creature beside him as his own? She was his wife for better or worse until death. He reached out a hand and stroked the fair hair twisted into a braid behind her back. Sharlyn's eyes opened, and he kissed her.

Twenty

Abbie ran her fingers through the long grasses as she sat on the hill beside Sharlyn. Monte had given in to Sharlyn's urging and shown her the way here, and she now made regular visits. For all her demure bashfulness, she seemed stubbornly determined to befriend her, and as a child picks a scab, Abbie let Sharlyn's talk of Monte rip open her wound again and again.

But looking at her now, sitting in the grass with her skirts circled about her, Abbie found that, even more than Clara, Sharlyn had connected with her heart. Was it because they loved the same man? Or was it just Sharlyn herself? Abbie drooped the chain of black-eyed Susans over Sharlyn's pale head like a crown. "There now, you're a nymph holding court. What will you decree?"

Sharlyn touched the blossoms. "I wouldn't have any idea. What would you?"

Abbie leaned back, feasting on the springtime around her. "I decree that the wind blow us an adventure."

Sharlyn laughed.

Abbie sat up again. "What shall it be?"

"Let's not have Indians."

"Why not?" She gestured up the hillside. "Right up that ridge is where I saw the Comanche braves. It was the most indescribable thrill when they came out of the woods on their mustang ponies, all dressed in beads and feathers."

"Were you really not afraid?"

"It wasn't a fearful thing at all. It was as though they were part of the mountains and I was, too."

"Have you seen them since?"

"Not since they brought me the rabbits. But I've looked." Abbie's eyes went up to the ridge. "Perhaps in the fall they'll return. Some bands still come through, and the Utes live up the pass south and west of here." She shook her head. "I've never been moved as I was by that hunter, and I hope . . . I believe he lives free, somewhere."

"I should like to see him, but I would not like him to see me."

"He'd think you were a vision from the Great Spirit."

Laughing, Sharlyn asked, "Why would he think that?"

"Because you're so fair and tiny." Abbie turned to her. "Perhaps he would think you were sent to lead them to a new hunting ground, unviolated by settlers who think their ways are savage."

"Are they not, Abbie?"

"Sometimes. But then so are ours. Even the ways of southern gentility can be cruel." Abbie spoke without thinking.

"Is that why you and Monte are no longer friends?"

Abbie bit her lip. "Why do you say that?"

"Isn't it so?"

"Of course not."

Sharlyn pulled the flowers from her hair into her lap. "I believe he's hurt you . . . and I know it grieves him."

Abbie turned away.

"I've known Monte since I was a child, and he can't bring trouble to anyone, especially one who was once, and must still be, dear to him."

Abbie wanted to shake her. How dare she defend Monte? "Really, Sharlyn. You think the oddest things." She pointed.

"Look, there's the eagle that nests on the bluff! Just look how magnificent!"

The bird circled below them, dove suddenly and grabbed a rabbit in its talons, then mounted up with powerful strokes toward the bluff. Life and death in one act. Life for one, death for the other.

Abbie stood and replaced her wide-brimmed hat. Sharlyn rose behind her. "Shall I come tomorrow?"

"I'll be at the mission."

"The mission?"

"The Franciscan brothers run an orphanage school." Abbie spoke as she walked. "Blake and I attended there. Blake hated it, of course. It's one of the only ways we're different. He was a naughty boy and wouldn't learn his lessons. Repeatedly, Father Dominic applied the rod and made him recite his lessons alone since he hadn't followed in class. I'd wait, and when he came out, he'd whistle like nothing had happened and then take my hand and run until he had worked out all the shame of it.

"I think I loved him best then, because he was so brave not to cry or rage or even complain. But then the next day or several days later it would be the same all over again. He never did learn much. He was too stubborn."

Sharlyn sighed. "I wish I could learn better. As hard as I try, I can't seem to decipher the words. They look different every time I see them."

Abbie stopped. "Are you telling me you can't read?"

"It's very difficult. That's why I like it so much when you and Monte tell me about things and people. It's like reading a story."

"I'll read to you if you like. I have ever so many books."

Sharlyn pressed her hand. "Would you, Abbie? Sometimes Monte reads aloud, but it's different kinds of things, and I think it frustrates him."

"Does he know your trouble?" She knew how highly Monte valued literary skills.

"I have alluded to it, but . . ." She sighed.

They entered the house and Abbie led the way to the study, opened the door, and relished the smell of the leather bindings. This was her favorite room in the house, and she silently thanked the Lord that He had not afflicted her like Sharlyn. "Would you choose one or shall I?"

"You choose, Abbie."

"Then I'll read you *Jane Eyre*. Have you heard it?"

"No."

"It's terribly tragic. Just like the author herself. Charlotte Brontë was sent off to a dreadful school for clergymen's daughters along with three of her sisters, and two of them died early, possibly because of that. Charlotte herself died in childbirth."

"Like Monte's mother," Sharlyn mused.

"I didn't know it was childbirth."

"Yes, and the infant son with her. Terribly sad."

"You've known him a long while." Abbie spoke half to herself.

"All my life, though I never dreamed he saw me. He was so . . . full of life and humor. And I . . ." She waved her hands. "Listen to me running on."

Abbie curled her feet under her in the window seat, willing the hurt to subside. The next three hours, she read aloud as Sharlyn sat enraptured by the tale, eyes glowing and mouth drawn up in a smile. She was surprised when Pa came home from work.

Sharlyn jumped up. "Can it be that late! What will Monte think?" She rushed to her feet, and they reached the door just as Monte rode up stern-faced in the buggy. What had it cost him to set aside his pride and come? How deeply he must care for Sharlyn.

"Thank you ever so much!" Sharlyn squeezed Abbie's hand.

Monte handed Sharlyn into the buggy. Then, climbing up beside her, he grabbed the reins. Abbie had her back to him before he said his stiff, "Good evening, Abbie."

♦♦♦♦♦♦♦

Abbie thought of Sharlyn as she listened to the young voices forming the sounds from the first primer. "No, Jeremy." She ran his finger back to the word he had mispronounced.

"Re . . . si . . . st."

"Good." She let him read on. Could she help Sharlyn? Part of her took a wicked delight in Monte's disappointment. Sharlyn's inability to study and discourse with him must be a thorn in his happiness. But a look into Jeremy's round face filled her with remorse. Would they trust her if they knew she was capable of such wicked thoughts? "That's enough. Pauline, read now."

Abbie knew little about Sharlyn's difficulty. She had read of studies on brain conditions that made learning difficult. She was not qualified to work with something like that. Perhaps the best she could do was satisfy Sharlyn's longing by reading aloud as she had. It was little enough.

Twenty-One

Blake led his gray mare close as Mack pulled a rope tight and grunted, "Sure am tired of strikin' camp." He checked the ropes again on the three mules loaded with provisions and gold coin, the proceeds from the sale of their mine. "Ready?"

"Yup." Blake mounted. "I can almost smell Abbie's cookin' already." He threw his head back and sang the chorus of "Oh, Susannah," but substituted "Oh, my Abbie."

Mack shook his head. "She'll be cryin' for you all right if you mean to keep up that noise."

Blake laughed. "Sure wish we were there. I got me a longin' down in my chest that ain't gonna give me peace till I take her in my arms. . . ."

"Yeah, yeah. I know all about that burnin'. But we ain't there yet, so cool it down."

Blake was sore and saddle weary from toiling over the Rockies. But every mile was one mile closer to home. The sun beat down, sapping his strength. "Sure am glad it ain't August." He wiped the grime from his forehead.

"Yup. It's already hot 'nough to singe a rattler."

The mountains were dry tinder waiting for a spark, except at night when the chill drove the heat away. It wasn't so much the heat but the sun bearing down on them without a cloud to thin it.

The regular plodding of the horse lulled Blake into silence.

It was funny. Here he was rich, and he didn't feel any different at all. Except he was a whole lot surer Abbie would have him. He wished she could have written him back, but he hadn't had an address for a while, tucked up into the slopes. He and Mack had kept clear of the busy camps, most of which housed the already producing mines. They hadn't the money for that kind of operation and weren't looking to work for someone who did. So they stuck with the old tried and true panning and sluicing, trying areas not already worked.

At least that had been the plan. Mack was right, though. They never would have got much that way. Finding the vein had been their redemption. Of course, that meant money to set up, machinery, men ... and a whole lot more know-how than they had. Once they'd picked clean all they could get at, it was time to hand it over to someone else. It took less than a day to find a buyer, and the deal they cut wasn't half bad. How Abbie's eyes would shine when he told her.

But they had ground to cover yet. In a day or so, depending on the mules, they'd be headed down the Ute pass, then skirting the base of the foothills along the eastern slope to Rocky Bluffs and home.

The sun finished its lazy arc and sank to the earth. Blake's back ached something fierce by the time they stopped for the night. He climbed out of the saddle and groaned. "I been too long doin' this."

Mack tipped back his hat. "That makes two of us."

They unpacked and watered the mules and horses at the creek they'd followed for the better part of the week. Mack stretched out against his pack. "You want a fire?"

"Nah. I'll jest fill my belly with jerky and sleep like a baby." Blake climbed into his bedroll and shuffled until he was comfortable. "See ya at midnight." Curled into the blanket against the cold mountain air, he watched the moon shrink from an amber globe to a small white disk as it climbed the sky. Overhead an owl whooshed and disappeared into the trees. Blake closed his eyes and imagined Abbie in his arms. Soon . . . soon.

When morning came, they broke camp and packed up the meager provisions they had left, redistributed the bundles on the mules, and started out again. To break the tedium, Blake urged his horse beside Mack. "You know the first thing I'm gonna do when I get back and marry Abbie?"

"Yup. The first thing any man does when he marries."

"I mean after that." Blake grinned.

"What?"

"I'm gonna take her up top of the lightning pine and have her pick whatever piece of land she wants, and I'm gonna buy it for her."

"Abbie's eighteen years old now. You ain't gonna git her to the top of the lightning pine."

"Wanna bet?"

"I bet you one hundred dollars you don't get her anywhere up that tree."

"Easiest hundred bucks I ever made." Blake laughed. "Abbie ain't worried what people say. She'll make it to the top, and I'll be right there beside her just like we used to."

Mack shook his head. "You always were a pair of wild ones."

"I couldn't imagine it any other way. Who'd want to marry someone who didn't do nothin' but cook an' clean and whimper all the time?"

"Nothin' wrong with cookin' and cleanin', Blake. If you plan to live in a house, that is. But maybe you and Abbie will just perch in some tree, eh?"

"No chance. I mean to build Abbie the finest house in all Rocky Bluffs. Finer even than Farrel's. What're you gonna do when you git home, Mack?"

"Take a bath."

◆◆◆◆◆◆◆

The lumberyard was filled with eager faces as the fiddlers stroked the strings and tuned, and Monte led Sharlyn past the tables laden with punch and cider, apple Betty, fruit and confections. In spite of his resolve, he searched the room for Abbie. She stood fresh and beautiful in a gown the color of her eyes, her hair pulled into thick sausage curls except for the ever present tendrils that teased around her forehead.

"Shall we join Abbie?" Sharlyn tugged his arm, following his gaze.

Jarred from his thoughts, he patted her hand. "You go ahead."

He watched them embrace in greeting. How ironic that the person who stood between them should be welcomed so warmly, while Abbie refused even to look at him. At first he had welcomed the distance. Being near was too painful. But now he hungered for something of what they'd had. Some small connection. Some indication that she felt more than loathing for him.

Laughing, she glanced his way. His chest lurched, but she turned her back so as not to repeat her error. He released his breath.

Joshua nodded, and Monte returned the gesture. No welcome there, either. You don't jilt a man's daughter without paying a price. He eyed the punch with disdain. Whiskey would be in better order, but the women's temperance were up in arms for every town function, Founder's Day included. Fortunately, Sharlyn wasn't militant about drink, as it had become a consolation. Of course, it was impossible to imagine her militant or even passionate about anything, except Abbie maybe.

What quirk of fate had knit them so closely? Did Abbie use Sharlyn to torment him? Did she encourage her to run on continuously over everything she said and did? No, that wasn't possible. Sharlyn was oblivious. He masked the need that fed on her recounting, but it was worse to have Abbie translated secondhand and know that were he present, she would grow cold and silent. One day it would drive him mad.

The caller climbed onto the crate and ordered the gents to find a lady to do-si-do. Monte waited until Abbie was claimed before he found Sharlyn and swept her into motion.

"Oh, Monte, we haven't danced in so long."

He felt a stab of remorse. She was lovely and eager to please. Sister to his closest friend, bound to him by honor . . . and love. It shone in her face and rang in the lilt of her voice. They bowed low to pass under the arms forming an arch above them and stepped backward, clapping, before he hooked his arm through hers and spun. Sharlyn was grace itself, as light as air on her feet. Had she set her hat for anyone, she would have had him. But she was his.

The square dances were lively, working off the exuberance of the gents, and, as Abbie once said, more like a stampede once the cowboys hit the floor. Near at hand, he watched as Cole claimed her.

"I declare, Cole, I hardly recognize you." Abbie curled her arm through his.

Cole ran a hand over his trimmed mustache beneath the slicked and parted hair. He was playing the part well. "I meant to git a dance with the purtiest girl in the room."

"I'd have danced with you anyway."

"I was hopin' it wasn't a beholdin' kinda thing."

"Of course not."

Monte frowned. What did Cole think he was doing, dancing with Abbie like that, his hold on her as sure as his confidence in anything else. The music came to an end with the two couples at arm's length. If Abbie noticed he was near, she hid it well. Cole stayed right beside her, not releasing her arm. "I've a mind to keep hold of you fer the next one, Abbie, if you'll have me."

"Well, I . . ." One of Monte's cowboys came up eagerly.

"Git lost, you mangy critter." Cole stepped between them. "Abbie ain't changin' partners."

Monte expected Abbie to protest, but she seemed amused. "Cole, that was terrible."

"I don't hear you complainin'." He swung her to the floor again.

Monte tightened his arm on Sharlyn. "Cole's making a fool of himself."

"Why shouldn't he dance with her?" Sharlyn asked, more aware than he suspected. "He's nice enough, and a good dancer from the looks of it."

"She's eighteen years old. He's probably twice that at least."

"Surely not."

Sharlyn rarely disagreed with him, and Monte raised an eyebrow. "Close enough. And he's not in her class."

"I thought everyone was equal here, that there were no class differences."

"Well, you're wrong. Abbie is . . ."

" . . . qualified to decide for herself."

Monte was at a loss. This was the closest to argumentative Sharlyn had ever come. Was she defending Abbie to him?

"If you're concerned," she added softly, "why don't you ask her to dance yourself?"

He quelled his anger, feeling suddenly empty. "She'd not have me."

Sharlyn's hand rested on his arm. "Why not, Monte?"

"Suffice it to say I'd be the last person with whom Abbie would dance."

Thankfully she didn't press him. He settled her with a cup of punch, then found Cole at the end of the long table. "Miss Martin's too young for you."

Cole turned, surprised. "What's got yer hackles up?"

"It has nothing to do with me." Monte frowned. "You could

be her father, for heaven's sake."

Cole grinned impudently. "I'd'a had to start awful early fer that. Besides, I don't hear Abbie complainin'."

Monte wanted to cuff the smug smile from his face. Where did he get off . . .

Sharlyn slipped her arm through his. "Let's get some air, Monte."

He let her tug him. Any more of this and he would come to blows with Cole Jasper. The man was a cocky scoundrel. The cold air felt good. Overhead, the stars were brilliant in the sky.

Sharlyn clasped her hands at her throat. "I've never seen so many stars in all my life. Why do you suppose there are more here?"

"There aren't more. You just see them more clearly through the thinner air." He said it gently, but Sharlyn's cheeks flared. He wished she were not so sensitive. He had to constantly watch himself. And as hard as he tried, he couldn't get past her simpleness.

He liked to be challenged, and Sharlyn was anything but challenging. He looked at her now, downcast and silent, and brushed her arm with his fingers. "It doesn't matter how few or how many. In the starlight you're lovely." He kissed her forehead.

"Oh, Monte, you're so kind."

Her words burned him. He would pay dearly for his falseness.

Another couple stepped out and walked a little way, barely visible in the shadows. Monte leaned on the railing and breathed the night air. Abbie's laugh caught him by surprise as her partner spoke something too softly for him to catch the words. But he caught her into his arms, laughing. "Jest as easy as ropin' a steer." It was Cole. Of course.

"You wouldn't dare." Abbie's voice held the playful tone

that Monte remembered so well. He watched as Cole immobilized and kissed her.

"Cole Jasper!"

He released her. "Next time don't dare me."

"I never did!" There was indignation, but not enough to dissuade a swagger like Cole Jasper, and when he leaned close to repeat his offense, Abbie put up little resistance. Monte's fist curled involuntarily as his teeth clenched together. His chest felt squeezed as he stiffened, grabbed Sharlyn's arm, and turned her back in.

Passing through the lighted doorway, he caught her expression, and his chest went cold. He could only guess what she had seen revealed in his face. He led her to the floor to the strains of a waltz. She was like a child in his arms. "My darling," he whispered into her hair. Sharlyn said nothing.

"Are you feeling well?"

"I'm tired."

"I hope you weren't chilled."

"No. Not at all. But . . . I'd like to go."

He gathered her wrap about her and settled her into the buggy. It was his responsibility to care for Sharlyn. And he did care, though he never declared a love he didn't have for her. Was it honor not to dishonor her with a lie?

They drove in silence. Soft lights glimmered from the windows of their home as he drew up near the entrance and stopped. He lifted her down from the carriage and led her inside. She was silent and pale, and he knew he had hurt her. He must be more careful not to betray his feelings. He would put Abbie from his mind. He must, God help him.

As he watched Sharlyn ascend the stairs, he handed her wrap to James, then went to the library and poured a snifter of brandy. The aroma rose up, and he allowed it to warm in his palm before it coated his throat. He stared at the wall. What had been between Abbie and him was past. One day someone else would claim her. Again the brandy coursed down his throat, and he closed his eyes. What if it were Cole? No matter. It would not be he. He refilled and drained another glass, then went upstairs to Sharlyn.

She was in the bed, eyes closed, but she did not look asleep. He undressed. Sharlyn was warm and still as he climbed in beside her. "Sharlyn?" he whispered. She didn't answer. He rolled over and slept.

Twenty-Two

Looking down the pass from the summit, Blake surveyed the narrow trail winding down Ute pass. It looked a wild, undisturbed country, the pines densely clothing the slopes on either side of the trail. His hand went to the pistol at his side, there, ready, should he need it. "Last leg, Mack. Let's make it a short one."

Leading the mules down the narrow, winding way, Blake kept his senses alert. Even so, when the rough, burly man lunged in front of them he was surprised. His horse shied, then steadied as he held tight to the rein.

Three more horsemen surrounded them from the woods, blocking the trail forward and behind. Blake's muscles tensed.

"Well now . . ." The swarthy man spoke. "You boys must be near tuckered out haulin' all that stuff over these here hills, I'd wager."

Neither Blake nor Mack said a word, and the pink-faced man beside the first chuckled. "You reckon we oughta give 'em a hand with it, boss?"

"Seems it'd be only neighborly. All we ask is a proper thanky kindly." He hooked his thumbs in his belt over the twin revolvers. "See, boys, we're gonna help you with them mules. Kinda take 'em off yer hands awhile."

Blake's temper flared. "We don't need no help."

Mack shifted in the saddle but didn't speak.

The man on foot looked up to the horseman behind him. "You hear that? This boy don't need our help."

"Don't seem neighborly to me," the pink man replied.

A voice from behind said, "Jest shoot 'em, Hollister."

Blake stiffened. He had already guessed as much, and he'd fight before he'd let Hollister have his gold.

The swarthy man glared. "We don't shoot no one we don't have to, Wilkins. Round here we hang 'em."

The pink-faced man flitted his eyes. "Look, kid, jest let go the mules and ride out."

Hollister spun on him, and he backed off. Then turning back, Hollister snarled, "Now, boy, you owe me an apology. An' then you kin ask real nice fer help with yer mules."

In the fiery rush of his rage, Blake reached for his gun. A shot blasted before his hand found the trigger, and Mack lurched in his saddle, then tumbled out. Blake froze as the shock registered.

"Mack!" He leaped to the ground.

"You done killed yer brother, boy."

Crouched in the dirt, Blake turned Mack and held his head in his lap.

"Don't fight 'em," Mack groaned. "Abbie don't need yer gold." Mack gripped his hand, face contorted, then he grew limp.

White-hot fury seared Blake as he lunged for Hollister. The impact of a bullet sent him sprawling to the dust. First the sting, then pain filled his side as nerves and blood vessels found the damage. He moaned, feeling the blood soak into his shirt. Opening his eyes, he made out a pair of boots and slowly raised his face. *Oh, God, forgive my foolishness. And make Abbie think well of me. I loved her the best I could. You know that, God. You know.*

The shot exploded through the quiet woods and echoed down the rocky canyon.

◆◆◆◆◆◆◆

Side by side with Clara, Abbie strolled the boardwalk.

"I feel like a hen," Clara said.

Abbie laughed. "You have a reason for your girth, dear Clara. At least you're not foolish enough to clamp yourself into a corset."

"Doc Barrow won't allow it. Any woman in his care caught wearing a corset past the fourth month is charged double."

Monte and Cole stepped from the saddlery before them. Cole tipped his hat, grinning broadly. "Mornin', Abbie, Mrs. Franklin."

"Good morning, Cole, Mr. Farrel." Abbie caught Clara's arm and pressed on.

"Abbie, how could you?" Clara whispered. "You were cold as ice."

"I was perfectly cordial." Abbie stepped into the street. Before she could cross, a wagon rolled past, driven by a man she didn't know, but with a start, she recognized the gray horse with three white socks and off-center blaze tied to the back. She gripped Clara's arm. "That's Blake's horse!"

As the wagon stopped before the marshal's office, Abbie rushed forward, but the driver stopped her before she could get close. "No, miss, you won't be wantin' to look in there. A couple o' boys got killed in the pass an' I'm bringin' 'em in."

Abbie's knees jellied. "What boys?"

"By their bill o' sale, Mack and Blake McConnel."

Blood pounded in her ears and a choking scream gripped her throat. Both Monte and Cole ran over, but it was Cole who reached out and pulled her to his chest. People rushed in as the news spread, and Marshal Haggerty's voice rose above the hue. "All right, everybody keep back. We'll be makin' a posse soon enough."

Abbie felt cold as Cole held her until Pa cut through the

crowd. She pushed free of him and of her pa and fought toward the wagon bed.

"Don't let her do that! They been dead fer some days."

Pa grabbed her back.

"I don't believe him, Pa! It isn't Blake. It can't be!"

He kept a hold. "You stay right here. I'll have a look." He reached in and lifted the canvas, and his face set as he let it fall. "Where's Wes?"

"He's been fetched."

Abbie's fists clenched at her sides. "Pa?"

"I'm sorry, Abbie."

Deputy Clem Davis was barking orders. One group would ride with him and one with Marshal Haggerty. Cole turned to Monte. "I reckon I'll ride out with the posse."

Abbie raised her chin. "I'm going, too." The men turned to her.

"No, you're not," Pa said.

"I am, Pa. I'm going to find who did this."

The crowd grew quiet. Cole circled his hat in his hands.

Marshal Haggerty strode over. "We gotta ride long and hard, Miss Martin."

"I can ride as well as anyone out here."

"Look, I got a job to do, and I can't do it lookin' after you as well. Joshua?"

"Come on, Abbie. The men will find them." He reached for her arm, but she pulled it away.

Her chest rose and fell. Tightening her jaw, she swung around, her skirts swirling behind. The crowd parted to admit Wes McConnel, looking suddenly old, and grew silent as hats were removed. Abbie wouldn't look at him, wouldn't view his grief. She would fight back. An eye for an eye.

She made her way to the stable. The buggy could stay, and she would use whatever saddle was at hand. Her limbs seemed to work of their own volition, because her mind had gone numb. She would not think of anything but finding Blake's killer.

She had the buggy unhitched and the saddle on Shiloh's back when Monte walked into the shadows. She didn't look at him but reached under the horse's belly for the cinch. He took the reins.

"Don't try to stop me."

"I have to."

She pulled the cinch tight and tested it, then reached one foot up to the stirrup. Monte grabbed her arm, and Abbie yanked against him. "Let go! If they won't let me go with them, I'll go myself!"

"You can't."

She tried to pry his hand off, but Monte grabbed her other arm as well. "Abbie, you'll only make it harder for them. They need their strength concentrated on the business at hand."

"I don't need their help!"

"Whether you need it or not, they can't help giving it. You'll only keep them from doing what they must."

She struggled against his grip. "Let me go! You can't stop me!"

"You can't bring Blake back, and endangering yourself won't prove your love." His voice was calm and cruel.

Abbie's mouth fell open. "How dare you!"

Monte held his grip. "I'm sorry, Abbie. I'm truly sorry."

She trembled. "Well, don't be. Don't be sorry for me, ever, do you hear?"

"I'll see you home."

"You won't."

"I promised your father."

"What's a promise to you? Kindly remove your hand, Mr. Farrel."

"Not until I have your word that you'll go home."

Abbie felt her defenses starting to crumble. *Dear God, don't* let me cry in front of Monte. "I'm going home." She swung into the saddle, slapped the reins, and the horse lurched forward.

Out in the open, Abbie turned the horse's head to the hills. If they had shot them down in the pass, would they make their escape to the west, away from the town and pursuit? But that would be expected. What would a twisted, wily mind do? She gazed back over the plain, crisscrossed by gaps and ridges. That's where a snake would go.

The horse was fresh, but she had no provisions. It could be hours before the posse was ready to go. What could she do alone? She could track them. She could track as well as any man out there, thanks to Blake. No, don't think of him. But she heard his voice, *The trick is to walk gentle. Don't mar what's left for you to see.* They had crept together following scratches so faint, a bent twig, crushed foliage. A pack of horses would leave much more.

Abbie raised her head. Once past the town, she would traverse the plain until she found the track. *Can't rush off half-cocked.* She had laughed at that. Blake telling *her*, when he was the one blowing off at anything. But in the woods or on the hunt he was like a wild thing himself, sly and still and wise. She would need water. But going to the homestead would seal Pa's orders.

She swung wide to the Maccabee cabin. With luck, old man Maccabee would be sleeping one off. Dismounting, Abbie looked cautiously about. Only a nest of wasps droned in the corner of the porch roof. She crept forward. The door rubbed against the rough floor as she made a space just wide enough to press through. Inside smelled stale and sour—sweat and whiskey and smoke. Her eyes grew accustomed to the dim. The single room was empty.

On the wall hung a pair of canteens. Two would be better than one, but Maccabee would more likely believe he'd misplaced one than both. She pulled it from the nail. This was almost too easy. Back out in the sunshine, she squinted. The mare stomped one hind leg. Abbie dipped the canteen past the rotting shelf of the well and brought it up soaked and filled, then hung it around her neck and mounted.

Stealth and speed together. Stay close to cover. Well, there wasn't much cover where she was going until she reached the gullies. So speed for now. The horse responded, leaping into a canter, and the wind brought tears to her eyes. She declared it was the wind. Her hair whipped her face. Skirting the farthest outbuildings of Rocky Bluffs, she held the horse to a canter and began crossing the plain in a series of passes. She concentrated on the southern reaches since the Ute pass lay that way.

Sweat spread between her shoulder blades under the noon sun as she kept her face to the ground. Mourning cloak butterflies flew up on black wings and a prairie dog scuttled to its hole. As the sun arced toward the mountains, she drained the last of the water and flung the canteen across her back to keep it from banging her chest. Her neck and shoulders ached. She had stopped twice to rest the mare and walked her frustration off. Herds of antelope, rabbits, coyotes, and varmints had left their mark, but no sign of horses.

Abbie kicked the dirt. Had she guessed wrong? Had they gone over the mountains after all? There was more cover that way, more danger and difficulty, but it was too obvious. An animal on the run switched back. She urged the mare farther south. Suddenly she reined in, pushing up in the stirrups. The ground was torn and trampled. She dropped to the grass. Hoof marks as deep as her second knuckle; the front edge dug in sharply. They were moving fast.

Her heart pounded in her chest. The marshal would be gone. They were starting at the pass, hoping to get the trail there. Maybe they'd follow it here, but how much time would be lost? Could she catch up to them? If she cut directly to the pass . . . but Shiloh was spent. Even now her head hung and her gait was rough. Abbie turned for home. The horse smelled the wind and perked her ears.

"Last effort," Abbie whispered and urged her past a trot to a canter. They'd make it to the homestead before dusk if she could keep this pace. Then . . . if Pa would not allow her to go . . . But someone would go when she told them what she'd found.

Before she reached the homestead, Pa met her. His face was drawn, but he said nothing when she burst upon him. "I found tracks."

"Your Mama needs you home."

A cold weight settled in her chest. "But, Pa . . ."

"The men are riding, Abbie. Women have another call."

"But . . ."

He turned his horse about. Pain washed over her. Hadn't she as much right to vengeance? What awaited her at home? Blake? No. She had sent him away, called him a fool boy for loving her. The mare plodded behind her father's gelding.

When they reached the homestead, Mama was on her way to the McConnels'. Abbie slipped off the mare and climbed into the buggy. Turning to Pa before he led Shiloh off, she said, "I found the track, Pa. They're not in the mountains. They're south of here and east, out across the plains."

He nodded. She and Mama rode silently.

Abbie entered the house where Blake had been raised and now awaited burial. She viewed the scene as from a great distance. Blake's sister, Mariah, stood with her hands against her face by the table that held the bodies. Mary, her mother, was removing the boys' clothes. Abbie's eyes found Blake, lying beside Mack. Blood crusted the side of his shirt, and part of his skull was gone. A trembling began in her spine, and the ache crushed her chest with iron bands.

She stepped forward once and again until she reached his side. The stench was foul, their bodies blackened and corrupt, but Abbie took a towel from the vinegar water that stood in the tub by the table. Slowly she wrung it out and rubbed it over Blake's face, over the sunken eyes and the lips that curled back. Behind her, Mariah sobbed and rushed from the room. Abbie mutely dipped the cloth and went on washing.

A strange and senseless act. This wasn't Blake. Blake wasn't here. Beside her Mary McConnel and Mama likewise tended Mack. The oldest and the youngest McConnel sons, together in death; no, not death. Abbie forced her arms to rub, her eyes to see . . . but her mind would not believe.

When they had been washed, the bodies were draped. Wes and Pa came and stood in the doorway. Wes slumped heavily in the jamb. Davy, the only remaining son, stood behind them with Mariah under his arm. Abbie brushed her finger over Blake's as she stepped back, her farewell unspoken.

◆◆◆◆◆◆◆

The bright morning sun cut sharp shadows from the mourners across the holes in the earth. Father Dominic in his brown hooded robe closed the Holy Scriptures and reached up in benediction. No one looked askance at the Latin, though many had never had any traffic with the brothers. Their grief united them, and their mute prayers reached heaven together.

Abbie stood silent and dry eyed as the pine boxes were lowered on ropes into the ground and Wes and Mary and Davy and Mariah dropped handfuls of earth into the depth. She watched them huddle together, felt her parents like sentries beside her, yet inside was nothing. Sharlyn came forward. "I'm so sorry. If there's anything . . ." Abbie nodded without really seeing her or Monte beside her. Sharlyn squeezed her fingers and passed by. Others murmured, touched, pressed her hands. They felt foreign and unreal.

The McConnels were gathered back to their home. Abbie walked, spoke, and responded through no effort of her own.

If she thought hard enough, Blake would walk through the door with his crooked smile and tell them all it was a mistake. *I'm home*, he'd say, tossing back his hair. If she thought hard enough she could see it. The waiting was terrible. If not today . . . when?

Pa told her word was sent of the track she'd found. No word said they'd heeded it. Everyone guessed it was Hollister they sought, and they knew the odds. With the newspaper Pa called them to war in their hearts and minds against the evil that lived and breathed within the shell of humanity that was Buck Hollister. But the men returned, robbed of vengeance and justice, like wolves that found no satisfaction for their hunger.

◆◆◆◆◆◆◆

Buck Hollister watched as the single rider sped over the rough terrain, doubled back through a crevice, and up over a ridge before turning into the gulch. He stood at the opening of the cave in the rocky wall, gun ready in his hand. He could smell the nerves of the men behind him. Recognizing Briggs, he relaxed and holstered his gun.

Briggs jumped from the animal. "Posse's gone home." He shoved a newspaper his way. "Thought you'd be interested in this."

Hollister stepped out into the sun and leaned against the rocky wall. His mood darkened as he read. The breath eased past his teeth in a low hiss. "No one calls me a coward. No one."

"We takin' 'im out?" Briggs asked.

He gazed out toward the blue ridge of mountains and the town of Rocky Bluffs nestled at their feet. "You recall that daughter Wilkins spoke of?"

The cold look in Briggs' eyes showed their thoughts matched. Hollister stretched a slow grin and found it returned.

◆◆◆◆◆◆◆

Abbie dropped to the ground on the grassy hillside beside the gravestones. Blake would never again appear in her doorway or walk at her side, his unabashed affection worn clearly on his face. Too soon, her feeble thoughts had given in to the truth.

In the two weeks since his death, memories of their days together had both tormented and comforted her, and she had found her way here repeatedly to sit beside the graves. The May sunshine warmed the slope through the needles of the pines above her, and a jay scolded from their branches.

Looking up, Abbie could almost hear Blake's voice calling to her from the top of the trunk. *That's it, Abbie. Grab that branch, take my hand . . . ain't this a view?* Was it all because she didn't love him well enough? Even now, she imagined him only as the friend he had been to her, but she hoped that now he understood.

"Oh, Blake," she murmured, "I miss you so. I wish we could have stayed children together. There are so many more trees to climb and streams to wade. And you never did tell Mama, did you? You kept all my secrets better than I did and loved me with all my faults." Her voice faltered. "Please forgive me for driving you away. I never meant it to come to this." Her shoulders shook with the sobs that finally broke through her hard denial.

What was God about? What manner of sovereign was He? Somewhere Blake's killer lived and breathed. Somewhere her love loved another. She shook her head. Her child's faith would not bring her into womanhood. How confident she had been in the providence of God. Was she wrong? Was it all a grand deception? Was Blake at peace? Was there peace?

Not here, nor hope. And yet, not to hope was to despair, to turn her back upon the Lord. Were dreams made only to be broken? Even if her dream were laid before her now, she would not take it up. To hope, to imagine, to love held more pain than she could stand.

Still, life pressed on, moment by moment, and she was a pawn to God's purpose. So be it. She would neither rebel nor embrace. What would come, would come. Rising to her feet, she walked down the slope to the McConnel house and tapped on the door.

Mary McConnel hugged her. "Thank you for coming, but I'm managing."

Abbie nodded. They were all just managing, going from one task to the next, one thought to the next. "I went up to see Blake. I hope you don't mind."

"You go anytime you like. He loved you so." Mary's rough palm brushed her cheek. "I thought you would become my own daughter one day. Even though Blake is gone, I consider you so."

Laying her head on the other woman's shoulder, Abbie wept again, but this time with relief. Her heart would not have been Blake's, had he returned. She was wrong to think they could have stayed friends. She would have destroyed this woman's hopes as surely as she had Blake's. She was not fit to love. She had given her heart wrongly, and God had condemned her.

Twenty-Three

Abbie walked the street, transformed by banners and swags of red, white, and blue, past the bandstand beside the square. People stood shoulder to shoulder along the walks as she pushed through. Sharlyn caught her sleeve. "Abbie, watch here with me."

She hadn't planned to watch the race, but Sharlyn looked so hopeful. They had been strained these last months, and she knew Sharlyn was hurt by her distance. Reluctantly, Abbie settled beside her as the men on horseback took their places behind the chalked line. Nine horses stomped and snorted, tossing their heads and straining against the bit. Cole caught her eye and winked, and she waved her good wishes. Beside him, Monte glanced up, then returned his attention to Sirocco, the black socked Arabian that stood hands taller than the others. Monte's horse was the swiftest, she knew, but it remained to be seen if he could run the course as well as the others without being disqualified.

Sharlyn clung to her arm, breathless with anticipation as Ethan Thomas lifted his arm and the gun shattered the morning. The people cheered as the horses leaped forward, vying for position down the rutted road and off across the plain. The crowd scattered.

"Where shall we go to watch?" Sharlyn asked.

Abbie shrugged. "I'm off to see Clara and the baby. You go

ahead." She wouldn't view Monte's triumph. Sharlyn gave no argument, and Abbie took the lane to the two-story frame house Marty had completed.

Clara was radiant. Beside her the round-cheeked infant dozed, and Abbie quickened at the sight. "Oh, Clara, he's beautiful. How proud Marty must be!"

"He is." Clara beamed. "He's like a cock crowing constantly."

"And with good reason."

Clara cupped the baby's head in her palm. "It was no easy thing bringing this one into the world, but ever so worth it."

Abbie dropped down beside her. "Just look at his tiny fingers. Have you ever seen anything so small? And to think they'll grow into great, strong man hands."

"Well, Marty's not of such great stature, nor his hands so large. Not like Blake's . . ." Clara's voice faded as she stroked the baby's downy hair. "I think of him still. Not as I used to before Marty, but . . . he was fine, wasn't he?"

"Yes. He was fine." Deep within, the memories gnawed. Too fine. She had not deserved him. But Blake would laugh at that. *Go on, Abbie*, he'd say. *You're my girl, ain't you?* No, Blake. I'm nobody's girl. I never will be.

"I'm so sorry for you."

Abbie startled. "You needn't be. Blake's a part of me. Sometimes I feel him here still. Maybe it's better that way."

"He loved you, Abbie. You would have been happy."

Abbie smiled. It was easy. Clara no longer knew her.

The baby made a tiny bleat, and Clara set him to her breast. Abbie turned away as voices outside broke the quiet. "Go, Abbie. Tell me who wins!"

She trudged heavily to the square, where people were already packed for the finish of the race. The sound of hooves reached them, and then a rider, far outdistancing the next two, came into sight. "It's Farrel!" someone yelled, and the cheers rose up. Abbie watched, but not with satisfaction, as Monte's steed flew over the finish line a full minute before the next horse. He did not rein the animal in but allowed its pace to slow and swung around, then walked it back into the midst of the hollering crowd as the other horses galloped through.

"Did you ever see a horse like that!" Marv Peterson called.

"Runs like a devil and strong." Ethan Thomas shook his head and whistled.

Perhaps Monte would find his market after all, Abbie thought. She watched him search the crowd and find Sharlyn like a sweet flower awaiting him. He led the horse there and lifted her in one smooth motion to its back. The cheers and laughter sounded hollow to Abbie. Pounding hooves raised the dust as the stragglers reined in and walked off the strain.

When all the racers had returned, the crowd shifted to the park and Monte climbed the platform.

"Ladies and gentlemen." Judge Wilson raised his arms for quiet. He held up his chin and put on an orator's voice. "One cherry of a race!"

The crowd cheered lustily.

"I say that in sincerity, even though my own Alabaster hadn't a chance against this foreign Sirocco." Laughter. Monte was probably the only one who could have merited that allowance from the judge. "Montgomery Farrel, you're a credit to our town." He presented him the trophy and the eighty dollar prize.

"Not that he needs it," someone muttered behind Abbie. She watched Monte give the trophy to Sharlyn, who had been pushed forward to stand beside him. He bent to kiss her cheek.

One man hollered, "He'll give 'er the trophy but not the prize money!" Monte made great show of pulling the bills from his pocket and placing them in Sharlyn's tiny hand. She blushed fiercely. Abbie made her way out of the crowd and back to Clara's home.

"Monte won. There was not another horse even close, but that's what I expected. His horse is unbelievable. He looked as though he could have gone on forever, hardly panting at all." She wouldn't say that Monte had sat strong and proud on his back, windblown and dirty, and still more handsome than any other. "They come from the desert, you know. Incredible animals."

"Did they present the trophy?"

"Yes. He gave it to Sharlyn."

"Abbie." Clara reached a hand to her arm. "You can't hate him so. It'll only hurt you."

"I don't hate him," she said flatly. "I feel nothing but the greatest disdain for him, and I pity Sharlyn for loving a man so false." Her own words surprised her. When had her longing become contempt?

Clara drew in a long breath. "Maybe he had a reason. . . ."

"Of course he had a reason," Abbie snapped. "Who does anything without a reason?"

"Then you'll give him the benefit of the doubt?"

Abbie smiled. "My dear Clara. Always the peacemaker."

"It's you I'm afraid for. Bitterness doesn't suit you."

"And there, you see? I'm not bitter. Aren't Sharlyn and I the best of friends, just as you and I?"

Clara sighed. "As you say. But, Abbie . . . God has His ways. . . ."

"Of course. But I won't keep you. You and little Del will nap now, I think." Abbie kissed Clara's cheek and went out. The last thing she desired was to return to the Independence Day festivities, but Mama and Pa would expect to see her there. They watched her now with furtive glances and wordless concern. For their sake she put on the face they hoped to see.

The booths were filled and the judging nearly finished. Martha Atwater had won the pie contest as always. The grand prize ribbon adorned her gooseberry pastry. Who else could win with gooseberries? And Granny Breck's quilt had beat out Althea Thorne's. Good for her. Althea could come down a peg or two.

Cole Jasper matched his stride to hers. "Lookin' purty today, Abbie."

"Thank you, Cole. You too." She giggled. "I can't help thinking so whenever you've slicked your hair like that."

His jaw dropped. Reaching up, he rubbed his hair ferociously, setting the curls free. "Better?"

"Yes." She laughed. "A cowboy may as well look like one."

"If I'd known you felt that way, I wouldn'a wasted my time slickin' it."

"What I think isn't important."

Cole swiped a bee from her hair. "You guess I give one wit what anyone else thinks? 'Course it was fer you. And then you go an' tell me I'm purty!"

Abbie laughed again. Cole had a knack for lifting her spirits. "I'm sorry. It's just I don't believe in people trying to be something they're not. I like you better when you've just ridden off the range than when you're trying to impress me."

Cole cocked his head. "Well, it's like this, Abbie. I never figured on givin' two hoots what any lady thought of me. But . . . you make it matter somehow."

Abbie stopped. "Don't get ideas, Cole. I don't mean to be unkind, but I'm not looking to be courted. I hope I haven't given you the notion I was."

Cole paused. "You been through a lot lately. Fergive my impert'nence."

"Not impertinence. You've been very kind. But . . ."

Directly before them, Marcy Wilson strolled beside Nora Thorne, tossing her head as she passed. "Seems since Abbie couldn't get Montgomery Farrel, she'll settle for anyone. Imagine, Abbie with a trail boss!" Nasty laughter followed in their wake.

Abbie gasped. "Oh, Cole. It's nothing like that at all. It has nothing to do with you. . . ."

"Don't fret."

Abbie swallowed her rage. "And . . ." She dropped her gaze to the ground. ". . . it has nothing to do with Mr. Farrel, either."

Cole raised her face to look at him. "I know what kind of lady you are." Then tipping his hat, he left her.

Abbie closed her eyes, fighting the angry tears. Did people think that she had set her hat for Monte and lost? Was she not even left her pride? Grabbing up her skirts, she rushed from the park. The street was bare but for a piebald mongrel and a pair of crows. Flying around the corner of the stable, she collided with Monte, and he caught her fall.

"Abbie!"

Raging tears came to her eyes as she wrenched herself away from him.

"Abbie, please let me talk to you."

"We have nothing to say," she hissed, her breath coming raggedly, her fists clenched at her sides.

"There's something you need to understand. My marriage to Sharlyn was a matter of honor."

"Do you imagine it's of any importance to me why you married?"

"A matter of honor, Abbie." Monte's eyes were fierce.

"Honor?" She struggled against his hold. "Honor is a word you use to excuse your dishonesty. Please unhand me. I find your touch singularly loathsome."

Monte released her arms. Lifting her skirts, she ran. She ran as long and hard as she could through the empty street and on over the plain, her lungs crying for mercy and her legs shaking with the effort until she collapsed on the ground and lay gasping. After some minutes, her breathing slowed, and she closed her eyes, regretting her cruel words and the disclosure of her heartache. What was she to do?

She should go back, apologize to Monte, and pretend every-thing was going to be all right. Lying in the grass, she allowed the silence to sink into her being. Once she would have prayed and imagined God cared. Clara was right. She had grown bit-ter, and it ate at her, claiming more and more of her spirit with each insult, each disappointment. Had she ever loved Monte? Or had she been a child, dazzled by his suavity? Could she hate him so deeply if she had not loved him equally so?

She grew still, thinking of Monte's words. What was he try-ing to tell her? What did he mean, a matter of honor? She draped her arm against the westerly glare.

What was done was done. Sitting up, she pulled the grass from her hair and shook out her brown curls, smoothing them with her hands. She stood a long moment, then walked away from town. She needed to be alone. Only the land could com-fort her.

Monte's soul stung with the venom of Abbie's words. *"Your touch singularly loathsome . . . a word to cover your dishonesty . . ."* What of his honor to her? Had his decision been wrong? What if he had told Nathan Bridges that he was already committed to someone? He would not have been expected to go through with it. But then what would have become of Sharlyn when she realized she was the cause of such destruction?

No, he had chosen as he had to, even though it cost him everything. Of the two, Abbie was stronger. She would recover in time. And the price he paid would be his silence. Allowing her to believe the worst of him would free her to care for some-one else. But did he have the strength? No. He had already failed miserably. For the first time, he turned to heaven with something near desperation. "Oh, Lord . . ." But he fell silent, struggling for control.

Through the war, through the desolation that followed, he

had become a man. He had given God his due, but he had not surrendered his strength. And he had begun again, made a new life, forged his way. Must he admit now that he had failed . . . failed Abbie, failed Sharlyn, failed Nathan . . . failed God. . . . He left the stable and returned to the park.

There he sought Sharlyn and tucked her hand into the crook of his arm. Even as he endured the hatred of the Yankee soldiers during the war to protect those in his care, so now he would endure Abbie's hatred to protect Sharlyn. Her face flushed with pleasure at his appearance. How many times he had neglected to give her the attention she deserved. He would do better. He would fulfill his honor even if Abbie believed him incapable of it.

Twenty-Four

Hearing the hooves, Abbie turned to the solitary rider. She didn't know him from town, though something about him was familiar. Slightly disquieted, she gathered the skirt that she had let drag and felt the empty pocket. No revolver. Suddenly another man emerged out of the gulch before her, and she stopped short. The rider behind kicked in his heels and was upon her in a moment, while two others came up from the road. She froze, and the swarthy rider dismounted.

"Miss Martin, I believe?"

"Who's asking?"

"Yer pa run the newspaper?"

Abbie straightened. "That's right."

"You're an awful long way out by yerself. S'pose I give you a ride. . . ."

"No, thank you." She kept her voice steady and started walking again.

Swiftly he lunged, grabbed her from behind, and covered her mouth with his hand. Twisting in his grasp, she bit down hard. He yelled and wrenched his hand away. She tried to run, but another of the men was instantly before her, and from behind the man struck her once, and then again.

◆◆◆◆◆◆◆

Monte pressed Sharlyn's hand in his. The reddening sky

blushed her cheeks, or was it his touch? How sweetly she responded to him. How uncomplicated her devotion. The evening cool was calming the air as the smoke from the barbecue rose.

"Hungry?" she asked.

"Famished."

"You've worked hard today."

"I've played hard."

Sharlyn smiled. "Does your body know the difference?"

"Probably not."

A scuffle caught Monte's eye as two youngsters broke through the tables. "Marshal Haggerty!" The girl clutched her side, obviously winded.

A boy caught up to her and bellowed, "It's Abbie . . . Abbie Martin."

Monte stiffened.

The marshal stood. "What's this?"

"Someone's got 'er! Out on the prairie. They hit 'er an'—"

"Whose got her?" Joshua pushed forward.

"Four men, maybe five. One of 'em had a white horse with one brown leg."

"Hollister." Marshal Haggerty's hand went to his gun.

Monte felt rooted, his whole body going cold.

Sharlyn's fingers trembled on his arm. "Go!" she whispered.

As though released, he ran for his horse with the others not far behind.

•••••••

Abbie banged against the chest of her captor, each jolt shooting pain to her head. Her thoughts screamed, but the speed of the horse and the number of men kept her silent. She controlled the urge to thrust her head back into his face. It would gain her nothing but pain.

All around them stretched the eastern prairie, broken by

smaller bluffs and arroyos. They dipped, and his arm closed around her. Abbie shoved it off, steadying herself with the saddle horn.

"Feisty little thing, ain't ya?"

"Why are you doing this?" She jolted and gripped more tightly. "Who are you?"

"We'll have us a chat shortly." He veered to the right and cut down into a dry, rocky bed, his horse struggling over the sharp, unsteady surface with the other riders close behind. Abbie feared for the horses, but they kept their feet and thrust themselves and their riders up the far bank and on again. The animals' sides were heaving, and she wondered how much farther the men would force them.

Approaching a cut, they thundered up to the edge, then veered sharply to the left. She saw that it was not a single gulch, but a series of deep, treacherous cuts. Her captor reined in, and she got a good look down the sandstone draw before he swung from the saddle, pulled the reins over the horse's head, and started leading it down. The horse's knees were stiff, braced against the decline as they descended, and she expected its hooves would slip loose any moment and they would go tumbling down. It was one thing to hide tracks, altogether another to die doing so.

But they reached the base without incident, and she saw a low cliff wall beneath the overhang, and in that, a narrow cave opening. It was hardly visible until you were upon it. From any distance away, this would be nothing more than a dry, stony gulch.

Only one rider entered with them, a fat man with the pink spider-webbed skin of a drinker. Were the others splitting off to confuse the searchers? Her chest lurched. Would there be searchers? Only Monte knew she had left, and he would think she'd gone to lick her wounds. It would be hours before the dancing and fireworks wound to a close.

They approached the crack in the wall, and her companion handed the reins to the other man, then yanked her from the saddle. She landed eye level with his grimy chest. His lip curled up.

"We ain't been properly interduced." He took off his hat and grinned. "Buck Hollister, at yer service, ma'am."

Abbie felt the bile rise in her throat. This was the man who had murdered Blake. Her throat constricted—not in fear, but in such an intense hatred that she could hardly contain it. She fought back the invectives that rose to her lips as Hollister directed her into the cave. The light was dim, but as her eyes adjusted, she saw a shaft far up in the ceiling that admitted some light and ventilation. Around the walls were piles of stores and loot, she guessed.

Hollister rubbed his chin. "You're as purty as I was told."

"What do you want with me?"

"Can't a man invite a purty woman over?"

"I'd hardly call bashing my head and abducting me an invitation."

"I see you're as mouthy as yer pa. But we're gonna see to that, ain't we, Conrad?"

Conrad snorted.

Abbie forced her thoughts to calm. "I don't suppose you'd offer a drink of water?"

"Now where's my manners?"

Hollister went to a barrel near the back and filled a tin cup. The water was stale, but Abbie was thirsty and drank it all. Now she knew where the water was, and her eyes found the canteens against the back.

Hollister jutted his chin at Conrad. "Git 'er somethin' to eat."

Conrad went to a rough crate and pulled out canned beans and jerky.

She hadn't eaten since that morning, but the thought

turned her stomach. "Thank you, I'm not hungry."

"Siddown." Hollister shoved her shoulder, and she dropped to the crate. His countenance darkened as he tossed the newspapers onto the rough table in front of her. "I reckon you kin read."

"Quite well." She matched his gaze.

"Then you'll no doubt recall thet yer pa said some dirty things 'bout me an' the boys."

"My pa records the truth."

"Yer pa slandered my name." He scowled. "That's a big mistake."

Abbie stared. "What do you think you are, a hero? You shoot down innocent boys and rob and steal!" Her anger took control. "You're no hero. You're not even a man."

His fist crashed against her cheek, and she fell to the floor, stunned.

"Tie 'er up," he rasped, then stomped outside.

◆◆◆◆◆◆◆

"We won't find anything in the dark, Joshua." Marshal Haggerty reined in.

"It's not completely . . ."

"If we pass something we may not find it again, and no tellin' what we'll muck up without knowing. Think with your head, man."

Joshua stared across the darkening land. How could he go home to Selena empty-handed? How could he leave off searching when Abbie wasn't found?

"We'll make a new search tomorrow. I'm sorry, Joshua."

He'd known when they'd mustered that time and darkness would be the enemy. Hollister had a good jump on them before they'd even got word. The sky was already reddening when they'd set off, and even though they had picked up the trail, it was soon confused and too dim to read. Marshal Haggerty was right. It would do them no good to miss something in the dark, but his heart wouldn't let go.

He raised his eyes to the night. "Oh, Lord, who are mighty in all things, protect and sustain the child you entrusted to me." With sinking heart, he turned his horse slowly back and followed the other men.

Tears streaked Selena's cheeks when he returned. "Where could she be? Why would they take her?" She covered her face and wept.

"They spoiled the press most likely because of what I wrote. I imagine now they've taken Abbie for much the same reason." He slumped in the chair. "I'd have never said a word if I had known."

Selena grasped his hands. "How could you not speak, Joshua? It's who you are."

"At what cost?"

◆◆◆◆◆◆◆

By the end of the second day, Monte rode home, weary and disheartened. Sharlyn met him in the yard. He caught her hopeful glance and shook his head. "Last night's rain obliterated any trail." He dismounted, handing the reins to Will, the stable boy. "We're shooting in the dark now, riding miles of rough, wild country that could swallow her up and leave no trace at all." He climbed the stairs, entered the house, and Sharlyn nodded for Pearl to bring refreshment. He sank to the sofa. "God help us, Sharlyn, we might not find her."

"I'm sorry, Monte. I know she means so much to you."

He looked up blankly. Everything was confused. What was Abbie to him? Hadn't he purged her from his heart? Hadn't she spurned his very presence in his life? Then why was it killing him to have her lost?

"I know what she means to you, too, Sharlyn." He straightened. "I don't want you going away from the house while I'm gone. Not for any reason."

She shook her head. "I won't, Monte. In fact . . . I'll likely be staying close to the house for some time now."

He watched the blush dawn on her cheeks.

"What would you think of Nathan Montgomery if it's a boy?"

Even in his distress, a thrill passed through him and with it a rush of compassion and tenderness for his wife. "Sharlyn! Are you. . . ?"

"I saw Doctor Barrow this morning."

He crossed to her, bent low, and kissed her cheek. "My darling wife."

Her breath caught, and tears sparkled in her eyes. "Oh, Monte. Are you happy?"

"How could I not be?"

She clutched his hand and laid it against her cheek. "I want to make you happy."

"And you do, Sharlyn." God help him, he would be happy.

◆◆◆◆◆◆◆

Abbie was shaking from lack of sleep, hunger, and a growing fear. She had underestimated Hollister's cruelty. After striking her, he had left her tied hand and foot for two days, letting her out only to relieve herself. Each time, Conrad removed the ropes from her ankles, then tied them again when she returned. At no time did they let her out of their sight.

When she refused food a second time, he did not offer it again, and she wouldn't ask. Her lips were parched, though Conrad brought her the tin cup of rancid water. After the first day, the hunger wore thin, but she knew she was getting weak. She looked around the cave—about noon, she estimated by the angle of the sun shaft through the opening in the roof.

The movement of her head caught Conrad's eye. Without a

word, he rose and brought her water. Even the brackish taste refreshed her now, and she drained it, but shrank back when Hollister stepped into the cave. He strode directly to her, wrenched her to her feet, and shoved her to the crate at the table. "Write."

With her hands tied at the wrists, she took up the pencil as he tossed a paper before her. In crude handwriting at the top was written: *Fer Mr. Martin to print ef he wants to see his dotter agin.*

He began to dictate. "Ain't no one hasn't heard the name of Buck Hollister, fastest gun in the territory. This here's the story of his life. At fourteen he robbed a stage and got clean away with no help from no one. Didn't kill no one cuz one look said he meant business, and no one tried fer his gun.

"It was easy as takin' candy from babies, and he hit three more stages the same year. 'Fore long men come askin' to sign up. Wanted posters don't do justice to his likeness no matter how they try."

At this the men laughed, and Hollister joined in with a cocky guffaw. Though insults rose to her lips, Abbie said nothing. Her wrists burned from the rope and she ached, especially her jaw, still tender from the blow. She wrote exactly what he said, though her stomach turned at the writing.

"It takes a man of unusual courage and smarts to outwit any number of sheriffs, marshals, and posses. In that, Buck Hollister . . . what's the word means does best?"

"Excels," Abbie spoke between clenched teeth.

"That's it, excels. Buck Hollister's the fastest, deadliest gun in the territory. Ain't no one he can't face, and no one dares face him. But certain acts of defense been charged against him as murder with no proof of such. Charges of cowardice are outright lies. This here's to set the record straight." He growled, "Sign it."

At the bottom of the page, she wrote her name, and he took

up the paper and read, then shoved it at the boy. "Take it, Wilkins."

Abbie looked at Wilkins, scarcely older than she, but he wouldn't return her gaze. What caused one so young to cast his lot with men like this? She watched him walk out in silence.

Hollister pulled a knife from its sheath. Slowly he thumbed the edge, turning it back and forth. Abbie jumped when he leaned close.

"I reckon you've learned to keep a civil tongue." He worked the blade under the ropes on her wrists. The skin rubbed raw and bloody before the ties fell free. She closed her eyes when he yanked up her skirt and hacked the rope from her ankles.

"Just so's you know, I ain't killed a woman yet."

If he expected an accolade he was disappointed. She looked away and drew a shaky breath. "When my pa prints this, you'll let me go?"

Without answering, he walked out. She could hear him through the opening. "You give it to the newsman, then git out."

"Maybe Briggs . . ."

"They got Briggs on a poster, bonehead. Now ride!"

Abbie glanced at Conrad. Of them all he was the least threatening. At least he saw to her needs the best he could. Now that her hands were free, he brought a plate of beans and a decent end of bread. She wondered if Hollister would rage if he saw, but she ate anyway. She was completely at their mercy and needed her strength. Hollister's shadow fell over her from the crack, but he only grunted and stepped back out again.

◆◆◆◆◆◆◆

Monte could hardly stand what he saw on Joshua's face as they sat across the fire in the moonlight: raw fear, yet dogged determination in spite of the pain. Once he would have reached out to the man, gripped his shoulder, and shared his despair. Now the wall between them kept him silent.

Only Cole and Wes McConnel shared the fire with them as night fell for the third time since Abbie's disappearance. He knew there were other fires scattered over the prairie, other bands of men gathered for the night, waiting for the dawn to light their way again. Would it matter? He fought the thoughts that said no. From the darkness, a horse approached.

"Joshua? Joshua Martin?"

The voice was Ethan Thomas's.

"Here, Ethan." Joshua stood.

Monte likewise jumped to his feet. Had they found her?

"We got word, Joshua!" Ethan pulled up. "Jacobs got a letter left for you at the paper. It's got Abbie's name on it!"

"She's safe?" Joshua demanded.

"That's all I know. They're passin' the word, tryin' to find you."

Monte stepped forward. "I'll ride in with you, Joshua."

Joshua nodded, snatched up his pack, and saddled Sandy. Beside him Monte turned Sirocco, and they started for town. Monte felt the silence between them. "Joshua . . . I feel I owe you an explanation."

"I'm sure you had your reasons."

"I can't tell them without violating the trust placed in me. But I want you to know that I never meant to bring Abbie grief. I truly never did."

"I believe that, Monte," Joshua said, then rode in silence.

Twenty-Five

Abbie looked up as Briggs entered the dim cave and tossed the newspaper onto the table before Hollister. From her place on the floor, she could see the flick of his eyes her way and pressed into the wall. He made her quake as much as Hollister.

Hollister took up the paper and pressed flat the front page. He read aloud the words she had written, the words Pa had faithfully recounted. How he must have cringed to put them into print, but she could see his jaw set, his fingers nimbly doing their work, and doing it well. He would not put principles above her life.

Hollister wrapped up his accolades and looked straight at her. "Listen up, girl. Yer pa's gonna beg." Then he read, " 'To Mr. Hollister.' "

The men laughed raucously. "Mr. Hollister, sir!"

"Shut up an' listen! 'As you have shown yourself interested in preserving your name, I trust you will not stoop to harm my daughter. I am asking you to return her to us. This will go a long way toward restoring your reputation, and I will personally be in your debt. Joshua Martin.' "

Tears stung Abbie's eyes. What had that cost her father to write? "Now will you let me go?" She bit her lip against her breaking voice.

Hollister eyed her but said nothing. Closing her eyes, she

fought the desire to beg. She had to get away! But how could she? Someone was always on watch, and she could not overpower any one of them.

The light from the hole faded, and not even moonlight replaced it. She lay restless, clutching the filthy blanket to her as the men took their places around the floor. Soon the snores marked their positions in the darkness of the cave, but she wasn't foolish enough to hope they all slept. Over the last few nights, she'd realized one was always awake, and they split the night in half shifts.

Still, she lifted her head. Movement at the opening revealed Conrad's attention. She dropped back to the floor. Tears threatened again, but she forced them away. This was not the time to quail; she needed to stay strong and alert. Closing her eyes, she forced her breathing to slow. She would need all the rest she could get.

It was mostly the smell that woke her, even before the rough, sweaty hand came over her mouth. Her eyes flew open as the man's weight pinned her. His hand groped over her clothing. Briggs. She tried to scream through the palm that was choking out air as well as sound and thrashed, freeing one hand and raking it across his face. He gripped her wrist and ground her arm into the stone wall. A shadow appeared above them, and she heard the cylinder of a gun turn as it cocked against Briggs' head. He froze.

"Git off," Hollister's voice rasped.

Briggs rolled to the side.

"Touch 'er agin and you're dead."

Abbie gripped her arms about her and tried to stop her shaking. She forced herself not to think, fighting the sob that rose in her throat. If Hollister hadn't stopped him . . . She pressed her eyes shut. It was small comfort to have Hollister as a protector. Only God knew . . . Drawing a shaky breath, she drew her hands away from her mouth. Did God know? Did He care? Everything in her cried yes.

"Oh, God," she whispered. "Help me now. I can do nothing without you." The shudders stopped, and though she couldn't sleep, she felt the ache of fear releasing.

She sat up with the dawning and remained calm, even when Briggs awoke and caught her in his steely glare. The red welts from her nails had raised up on his brown cheek. Hollister stood and kicked Wilkins awake. "Git the horses."

Abbie's heart lurched. For once she was left alone in the cave, and she pulled herself up. She could hear them just outside. Conrad came in and filled canteens. Were they taking her home? Again she was alone. "Dear Lord," she murmured, "Though I turned my back, you have not forgotten me."

Hollister came in and took her by the arm. Outside he mounted and pulled her up in front. As his arm went around her, she felt a dreadful loathing. The touch of a murderer.

"You sit still, and you stay free. You try anything, and I'll tie you up agin, got it?"

She nodded. At the back, Conrad took hold of a remuda of spare horses. Had they obtained them since bringing her there, or had they been tethered somewhere out of sight? And what was their purpose? To ride hard and far with plenty of change horses? They started out, keeping to the gulch until it ended, then turned and followed a narrow path up the side and onto the plain. Abbie could tell by the distance of the mountains that they were far from town and not heading that direction. Her spirit sank.

"Please take me back. You got what you wanted. Just let me go. I'll find my way."

" 'Fraid I can't do that." His tone was cold.

"But my pa . . ."

"You're gonna see yer pa, all right. He'll come fetch you. But I reckon you may as well know . . . Nobody calls me a coward an' lives."

Abbie's whole body went weak. "Please, please don't hurt my pa. He was only doing what he thought was right." For Pa, she would beg. She would do anything.

Hollister didn't answer.

They changed horses several times, resting only a short time at each break. Abbie saw that they were circling the town in a wide loop. Were there searchers out there? Was there anyone to see them? By nightfall they neared the foothills and stopped beside a smaller bluff that rose up from the prairie. Tucked against the wall was a cabin. Conrad crept forward alone, then returned, nodded shortly, and Hollister dismounted, pulling Abbie with him. She made herself limp in his arms, staggering a little as she landed. It wasn't hard to act it. She felt almost that weary.

Furtively she searched her surroundings. She'd never been this far south, but she had her bearings now, and if she was going to help Pa, she would have to break free before he walked into the trap.

Inside the cabin, the others slept while Wilkins kept watch. Abbie saw him sitting at the edge of the stoop directly outside the open door. She slipped off the rough bunk they had given her and made her way across the room. Startled, Wilkins spun, but before he could make a sound, she stepped outside and whispered, "I'm not feeling well. I need to . . ." She indicated the patch of trees where they had allowed her to relieve herself.

Wilkins grunted, "Be quick about it."

"I'll do my best, but . . . I'm feeling poorly. Please be patient." She made her voice faint and plaintive. He shrugged and looked the other way. Thank God it was Wilkins. Abbie slipped into the shadows. Except for the fringe of trees at the base of the bluff, the land was open all around with little shelter but gullies and rises and occasional clumps of scrub oak and mahogany.

By the light of the fingernail moon she could just make out

the silent form of Wilkins on the porch and counted on his embarrassment to give her time. With a shaky breath she hitched up her skirts and pulled off the narrow hoop. This she hooked over her arm and slipped around the back side of the tallest ponderosa. In the daylight it would not have been dense enough to hide her, but she was praying that the darkness would prove sufficient.

Stretching, she grabbed the highest branch she could reach and pulled herself silently up, tucking her foot in the notch. The first branch was the hardest because she had to swing her whole weight up. She reached for the next. Hand over hand, she scaled the trunk until the branches thinned. She didn't want to lose their cover, but she had to be high enough that no breath, no move would alert anyone.

Through the branches, she could see Wilkins straining her way. He unfolded his legs and stood, stretched, then strode a little way toward the trees. "Hey, you!" He kept his voice muffled. "Hurry up, ya hear?"

Abbie didn't answer.

"I'm talkin' to ya." His voice was louder this time.

No answer.

He exploded with an angry curse, ran for the cabin, and banged through the door. "She's run off!"

"Oh, dear God . . ." Abbie whispered. "Hide me now." *Hide me under the shadow of thy wings. From the wicked that oppress me, from my deadly enemies, who compass me about . . .* Within seconds they were out the door.

"Spread out," Hollister bellowed. "She ain't gittin' far out here."

She clung motionless when Conrad passed directly under the tree. Hollister cursed loudly. "How much head start did ya give 'er, bonehead?" He gripped Wilkins' collar.

"She said she was poorly!"

Hollister spat. "Poorly! She's as strong and twice as smart as you!"

Wilkins cowered.

"Git the horses!" Hollister cuffed his head. "She's gonna git more'n a taste of my fist this time."

Conrad hurried back beneath the tree, but his focus was ahead. He helped Wilkins with the horses, and Abbie strained to hear Hollister's directions. If they scattered now, her work would be harder . . . but to her relief they all fanned in basically the same direction. North toward town.

Abbie let herself down from the tree, ignoring the scrape and tear of the bark against her palms. She pressed through the foliage to the wall of the bluff and climbed. Her legs were shaking by the time she reached the top and started across the surface through the windblown trees and underbrush. She crept with as much haste as she dared while trying not to alert anything that would give her away by a sudden flight.

The daylight was growing before she reached the base of the far side. She pressed on, praying they hadn't already captured Pa. Once in the foothills, she felt the familiar lay of the land and wound her way up and north, wishing she could have taken a canteen. Well, there would be a stream or spring some-where along the way. Her skirt caught on a branch of scrub oak and she tore it loose, then hurried on. It would not be long before they realized she was not on the prairie heading for town. They were smart enough to know she couldn't fly, and their search would not go farther than she could feasibly get. Would they guess she had gone over the bluff?

Her lungs began to ache as did her legs. To the east, the sun rose like a great glaring eye, gracing the earth with sight. Lean-ing against a tree, she caught her breath, then pushed on.

◆◆◆◆◆◆◆

Hollister reined in and squinted over the broken, treeless

land. He took off his hat and smeared his hand across his face. "She ain't gone this way. I shoulda knowed right off."

Conrad pulled up beside him. "What now?"

"Cut over to them hills. I'm thinkin' she got herself some cover."

"Git the others?"

"Yeah, an' tell Wilkins ef he wants to live through this, he better find 'er quick."

Twenty-Six

Abbie had to rest. The afternoon sun baked the land, and she wiped her arm across her face, then dropped into the shelter of a spruce, its bed of pointed needles pricking her legs through her skirt. There were a hundred places she could hide. But that wouldn't keep Pa from coming to the trap. Closing her eyes, she moaned, "God, please help me! Please don't let them find me or hurt Pa! Please, please help me!"

She forced herself on and nearly cried out when she stumbled against a root, lost her footing, and came down hard on her knees. She stayed there a long moment as the pain ebbed. No words came, but her heart reached out for God, and she found the strength to go on. Coming at last to a small rocky stream, she fell to her knees and splashed the cold water over her face, then drank. Around her were only the wild sounds of the mountain. Had the men turned to the hills?

She had to keep going, had to push on. Thinking of Pa, his humor and wisdom, his quiet strength, gave her courage. She had to get word to him. Suddenly she came upon the wide base of a trail and looked up the mountain. Was this the pass where Blake was killed? A terrible pain stabbed her, and she stifled a scream. *Oh, Blake . . .*

The pass seemed to echo his voice. *I'm comin' home, Abbie.* She could hardly force herself into the open. It seemed to hold her back. Drawing a deep breath, she swiped at the tears and went through. Just as she reached the trees, Briggs stepped out before her, and she shrieked.

"Lost yer way back?" He sneered.

Hollister came from the woods with murder in his eye, both hands curled like claws.

Abbie froze.

"You're causin' me trouble."

In the wake of her pain, Abbie's fury flamed. "I guess I could say the same. But you can't see past yourself, can you? You're so mired in your own filth you can't even smell the rest of the world. You're an animal!"

His fist sent her into the dirt and she scraped her face as she fell. He yanked up her head and slapped her so hard she was stunned. "An animal, eh? We'll see about that!"

He crushed his mouth to hers, and Abbie fought as he pinned her down. With all her strength she forced him back, and he raised his hand to strike. She cringed, but he stiffened, hung there still and stunned, then fell to the ground beside her with three arrows in his back.

The others ran, screamed, and fell. Wilkins landed only inches from her face, and as she watched the life leave his eyes, a brave straddled him, yanked up his head, and sliced off a piece of scalp. Blood rushed to replace it. A few feet away, Conrad moaned, then grew still, his own face running with blood from the slash across his crown.

Briggs tried to escape into the shelter of the trees, and Abbie shuddered as a war club split his skull. The brave who wielded it leaped onto Briggs' back and uttered a war whoop that rang against the rocky sides of the pass. Abbie covered her face with her hands.

Then it was silent. Her breath echoed in her ears. Slowly, she removed her hands and looked up into the face of the Comanche brave. His eyes still held the fire of the kill, something raw and ancient. There was blood splattered on his bare chest and forearms, and a smear across his jaw. A bloody pair of scalps hung from his belt. Conrad's and Hollister's, Abbie guessed, shuddering. But he held out his hand, and she took it.

Riding saddleless on his mustang, she leaned weakly against his back, letting the rhythm of the horse lull her. How long had it been since she slept? Her body no longer felt like her own, but a weight of baggage only. Her eyes were already closed when the brave dropped her to the ground. She lay where she landed and slept. The sun was sinking when she woke beneath a hide suspended on poles. She sat up.

There was no sign of the braves. Two women tended a fire roasting what looked like rabbit or squirrel. One of them saw her and brought a waterskin. Abbie drank, then handed it back. The woman returned with a basket of flat bread baked with berries. Abbie felt her stomach grumble. The bread was tough and bitter but had a wholesome smell. She finished it.

The other woman was thicker and worked a fresh hide—mule deer from the looks of it—with a sharp-edged stone. Seeing Abbie watching, she indicated the ground beside her, and Abbie came and sat. Both women treated her with deference, though she could only wonder why. Was she captive or friend?

Abbie knew well enough the usual treatment of a female captive by Comanches. She had heard the stories of torture, rape, and disfigurement. She knew also that it depended on the temperament of the particular chief of the band. If the brave who had brought her in was chief, she had hope he would not harm her. But would he set her free?

At any rate, even if she were captive, she was in better hands than before. She shuddered and felt her stomach turn. Swiping a hand over her mouth, she ached to be clean of the kiss of Blake's killer.

The younger woman removed the meat from the spit, wrapped it in cabbage leaves, and laid it on a board. She had ground corn into meal with a pestle in a stone mortar, then mixed it into a watery gruel. This she poured into a hide suspended over the fire and dropped hot stones from the ashes into the mixture.

Abbie looked up. The braves had returned, stepping their ponies silently into the clearing. They swung their legs over the horses' backs and leaped down. Abbie stood and waited for her rescuer to approach. He stopped an arm's length from her, then reached out and pointed to her scraped and swollen cheek. He barked something, and the woman who had been tending the hide came forward with a bowl of ointment. She applied it to Abbie's face. It was smooth and soothing, though something in it stung, and she guessed it had medicinal qualities.

The brave spoke. "Men gone."

Abbie's mouth dropped open. "You speak my tongue!"

"White men speak. Gray Wolf hear."

"You saved my life . . . Gray Wolf. Thank you."

He touched her forehead. "You . . . wise one. Not afraid." He turned from her and spoke to the women in Comanche, then sat on the ground. The other braves sat with him. Abbie backed away, feeling dismissed but uncertain what to do. She sat again in the shelter of the hide on poles. The squaws served the men meat and corn mush in bowls. Then they brought it to Abbie. She sat alone and ate with her fingers.

The women sat together across the fire from her. As they ate, they spoke in low voices, seemingly careful not to disturb the men, who laughed and chattered, waving their arms and gesticulating. By the motions, Abbie guessed they were describing the fight and relishing their victory.

All of Hollister's horses were now added to the Indian ponies, including the remuda left at the shack when they rode off to search. Abbie guessed the braves had raided the cabin after leaving her. The horses were laden with Hollister's supplies and his weapons. It had been a successful raid, indeed, and she still didn't know whether she was part of the plunder.

As she mopped the bowl with her fingers, she thought of Monte's fears for her, his warnings against these very same Indians. It all seemed so long and far away. She was not even the same girl anymore. She drank from the waterskin and set aside the bowl.

Her body ached and fatigue overcame her. It had been too many fear-filled nights, too hard a trek. She lay back on the blanket and closed her eyes. Her breathing slowed and the languid warmth of sleep stole over her. The last thing she remembered was the soft caress of fur against her cheek.

The morning sun warmed the blanket under her face, and she woke. A soft fur had been laid over her, and she was tempted to snuggle down again into its thickness, but she saw that the others were up. The smell of the fire and frybread called her even more strongly. The younger woman brought her a loaf and she ate, then quenched her thirst with water from the skin. Had anything ever tasted so good?

She made her way to the stream below and washed with a soft hide and a root, which she guessed to be yucca, that made suds when rubbed against the hide. She dared not remove any clothing but pushed up her sleeves and scrubbed her arms, neck and face. The ointment had helped her face immensely. Though the scrape remained, it had not swelled or festered.

Looking up, she saw Gray Wolf astride his mustang. He motioned, and she crossed the water. Without a word, he pulled her up behind him. The mustang wore no saddle, only a thick woven blanket with patches of fur, and a halter-type bridle. She noticed the horse's split ears, a Comanche marking. That, and its gaunt condition, told her this horse and rider had been together a long while.

Gray Wolf swung the horse around, expecting her to maintain her own balance. Abbie flashed back to Hollister's hold on her and shuddered. But he was dead. They were all dead.

She had no idea where Gray Wolf was taking her or what his intentions were, but she felt little fear. If he had meant to harm her, surely last night would have shown it. Though she sensed his closeness, he didn't intrude. Like her, he was part of a larger plan. Who but God could have placed him there like an avenging angel? Had the very ground cried out with Blake's blood? Had violence bred violence? She was surprised to feel relieved but not elated. Vengeance was, after all, God's.

The sun caught the dew on the needles of the trees. Everything seemed brighter, greener, more vibrant. She drew a long breath, feeling deeply, richly alive. A bird trilled from a treetop as they passed beneath. It echoed her spirit.

They kept to the foothills and maintained a moderate pace, not the bone-jarring rush of the previous day, but steady. Was it only yesterday she was fearing for her life and Pa's? Only a handful of hours since she was so desperate to escape that she hatched a reckless plan and scrambled up the tree? Only a sun's setting and rising again since the men who murdered without guilt were themselves cut down in their own blood?

When the sun centered above them, Gray Wolf halted in the shade of a mossy crag. He swung down but didn't reach for her as a white man would. She didn't mind. She slid off and sat where he indicated while he led the horse to water and left it loose to graze. From the pouch at his side, he took strips of dried meat and offered her one.

It had a peppery tang and was a gamy meat. She hoped it was venison or buffalo and not dog or any of the other critters she'd heard Comanches ate. Still it was heartening and her appetite awakened. She chewed eagerly. They drank from the skin, then started out again. Gray Wolf didn't speak, and she dared not question him, though her heart beat faster the farther north they went.

As the western sun ignited the sky, Abbie caught sight of

the homestead nestled into the lower hills. Her breath caught as her heart swelled. Gray Wolf reached behind and pulled her arms around his waist, then the horse leaped forward at his word. The wind rushed in their faces. Had he sensed her need?

They stopped at the yard, her own yard, her home. With one arm, he swung her down. She stood speechless. How did one repay a life?

Slowly, he raised his hand. "Wise one."

She repeated the gesture. "Gray Wolf." Her voice caught as she watched him spin, dig in his heels, and gallop away.

Mama stood in the kitchen swinging the broom as Abbie rushed in. "Mama!" She threw herself into her mother's arms. The broom smacked the floor.

"Abbie! Oh, child." Her voice broke.

"Mama, please, don't cry." Abbie squeezed her tighter. "Where's Pa?"

"Looking for you. When writing the article didn't bring you back, he and Cole and Monte took up the search again. Oh, Abbie! What . . ."

"Please don't ask. I don't think I can tell it twice." She pressed her mother's hands. "But, Mama, I know now that nothing is beyond God. I doubted . . . when Monte . . . but who else but God could have brought me through?"

Mama placed a hand to her cheek. "Who indeed?"

◆◆◆◆◆◆◆

The light was soft through the white organdy curtains as Abbie opened her eyes to the familiar blue feathered wallpaper. The warmth of her own bed was a piece of heaven. She ran her hand over the quilt she and her mother had pieced when she learned to work a needle. How much she had taken for granted. The aroma of hotcakes and bacon wafted in. Her stomach tightened. She swung her legs over the side of the bed and went to the washstand.

Last night she had bathed. Even the memory was delicious. Now she dipped a cloth in the bowl and rubbed her face and neck, then hung it to dry and brushed out her hair. Horses in the yard brought her to the window, and with a gasp she spun and ran outside. "Pa!"

"Abbie!" He caught her against his chest so tightly her breath stopped. "Abbie, how . . ."

"Oh, Pa, I was so afraid! It was a trap. They wanted to kill you, and I had to get away before . . . But then Hollister . . . Oh, Pa, I can't tell you how dreadful he was. And the others . . ."

"Abbie." He squeezed her close again, then glanced up at Cole and Monte still astride their horses. "Give us a minute to wash. We've been out all night."

"I'm so sorry, Pa." She looked past him. Monte's face was haggard, his white shirt limp and dirty. Why was he here? Had Pa asked his help? Surely he could have refused.

Cole swung down and slapped the dust from his pants. He might have just come from the range. His eyes weren't haunted like Pa's and Monte's. He looked almost amused, and she felt a smile inside. He probably thought she got home single-handedly. "Mama's making breakfast."

Pa released her. "We'll wash first."

They gathered at the table, and Pa prayed. Tired as he was, he couldn't keep the tears from his voice as he thanked God for His goodness. He looked right at her as he said, "Amen. Now tell us."

"It was Hollister, Pa. He took me to get you. He said no one calls him a coward and lives. He meant to kill you after you printed his letter." She rolled her eyes. "Oh, heavens, Pa, did you ever hear anything like it? It turned my stomach to put it in writing. I can imagine how you felt. . . ."

"Abbie." Pa laid his hand on hers. "Tell us what happened. Where were you? How did you get home?"

"First they took me to a cave in a gulch on the prairie. It

was full of stuff. Must have been a regular hideout. We were there . . . I'm not sure of the days . . . three maybe." She rubbed the red rings on her wrists, then caught Monte's eye and dropped them to her lap. "After I wrote the letter, I thought they'd let me go. But they took me to another hideout south of here a day's hard ride. That's where they meant to bring you. I had to get away before they sent for you."

Cole leaned forward. "How'd you manage that?"

"I fooled the boy into letting me out. I had just time enough to climb into a tree before they started looking. Don't frown, Mama. Some things are good to know. I went over the bluff to the hills and all the way to the pass. . . ." She drew a long breath. "That's where Hollister found me. I don't care to think what would have happened if Gray Wolf hadn't come."

"Gray Wolf?" Monte's voice was low.

She looked directly at him. "The Comanche brave I met in the woods." It was too difficult to hold his eyes. She turned away. "Hollister's dead, he and his men. The Comanches killed them. Then Gray Wolf brought me home."

Cole whistled. "Now that's a tale. I can see the Comanches fightin' for ya, but I don't get them settin' you free on yer own doorstep. You musta had some powerful medicine over that brave."

"I don't know about that." Abbie pushed him the hotcakes. "Now eat. You look as hungry as I feel."

"You reckon they got the McConnels' gold in that cave?"

She froze. A sudden ache seized her. "I hadn't thought that . . . some of those things might be Blake's and Mack's." Tears surprised her eyes. "I know murder's wrong, Pa, but I can't help the satisfaction I feel after what they did to Blake. . . ."

Pa laid down his fork. "I guess the Lord'll forgive us this one. Had they been caught, they'd have hung anyway. I suppose the Comanches just saved us the trouble."

✦✦✦✦✦✦✦

Abbie was surprised how well she remembered the nightmare ride to the cave. She could almost smell Hollister behind her as she rode. She glanced at Pa on Sandy. Behind them rode Marshal Haggerty and Wes McConnel. Abbie turned toward the cut down to the cave in the gulch and led them through.

She heard Marshal Haggerty whistle. "Hollister knew this land like a wild coyote." He spat and dismounted.

"The cave isn't deep, and everything's packed in the back." She stood outside with Pa. "Not for anything will I go in there again."

Pa closed her shoulders in his arm. Wes McConnel dragged a crate and barrel out, and Marshal Haggerty followed with more. Abbie dropped to the earth and pulled open one of the packs. It held no gold, but clothing and a roughly bound journal. She opened the cover.

Mack and Blake McConnel. This here's to account for our time prospecting....

The writing was Mack's, neat, methodical. She flipped the pages and found one written by Blake: *Mack's gittin' discouraged, but I ain't goin' home without what we come for. I mean to bring Abbie all I promised her.*

Tears blurred her eyes. Why, Blake? Why? Only one other entry was his.

We're settin out for home tomorrow. Mack's tired of hearin' how I miss Abbie. He said don't dare write it, but I never listen to him much. I'm comin home to her. How's a man keep that quiet? I feel like hollerin' it all across the country. Abbie, I'm comin' home!

Abbie pressed the cover shut and wiped her hand across her face. She found Wes at the entrance. "Mrs. McConnel will want this." He took the journal in his big hands and nodded.

Pa took her elbow. "The men'll finish here. Let's go home."

"What'll Mr. McConnel do if they find the gold?"

"I reckon he'll put it to good use."

Abbie shook her head. "Is it worth it? To lose your life for gold?"

Pa took her hands. "I reckon it was more for a dream than the gold itself. Give Blake more credit than that."

She turned away. "Then it hurts too much."

"I reckon it does."

Twenty-Seven

Abbie tethered the horse outside Monte's house and pushed her hair back from her damp forehead. She didn't want to be there. The heat was oppressive and her nerves were ragged. The memories connected to this day made her tense and sad . . . last year's dance in her honor, Blake's proposal, his good-bye, Monte's waltz . . .

It was hardly a birthday mood. But she couldn't refuse Sharlyn's invitation, not with Mama hovering over, looking for any cause to worry. And not after Monte had searched so long and hard.

That thought only confused her more. Why had he been there at her homecoming? Why had it been he who saw it through with Pa? Yes, Cole had done as much, but why Monte? Why had his face revealed an angst and weariness that pained her to see? She pressed her eyes shut and banged the brass knocker. James showed her in.

"Abbie." Sharlyn swept toward her, elegant in a rose taffeta gown with empire waist. The lace overlay trailed inches behind her. "Happy birthday! I'm so glad you could come."

"Thank you, Sharlyn. It was kind of you to have me." She felt and sounded stiff. Where was the easy love she had for this woman? Doctor Barrow had warned that her moods might be unpredictable for a while, but until today she had scoffed.

Sharlyn ushered her into the parlor. There were the pictures

251

of Monte's parents on the mantel, the marble clock and candlesticks, the claret velvet curtains over the lace. The air felt thick and cloying. If she could gracefully turn and run she would.

Sharlyn sat and patted the sofa beside her. "Pearl's oiling the morning room, so we'll have tea here if that's all right."

It wasn't all right. Unexpected emotion choked her. "Of course." Abbie sat.

"I can't tell you how good it is to see you." Sharlyn lifted the cozy from the pot and poured the tea.

"And you, Sharlyn." Abbie took the cup, wishing it were iced—something she could pour down the ache of her throat.

"Are you . . . are you all right? Oh, Abbie, Monte was so worried for you. If you could have seen him . . ."

"Of course, I'm all right. It's been over a month now." Vaguely she wondered why Sharlyn hadn't come to visit. It was unlike her, especially as involved as Monte had been.

"We'll catch up now." Sharlyn smiled, sipping her tea. Every movement was dainty and soft, like that of a butterfly. She loved watching her. Why today did it make her cross?

"Have you heard of my brother, Chandler Bridges?"

She had. The one to whom Monte was devoted. But she hadn't made the connection to Sharlyn before. "I've heard mention."

"He sent us a letter. He's getting married to a lovely girl, Maimie DuMont. Monte's not met her but I have. She'll be so good for Chad."

"That's wonderful news."

"How I wish we could be there. He wanted Monte for best man."

Abbie shrugged. "Well, you could, you know. By stage to the railhead."

Sharlyn blushed. "That's not possible. Not now." She folded her hands. "You see I'm . . . I'm expecting . . . a baby."

Monte's baby. The words were like a knife, burning Abbie's chest and abdomen, proof of his devotion to his wife, proof of their love. The emotion she had seen in his face at her return was nothing but artifice, deception. Abbie's throat felt tight, and she forced her breath through, hardly caring to shield Sharlyn's seeing.

"Please listen, Abbie. I asked you here because Monte won't let me ride now that the baby's coming. He's terribly protective, and I don't fault him it, but I had to talk to you." Her eyes were pleading. "Your friendship means so much to me. Without our time together my days would be so lonely."

Your nights are not lonely. Abbie was ashamed of the thought. Surely she didn't carry the hurt still, surely all that had happened had purged the smallness from her. The last weeks had held a halcyon sweetness, a peace and thankfulness to be alive and home. Even the pain of finding Blake's things had been kept at bay, not reaching inside where she was vulnerable.

Sharlyn's voice softened. "Abbie, I know of your affection for Monte . . . and his for you."

The room closed in. She wanted to run. Was Sharlyn blind, stupid not to see what she was doing to her?

"I've seen it in his face, heard it when he speaks your name. I know he didn't marry me for love. But I will try to make him happy, because I love him. And he is very good to me."

"Why are you telling me this?"

"I feared that when you learned of the baby, you would not bear my company. I know it's painful. . . ."

Something snapped inside. Abbie clenched her fists. "How do you know? What have you ever suffered to understand my pain? Have you lost those who meant the most to you in all the world? Have you lived with the rejection of someone to whom you trusted your heart when it was new and able to dream? What do you know of pain, Sharlyn? Nothing! You know nothing!" Abbie flew from the room and through the doors.

The heat hit her as she fled across the yard, leaped astride and kicked the startled mare, then galloped for home. Shame and remorse filled her, but she rode on until she reached her own barn and unsaddled the horse, turned her out to pasture, and stormed from the barn to walk the land. She felt little and mean and wretched. Sharlyn had begged her understanding, but she had not understood. How could she? She dropped to the grass and gave vent to tears of frustration.

✦✦✦✦✦✦✦

Through the window, Monte watched Cole take the porch steps two at a time. In a moment the knock came at the door. "Come in."

Cole removed his hat as he entered.

"What can I do for you, Cole?"

"Well, Mr. Farrel, it's like this. Tomorrow night I'm askin' Abbie to marry me, and I'm needin' to know if that'll risk my position here."

He wasn't surprised. Cole had spent many evenings out, of late. It wasn't hard to figure where. "No, Cole. It won't risk your position." His voice was steady. "But she won't have you."

"Why not?"

He took up a decanter and poured the brandy. "Abbie has a dream that, perhaps, no man can fulfill. She won't settle for less." He handed Cole the snifter. "She's very young, Cole."

"She's nineteen. That's old enough to decide if I can make her happy." He swallowed the brandy like a shot. "Seems to me, Mr. Farrel, and no disrespect, but you had yer chance."

Monte swirled the liquor in his palm. "I suppose you're right."

Cole replaced his hat and left. Monte sipped the brandy. He was prepared to let Abbie go, but only for her happiness. What kind of life could Cole give her? What kind of love, sixteen years her senior? Would she marry Cole to spite him? She was headstrong enough that it was possible. But what could he do? She'd taken after him like a she-wolf the last time they'd spoken alone. Still . . .

Taking his coat, he stepped out into the cool evening air. Sirocco high-stepped until Monte kicked his heels. The path was well worn between their homes from first his and then Sharlyn's comings and goings. He reined in and tethered Sirocco.

Abbie pulled open the door and stepped back. "Pa's in town with Mama."

"It's you I came to see." His throat was tight. "Will you walk with me, Abbie?"

"I'd rather not." Her voice was soft, not cruel. "Come in if you like."

Monte stepped into the front room, and Abbie offered a chair, but he shook his head. "I don't know how to begin. There's so much I would say, and so much I cannot."

She said nothing. Once she would have coaxed and demanded what he withheld. Now she merely waited. How much she had changed. Did he even know her anymore? Had he ever?

"Cole's coming tomorrow to ask for your hand." He saw the flush of anger in her cheeks.

"What has that to do with you?"

"Abbie, I know well what you think of me, and I don't blame you for it, though there's much you don't understand. But you must know I want for you to be happy."

Her chin came up.

"Cole's a good man, but . . . I don't believe you love him."

She stiffened. "What can that possibly matter to you?"

"You know it does. I can't bear the thought of you in a loveless marriage. Not when you had such hopes, such a dream . . ."

"That dream is dead—and good riddance." She stalked to

the window. "What does it matter if it's Cole or anyone else?"

"Abbie, please . . ."

"I'm sorry, Monte. I've not yet acquired that subtlety in which you found me so lacking and pretended it didn't matter . . . before you went home to find a proper wife."

"Is that what you think?" Monte gripped the chair back.

"It doesn't matter what I think."

"It matters more than you know."

"How dare you come here and speak so? Are you happy only when you think I'll long for you to my grave? I swear I will not!"

"I don't want you to! But think, Abbie, what it would mean to spend your days with someone for whom you have affection, perhaps even tenderness, but not love. You need more."

"You no longer know what I need, Monte. Nor do I." She softened. "Thank you for your concern. I'm sure you're sincere."

"I am sincere." He willed his arms to remain at his sides. "I want you to be happy. I truly do." He picked up his hat and left. He had done what he could. The rest was up to her.

When he had gone, Abbie sat alone in the dark. Why had he come? Did he mean to keep her from marrying Cole? She sighed. She had allowed Cole's visits, enjoyed them even. He asked so little. He made her laugh, and she truly liked him, but she had hoped . . . allowed herself to hope that it was nothing more for him. Why had she believed he was not courting her? Because she had wanted to. She had needed to.

Why had Monte come? He with the expecting wife? She closed her eyes. "Please, Lord . . ."

✦✦✦✦✦✦✦

Cole arrived the next evening, clean shaven but for the trimmed mustache. Thankfully, though washed, he had not slicked nor dressed for the occasion. Abbie met him on the porch. "I'm afraid you're too late for supper, Cole."

"I already ate. I was hopin' we could talk."

She pulled the shawl from the hook and joined him. The night was warm for September, but she felt chilled.

He set an easy pace. "Sure is a purty night."

"Yes."

"Nice ta spend it with you."

Abbie forced a smile, dreading what would come next. But maybe Monte was wrong. Cole wasn't nervous, nor overly eager. They wandered a bit as always, enjoying the air, the scenery.

He stopped walking. "I ain't real good with words fer this sorta thing, so I'm just gonna say it." He reached for her hands. "I love you, an' I want you fer my wife."

Even though Monte had warned her, she was touched. She didn't think Cole was a man to say that lightly. She wished he hadn't. It would change things, and he didn't deserve the rebuff. She tried to be gentle. "It means so much that you would ask, Cole . . . but I can't. I can't pretend something I don't feel."

He looked past her. "That's about what Farrel said."

"Monte spoke to you?"

"More like I spoke to him. I needed to know where I stood if you accepted."

"Cole . . ."

"No, listen. I know I ain't Farrel, but I'd do my best fer you, Abbie."

The tears stung her eyes. "I know you would. You've already done so much. . . ."

"I wasn't meanin' that."

She drew a shaky breath. "Cole, I don't know what I expected from life, but . . . I can't marry you. I can't marry anyone. It wouldn't be right."

"You weren't meant to be alone."

"There are worse things. Being alone doesn't frighten me. Maybe one day it'll be different, but . . ."

"I'll be gray by then."

She smiled. "Thank you for asking, Cole."

Cupping her face in his hands, he kissed her. "Sure you won't change yer mind?" He kissed her again.

To be held by a man again, kissed, cherished . . . "I can't."

Watching him walk into the night, Abbie wrapped herself in her arms. With any encouragement, he would be back. So would any number of others, but she would not marry one she didn't love, and Monte had known that. He had come to remind her of herself.

She stopped on the hill and lay in the grass, watching the clouds scud across the stars. Her thoughts ran back through the past year, touching every good and painful memory alike; Blake's devotion, his death, her capture and rescue, Gray Wolf, and lastly . . . the awakening of love in Monte's arms, in the sound of his voice, the touch of his lips, and the pain of his betrayal.

Was it betrayal? Had he been false? She touched the memory. He had promised nothing. Never had he spoken for her, nor broken a pledge. He had done what he must, chosen as he was born to choose. It was done, and she must forgive. But why had he not even told her? If it was a matter of honor, why had he not explained? Did he think her too petty to understand, too small to forgive?

She was too small to forgive. Look at the time that had passed, time she had used to feed her grudge, time that had made her bitter. What was his offense? Finding her attractive and letting her know? The pain lashed out inside.

Yes, there was offense, betrayal, trust broken. Yes, he had urged a love from her, then turned his back on it. Perhaps his reason was compelling. Would she have listened had he told her? Would it have lessened the hurt?

But the wound had been bound long enough. It was time to let it heal, and that wouldn't happen while she washed it in the poison of unforgiveness. Abbie sighed. She hadn't the strength.

But God had proven more than strong enough. What had Father Dominic told her? *Where the heart is willing, God will provide the strength.* She pressed her eyes shut, saw in her mind Monte's earnest face.

He regretted her unhappiness. She believed that. He had concern for her. Maybe that was all there had ever been, concern and caring. She'd been wrong to expect more. *Oh, God, help me.* She dropped her face into her hands, but no tears came. Perhaps a lightening of spirit, perhaps her heart was less pinched ... With a strengthening of her will, she drew a long, painful breath and released him.

◆◆◆◆◆◆◆

Abbie folded Tucker's hands behind him and straightened his shoulders. "Okay. Try it now."

" 'All things bright and ... beautiful, All creatures great and small ...' " He worked his mouth around the Ls, but it still came out *smaw*. " 'All things wise and wonderful ... the ... Lord God made them all.' "

She smiled. "All right. That's good for now. Whom shall we hear next?"

As she listened to them recite, she felt the bond that connected them—the rejected and unfortunate, children of affliction, maligned and forgotten. But not here. Here they found a haven, and her soul fed on being part of it. They were bright, eager, and affectionate, and they tugged at her heart as no one else.

The night was deep when she unsaddled Shiloh in the barn, and Pa joined her with a lantern. "You're coming in pretty late these days."

"I have so much to do. Father Dominic's given over the middle students to me for reading, letters, and history, and I've started recitation for them all." She heaved the saddle over the rack. "Even Silas."

"Don't you think you're pushing a little hard?"

"They enjoy it. You should hear them. I can hardly make them stop when I have to leave." She filled Shiloh's box and slipped through the stall.

"I meant you."

"I love the work, Pa. You understand that." She blew out her lantern, and he lifted his from the rail.

He pulled open the barn door. "Abbie . . . Monte's not the only man."

A shadow touched her. "Of course not, Pa."

Twenty-Eight

A buggy was leaving toward town as Abbie crested the rise over the Farrel ranch. She hoped she had not missed Sharlyn, but then she doubted Monte would allow her out in her condition with it threatening to storm. She'd spoken with neither for the last two weeks, hoping Sharlyn would visit, but it was a vain hope. Sharlyn had said Monte would not allow her to drive. Besides, it was not Sharlyn's duty to right things.

She left Shiloh at the stable with the boy and fought the wind to the porch steps. Monte had the door open before she could knock, and his face was haggard.

What now? "I've come to see Sharlyn."

"I'm sorry. Doctor Barrow said no one's to be admitted."

"What?"

"Scarlet fever."

Abbie stared. "Sharlyn? Scarlet fever's a disease for children, Monte."

"Perhaps, but not in this case." He looked away. "She . . . the baby's gone."

"Oh, Monte!" She gripped his hands without thinking. "I'm so terribly sorry! Truly I am. Oh, I must see her."

"You can't come in. We can't risk it."

"I must see her, Monte. I must!"

"Please, Abbie . . ."

She pressed past him and, picking up her skirt, hurried up

the stairs. Pearl carried a tub and towels from the large bedroom in which the massive four-poster dwarfed Sharlyn like a tiny doll, a crushed blossom. Her eyes had an unnatural brilliance as she turned, and her skin was crimson and peeling. "Abbie . . ." she whispered.

"Dearest Sharlyn, can you ever forgive me?" Abbie dropped to her side.

"Yes, Abbie, of course."

Behind her, Monte hunched against the doorframe.

"I'm so very sorry for my awful words. I'd take back every one if I could."

Sharlyn smiled faintly. "You spoke only the truth. You shared your heart with me at last, and I'm so grateful."

Abbie took the fiery hand and pressed it to her lips. "I'm sorry about the baby. But there'll be others, and when they come, I'll be so happy for you. And as soon as you're better, we'll walk and read together. See, I've brought Tennyson, and if you like I'll leave it with Monte."

Sharlyn breathed, "Oh yes, I love it when he reads."

"Of course you do." She tucked the book under Sharlyn's hand. "Then I'll leave it and check back tomorrow. Rest now." Sharlyn's eyes were already closing.

Monte walked her out, shielding her from the wind. "I can't see you home."

"I'll be fine."

"Abbie, you mustn't come again. Doctor Barrow will be back soon, and he won't admit you. I'll stay by Sharlyn and read as she likes."

"I told her . . ."

"I'll explain."

"But—"

"Abbie! Must I beg?"

She sagged. "I'm sorry. You'll send word?"

"I'll come for you myself."

After watching Abbie ride away, Monte returned to the bedchamber. Sharlyn lay holding the book against her chest, and he sat by her side. Gently, he took it from her but did not open the cover. "Sharlyn dear, there are so many things I should have done for you, so many ways I've not made you happy."

"No, Monte. You've been so kind."

"I brought you here away from all you knew, away from your family, your friends . . ."

"You're my family, and I have new friends. You gave me Abbie, Monte. And I love her, even as you do."

He winced.

"I know what was between you. Though in your kindness you would keep it from me, I can't help but see." She drew a ragged breath. "I guessed long ago that it was at Father's request you chose as you did. Yet I realize that this in itself is love, that by your honor you were bound to me, but you never revealed the cost. You've loved me well, Monte. Better than you know."

Her hand burned in his, and he feared for her. "Darling Sharlyn, when you're strong again, we'll start new, no secrets between us. What was will no longer keep us apart. I swear it. You are my wife and will bear my children, many children for the one we've lost."

Sharlyn closed her eyes and nodded. Monte opened the book and did not leave her side until she slept.

◆◆◆◆◆◆◆

Why did Monte not come for her? Abbie knew with severe cases of scarlet fever it could be weeks before the patient's strength returned, and even then only if pneumonia didn't set in. But surely the contagion was passed. If not for his desperate appeal, she would ignore her promise and go. "Lord, speed Sharlyn's healing and make her strong again."

She actually ached to see her, to make good her promise.

Her heart longed to comfort Sharlyn in her loss. She thought of stories she could read to take her mind from the baby as she gained back her strength. Any number of hours in Monte's house would be worth even one of Sharlyn's smiles. And somehow Sharlyn's knowing the truth had removed the last vestige of a wall between them.

Now they could be wholly friends, devoted not just by the good times they shared, but by a shared and understood pain. And even the pain seemed to have diminished. It would fade and pass away, but their affection would thrive. Abbie longed to tell her this. If only Monte would send for her.

She started back across the street for the smithy, where she'd left Shiloh to be shod. Clouds masked the September sun, bringing a chill and midday gloom. As she came upon the clinic, Doctor Barrow climbed down from his buggy, and she hurried to him. "Doctor Barrow. How is Sharlyn Farrel, and when may I visit?"

Slowly, Doctor Barrow turned to her. "I'm sorry, Miss Martin. Mrs. Farrel has passed on."

◆◆◆◆◆◆◆

Monte stood, hands folded in front of his long black coat. Before him yawned the hole, chiseled from the ground that welcomed the small coffin being lowered. Wes McConnel and Joshua Martin barely strained with the weight. The Reverend Winthrop Shields presided at his first official duty. Monte glanced at him as he stood with the Bible now closed in his very thin hands. The casket came to rest with a final grating thud.

Slowly Wes pulled the rope free, and Monte stepped forward. Reaching down he lifted the cold earth into his hand and allowed it to filter through his fingers onto the casket, then turned away and started for the house in silence.

He had instructed Pearl to lay a meal for the townspeople,

but he didn't join them. He went instead to his bedchamber, opened the wardrobe, and pulled out two large carpetbags. These he loaded with clothing and personal items, then he slipped out the back and went in search of Cole.

As he guessed, he found him alone in the bunkhouse.

Cole stood. "I'm real sorry, Mr. Farrel."

Monte nodded.

"I saw you slip away and figured you'd be wanting a word."

"I'm leaving for a time. The ranch and my affairs, I'm placing in your hands."

"Yes, sir. You mind my askin' where yer goin'?"

"Charleston. I'll be staying with my sister."

"You'll be stayin' awhile?"

"I don't anticipate my return." He pressed his hat brim and returned it to his head. "Rather, I'm not certain at this time of my plans."

"Mr. Farrel . . . does Abbie know yer leavin'?"

He drew a long breath. "No. I left a letter for Joshua in town."

Cole kicked the toe of his boot in the dirt. "I ain't plannin' ta run this place forever."

Monte felt a ghost of a smile. "I'll keep you informed."

♦♦♦♦♦♦♦

Jostling in the stage, Monte was glad to travel alone at least to the next stop. Solitude was a gift. He wouldn't inflict himself on anyone with such dark thoughts as filled his mind. Even Sharlyn's gentle words could not purge them. It was better to be alone.

The thought of Frances's ministrations made him cringe, but she was most insistent he come. And perhaps she was right. Every room in his house condemned him, and none more so than his own bedchamber. There he had taken of Sharlyn's sweetness, then in his sleep dreamed of another and wakened with longing. And in that bed, Sharlyn had died.

Perhaps his actions had been kind, and he hoped this was so, but his heart had been false. He bumped against the side and shifted over. In the letter to Joshua he had included the legal note to their partnership. With that dissolved and the ranch in Cole's hands, he could stay away.

He thought of Sharlyn's words. How long had she known? How had she borne it? Hers was the honor, to give love in return for his lack. In the end her heart proved as strong as he had believed Abbie's to be.

Abbie. At the funeral they had stood silent and separate in their grief. Though he no longer sensed her contempt, he felt the distance between them. It was better to go. He needed to find where, indeed, his honor lay.

Twenty-Nine

Pa caught her at the kitchen door. "Hold on a moment, Abbie."

She buttoned her coat and reached for the milking pail. "What is it, Pa?"

"Monte left a letter. He's gone to Charleston."

She waited. Pa's eyes said there was more.

"He returned full ownership of the paper to me."

"Then he's not coming back."

"I don't know that. He's not sold out, but he left the ranch in Cole's charge."

She nodded and took up the pail. In the barn, Buttercup chewed placidly as Abbie ran her hand along the bony ridge of her back. She tried to imagine Monte gone. Even married to Sharlyn, he had been part of the fabric of her life, but perhaps it was best he didn't return. She had released him from her heart and would not dare invite him in again.

Walking back with the warm milk frothing up a steam into the cold air, she set the pail on the cupboard.

Mama glanced up. "I'm hoping to dye the last of the wool today, Abbie."

"I'll help." She poured the milk into the skimming trays. "But after that I'm going to the mission."

"It's so far to go every day, Abbie. And dark before you return."

"I know my way blindfolded. Besides, I'm working on a Christmas benefit recitation. They're in need of so much. All the children are learning some little thing, and some of them a good deal."

She took up a cloth and wiped the drops of milk from the table. "The new reverend is a kind man, but I'm not sure he's suited to exhorting the tough hides of his western flock, even if he'd the notion. Not like Reverend Peale. No, we'll have to come up with our own ways to remind people of the orphans' needs. And the recitation is the first. I know it will move folks."

Mama shook her head. "I don't doubt your success. I just worry. . . ."

"Well, don't. There's no need. Now, shall I get the pot to boil the dye?"

"I'd rather you went now to the mission and returned before dark."

"Can you manage?"

Mama laid a hand to her cheek. "Wrap warmly. There's snow in the air."

As she drove to the mission, Abbie tested the feel of Monte's absence. With the loss of Sharlyn, it was only one more ache. At least somewhere he lived. His roots had not gone deep enough to keep him here, in the place he had thought had held his destiny. She looked over the endless spread of grassland, brown field after brown field.

The land remained, oblivious to their losses. People came and went, but the world remained. She passed a fence post, broken and sagging. Perhaps it would collapse, perhaps a range rider would find and repair it. Either way, in a hundred years it would be gone, as would the rancher who now claimed the land.

One day even the land would pass away. Nothing was forever. The weight of hopelessness bore down upon her. What was the use? She felt the smooth leather of the reins in her hands. Why continue on? Why trudge the prairie to the orphanage when its charges would soon be grown and gone, its brothers grown old, its buildings barely withstanding each onslaught of weather? What was the point?

She imagined Tucker's face each time she came, felt the pressure of his little arms around her. He was the point, he and all the others. Their needs were real, if only for the day. If for one day she could reach out, broaden their minds, build their spirits, touch their hearts ... then that day had not passed in futility. No matter how small, how fleeting the life of every person, it must mean something.

Maybe she didn't understand it. Maybe she never would. Sharlyn so young, so good. But there had to be a purpose. A purpose larger than herself. And that drove her on through the wind that indeed smelled of snow. It wouldn't be much this early in the year, and the ever greedy ground would receive it, leaving hardly a trace. But it would have done what it was sent for. Roots that were shrunken would swell and pump life into stem and branch.

The mission buildings came into sight, the bare trees weeping the last of their leaves in the wind, the juniper mounds bowing like tired green sentries. The mission was small in the vastness of the plain, but it clung to the earth with the tenacity of the sagebrush, unmoved by the wind, undaunted by Indian fire, unbeaten by killing hail.

Here was her strength, that what God had established would not fail. Though their numbers were small, though their original purpose to bring Christ to the Indians had passed, as long as there was need, there was purpose. And with purpose came hope, with hope determination and assurance of God's provision.

To fill the children's minds with thoughts beyond themselves and enable them to think for themselves meant as much as filling their stomachs. To that task she would commit her energy. She reined Shiloh in and slipped from the mare's back. The blast of wind that sucked away her breath couldn't keep her from the warmth that waited within.

◆◆◆◆◆◆◆

Icy pellets rattled against the window panes of the town hall as the children shuffled nervously behind the makeshift curtain drawn across the room. Abbie held the small ones against her skirt. Silas stood aloof, but she could tell by the flush of his cheeks that his nerves were as tight as any. She nodded to Ben and Michael, who pulled the curtain.

Little Tucker Bates stepped onto the riser. The room hushed. "'The Creation,' by Cecil Frances Alexander, as recorded in *Hymns for Little Children*." He hooked his hands as she'd shown him. "'All things bright and beautiful, All creatures great and *smaw . . .*'" His voice was sweet and clear in the packed room. People who never thought of the orphans' needs had come to hear them perform. There was little enough entertainment, especially in the cold winter months.

Abbie silently congratulated herself. Father Dominic hadn't been easy to convince. Only their need for medicines and warm clothing had won him over, and even then he refused to charge a ticket fee, but agreed to accept donations. She had collected a twenty-five-cent donation at the door from every adult and a nickel from the children. That she had posted the minimum donation amount in the previous week's newspaper with the notice of the event, he didn't have to know.

The room erupted with applause for Tucker, and he bowed a second and then a third time before she snagged his shirt and tugged. Pauline took his place, and then each child in turn. Abbie bit her lip, smiling, as Silas rendered Edgar Allen Poe's *The Raven*, making his voice gravely at, "'Quoth the raven, Nevermore.'"

At the last, Felicity Fenham took the stage. "The Christmas

story as recorded by St. Luke in the Holy Scriptures." Turning her serious eyes to the crowd, she quoted the nativity passage, then closed, saying, "And all the good things we do are to honor the child born that night, for it is in this that we find joy."

Abbie felt the collective breath before everyone clapped, rising to their feet. Behind the curtain, she silently locked her hands across her chest in congratulations as they did on real stages and opera houses. A rush of pleasure and relief flooded her. As the curtain opened again, she pushed the children forward, and they all bowed together. Then Silas reached back and pulled her up with them.

She faced the crowd. Marty and Clara with baby Del sat directly in front. She didn't see a sour face anywhere. "I'm so glad you enjoyed the evening's entertainment. Much work went into each one of the presentations, but we had a lot of fun as well. Next spring, we'll be challenging any and all to a debate night. But be warned, if the arguments they use to escape their lessons are demonstrative of their disputation abilities, you'll have your work cut out for you!" She laughed, and the crowd cheered again.

She was heady with success as the Franciscan brothers loaded the children into the two ox-drawn wagons and covered them in wool blankets. Abbie waved. "You were all wonderful!"

Father Dominic smiled. "A true charitable event." He waved back with the newspaper, and Abbie caught her breath.

Beside her Pa chuckled. "It's hard to pull one over on a man of God."

The children's voices raised in hymns as they drove into the night through the falling snow. Abbie watched until the darkness hid them.

"Well, Abbie, you did a splendid job of that." Pa squeezed her shoulders, then handed her into the buggy beside Mama. "I had no idea the children would do so well!"

Mama pressed her knee. "They had a good teacher."

"Well, I did keep them excited. But really, I think I enjoy it all more than they do."

"That's the sign of a great teacher," Pa said and clicked his tongue to the horse.

"I was thinking that if Mr. Pemberton is going back to Ohio at the end of the term, maybe the board would consider me for the Rocky Bluffs school."

Pa cocked his head. "I'd guess after tonight they'd more than consider you. You'd have the job hands down if that's what you really want."

"I'd have to know the mission children would be accepted there."

"I don't think that's an obstacle you can't face."

Abbie laughed. "Well, heaven knows I'm not qualified for many other things, unless you want to give me a job at the newspaper."

"I just might at that. But let's think on one job at a time, shall we?"

✦✦✦✦✦✦✦

After Abbie disappeared behind her bedroom door, Selena turned to Joshua and sighed.

"What?" he asked.

"Abbie's no longer a little girl."

"No, she's a fine young lady."

Selena hung her wrap. "How I worried about her. She was so carefree and enthusiastic, overly so."

"She's still enthusiastic. Look how she tackled this night."

Selena dropped into the chair. "Yes, but there's a difference now. The dreamy, spirited girl has become a pragmatic young woman." She looked up. "I can't help hoping the Abbie of old lingers somewhere inside."

Thirty

Monte stood at the window watching the traffic on the street. The mud bogged down the carriages, and the people on foot raised their legs like cranes. It was almost comical the pains they took to avoid the puddles, only to slip through the sludge instead.

"Goodness, Monte." Frances hurried down the stairs. "Didn't you hear the door?"

"I wouldn't presume."

"Presume, presume! This is your home, too." She pulled open the door.

"A message for Mr. Montgomery Farrel."

Monte took the note and recognized Chandler's writing. "Looks like the honeymooners are back." He pulled it open with mixed feelings.

> *My dear Monte,*
> *Imagine our delight to return and find you still among us. Maimie and I would enjoy your company for supper at your earliest convenience.*
>
> *Most sincerely,*
> *Chandler Bridges*

"It seems I'll be offering congratulations in person."

"Not tonight surely. It's dreadful out, and I've planned ..."

273

"No, not tonight, but soon." Monte folded the note.

Kendal burst in through the back door. "Incompetence!" He slammed his crop onto the stand. "I'm surrounded by incompetence! Frances!"

She turned.

"I've let that worthless darky go. Sent him packing on his backside."

"Not Moses!"

"Not Moses," he mimicked. "Of course Moses. How many darkies have we to let go? Ah, Monte. Pour me a whiskey, will you, while I wash. It's a hog bath out there."

Monte poured a pair of whiskeys and waited for his in-law. Of late, he'd limited himself to one, though Kendal had no such restrictions.

Kendal reappeared in clean breeches and knee-high boots. "I tell you, Monte, there's a time for the whip."

"You used your whip?"

"Crop actually."

"What was the offense?" He handed Kendal the drink.

"The horse stood for three hours after the rain with no cover nor rub. Do you know where I found him? In the tack room, reading."

"The horse was reading?" Monte cracked a wry smile.

"The groom, man. The groom was reading. Reading!"

"What was he reading?"

"You ask? I threw the book to the fire. I don't pay him to read."

"I wonder where he learned."

"In hell for all I care." Kendal dropped to the chair.

"Come, Kendal. Find yourself a new groom and be done. I'll ask about if you like."

Kendal frowned. "I'll ask about myself."

"As you like. Though I doubt you'll find many leaping for the chance. You're making a name for yourself."

"As you're quick to point out." Kendal poured a refill and downed it.

Monte said nothing. Kendal's labor problems were his own. Frances managed with Dilcey, baby Jeanette's mammy, and the young maid, Rilla. It shouldn't prove too difficult to replace a groom ... though he did wonder if Kendal's finances were quite what they seemed. Else why hire Negroes when he felt a white groom would better suit?

Frances was clearly piqued. At the table she returned Kendal's comments crisply and offered none of her own. Monte looked from one to the other. Their sparring was growing tedious. Kendal held forth on the ills of the ignorant, freed Negro. He didn't consider that it was his particular Negro's lack of ignorance that had so infuriated him.

Monte didn't point it out. Frances's eyes held a dangerous glow, and he didn't want to be caught in the cross fire. He wiped his mouth with the linen napkin and tossed it in his plate, then smiled as Dilcey removed it. "Very good as always, Dilcey." He jumped when Frances threw her fork onto her own plate and faced Kendal.

"You shouldn't have relieved Moses without consulting me. I depend on him."

"Well, I'll replace him."

"As you replaced Rawley? And Joseph? Am I to harness the horse myself as I answer the door?"

"Rilla can answer the door."

"And saddle the horse? Or will you be in the stable to do the honor?"

Kendal pushed his chair back. "Have a brandy with me, Monte."

Monte glanced at Frances as she fought to contain herself. She waved him away. He followed Kendal to the library and watched him pour two fingers into the snifters.

Kendal handed it over. "You see how she fusses?"

"Now, Kendal, she is my sister."

"And that's the bite, isn't it? To be held up and compared to her impeccable brother. *I'm* her husband."

Monte swirled the liquor. "Perhaps I've worn my stay thin."

Kendal took the wing chair and stretched his legs before him. He shook his head. "Forgive my deplorable manners. It's been a rot of a day."

Monte raised the glass. "That . . . I understand."

◆◆◆◆◆◆◆

The roads had dried considerably when Monte made his way to Chandler's plantation. Kendal's contrition had extended to use of the carriage for the night, and he'd not had to hire a rig. He left the horse at the stable and crossed the spongy ground to the house. Chandler himself opened the door, with a frowning Benton behind him. "Forgive me, Benton."

"Yessuh. I must be too old to ansuh the do'."

Chandler smiled. "I'm scolded in my own home. He would never have spoken to Father that way."

"Mastuh Bridges knew his place." Benton turned his back.

"Come in, Monte." Chandler showed him to the study. "What can I get you?"

"Nothing, please. I'm nearly sloshed every night keeping up with Kendal."

"Good, then I'll not, either. I think my veins are running wine after six weeks in Italy."

"Ah. My deepest congratulations."

"Wait till you meet her, Monte. She'll be with us shortly. She's making herself beautiful."

"Really, Chad." Maimie swept in, a compact package in green watered silk.

"Monte, may I present my beautiful wife, Maimie. My dear, my incomparable friend, Montgomery Farrel."

Monte bowed low over her hand. "I'm delighted."

"And I. Chandler's told me so much about you."

"My reputation will never stand it."

"On the contrary. But you two have catching up to do. I'll see to supper." Her skirts swept the floor behind her.

Monte watched until the door clicked. "She's a prize, Chandler. I congratulate you again."

"As you have in excess. Your wedding gift was far beyond generous."

"Nonsense. It was opportunity only. I trust you've made good on it?"

"And more. With those profits and the modest profit the tobacco is turning, I'll have Father's loan paid off by the end of the month."

"That's very good news. Your father would be proud of you."

"And of you." Chandler came around the table. "If not for you, who knows how things would have turned out for Sharlyn, for any of us."

Monte frowned. He wished the conversation had not so soon turned that way, yet he had expected it, avoided it, put off coming as long as he could.

"My family and I are forever in your debt."

Monte's chest felt tight. "It's no more than any of us would do."

"Isn't it?" Chandler went to the desk in the corner. "Here, I've something to show you." He pulled out an envelope that Monte recognized as Sharlyn's stationery, monogrammed with her initials S.B.F. He held it out.

Monte reluctantly took it and removed the letter within. The writing was painfully deliberate, and he realized just how severe her affliction had been.

Deerest bruther,

I am overjoyed by the news uv your impending marrige. There is no happyer state, I assure you, for I am most sublimely content even though I hav discovered, not by Monte's telling nor by any action on his part, the nature uv his proposal to me. Did you know, I wunder, that he loved another? For I dout he made menshun uv it.

But you see, by his sacrifice, I am made doubly preshus, one that he wud accept Father's request, and two, surrender his own hopes in order to save me, I am guessing, from the truth of whatever happened that day. Do not be surprised that I know, tho Monte never revealed the reason. There must be one or why ask such a thing of Monte?

But he is kindness itself to me, and I love him better for knowing than I did before. There is no man born uv higher honor. I tell you this in the hopes that your marrige will be uv the same kaliber of joy to you.

Lovingly,
Sharlyn

Monte stared at the page trembling in his hand.

"And so you see, my dear friend, I know what you did for my family." Chandler laid a hand on his shoulder. "And as I recall, I saw it then in your face, though I failed to understand. Why didn't you speak, man?"

"I thought I saw my way."

"How dark it must have looked."

"Not so dark as I made it."

Chandler's grip tightened on his shoulder. "What is it that keeps you here? Is this person lost to you?"

Monte shook his head. "I don't know. She was grievously hurt and believes I betrayed her. After ... Sharlyn's death, I thought it best to sort out our feelings separately." He handed the letter back. "In truth, I ran. I needed to know if indeed I am a man of honor or if I deceived even myself."

"That's not what I read here." Chandler held up the letter. "Sharlyn was deserving of so much."

"And received so much . . . at your hand, Monte." He reached into the drawer again and pulled out a paper folded once and sealed. "Do you recognize this? I found it among Father's things."

Monte waited as Chandler slit the seal and opened the paper, then held it out. He saw what he expected, the sprawling script of Nathan's hand and signature, his father's beneath it, followed by his own. He remembered the solemn responsibility he had felt as he penned his name that day.

Sharlyn's name did not appear on the pledge. She wasn't party to the arrangement. Monte had not stopped to wonder whether she would accept if the time came. It was simply a pledge to do the honorable thing if called upon, his word given as a man, though his voice had only just settled into its baritone the summer before.

He drew a long breath. "I could not love two at once."

"No, you could not. But Sharlyn's words are true nonetheless. Love is bound up with honor, that serves without reward. You have fulfilled your pledge, Monte. You've kept it well."

Monte was silent. Perhaps that was so. Perhaps.

◆◆◆◆◆◆◆

As he lay sleepless, Monte turned and eyed the paper lying open on the stand beside the bed. His immature hand had penned his name with no idea the impact it would have on his future, only that he had felt called upon to serve, even as his father and Nathan Bridges were called. He had even been proud of it. And what had it gained him?

He fought the memories, each stricken expression of Sharlyn's when he was sharp or impatient, each painful encounter with Abbie, every guilty longing. He had thought to choose truly and follow his honor, but in the end proved powerless.

He had tried in his strength to do right but had not surrendered to the one who held life and death, love and sorrow.

"Oh, Lord . . . I'm a sinner and a fool. All that I do goes awry. But I surrender to you now, not in shame without honor as one man to another, but as one coming to my senses. The war's already been fought, the victory won by your blood on the battlefield of the world. Please take what I am and bind up what I've broken."

He took up the paper, ran his eyes over it in the moonlight, then folded it twice and tucked it into the pocket of his nightshirt.

Thirty-One

Vestiges of snow clung still in the shady crevices, but the ground gave off the rich earthy scent of spring. Beside the grave a cluster of wild crocus put up its heads to the May sun filtering through the tall ponderosas that overlooked the hill. Abbie was glad Monte had chosen this place to lay Sharlyn to rest. It was like her, filled with a quiet beauty and dignity.

She sat on the grassy slope beside the grave and looked at the fairylike angel on the tombstone that resembled Sharlyn in form. The words beneath were more than words to anyone who knew. *Love beareth all things.*

Since Monte had gone, she was free to come to the grave as often as she liked, though only now had the weather permitted her to stay. Closing her eyes, Abbie listened to the chirping of the chickadees and finches hopping about the branches of the trees. It was the sound of spring, of new beginnings, of awakenings.

Sensing the shadow that crept up behind her, Abbie opened her eyes but didn't turn.

Monte spoke low. "I tried to love her. I tried with all that was in me."

She remained still. "I know you did."

"She deserved to be loved. She was . . . very good."

"You made her happy, Monte. You have nothing to regret." With her eyes, Abbie sought the mountains, hazy in the late afternoon light, their tips enshrouded by clouds. Had she known he would return?

He took one step and stood over her. "I hope that's so. But it seems regret has become my constant companion. Each moment holds myriad choices, and one that seems right may never be remedied. Who can say what might have been had the choice never been made."

"I don't know." She looked up. He was thin, even a little gaunt. "Do you remember when you moved my place to the wrong end of the table, and I told you that I say what I think and do what seems right?"

A smile touched his mouth. "I remember."

"I think that's all any of us can do."

"And let God pick up the pieces." He raised her to her feet. "Abbie, would you do me the honor of staying for supper?"

Shaking her head, she laughed bleakly. "I think I'm coming to hate that word . . . honor."

"We have to have honor, Abbie. We can't live without it. It is the backbone of all that is right and just and good."

"Can you say that still?"

"I must say it, or everything I've done, all that I've been is for naught." His voice thickened. "On my honor, Abbie, I love you with all my heart. Do you think you could ever care for me again?"

Abbie heard his words as from a long distance, removed and muted. "I don't know, Monte. I honestly don't know."

He smiled wryly. "But you no longer despise me."

"No, I don't despise you."

He hesitated. "Then I may call?"

"If you like. Pa would enjoy that, and Mama as well. They've both missed you, I know. But the little lamb on the hill is all grown up now and doesn't bleat anymore."

"Yes, I see that."

Abbie walked over to the mare and mounted. "Good afternoon, then."

"Good afternoon, Abbie."

He watched until she was out of sight around the bend of the slope, then dropped his gaze to the gray marble stone and ran his fingers along the delicate carved angel. Silent, he stood, then spoke softly. "I hope you understand, Sharlyn. . . . You always did."

◆◆◆◆◆◆◆

Monte made his way over the once familiar and cherished ground between his home and Abbie's. Only two nights had passed, and probably he was a fool, but he went nonetheless. Sirocco tossed his head as he pulled up to the house, and Joshua came out to the porch.

"Come on in, Monte. We heard you were back, and you've been too long a stranger."

"Thanks, Joshua." He swung down. "Abbie said I might call."

"Good. She's been too long a stranger, also. It's time she came back to life, I'd say."

Monte shook his head. "I don't know that I'll have a part in that. I must tell you, her invitation was less enthusiastic than I'd hoped."

"Well, the good Lord knows His plans; it's our part only to obey. You're welcome in our home, Monte, as you've always been. And if Abbie sees fit to entertain you, so much the better." He gripped Monte's hand powerfully. "But I'm afraid if you want to see her first, you'll have to find her in the hills somewhere."

"That, sir, I am accustomed to doing."

Abbie saw him coming, his tall figure cutting across the

field toward the hill where she sat. Something stirred inside
her at the sight, and she sat quietly, exploring the emotion. She
looked up as he strode to where she sat, towering over her.
"May I join you?"

"You may."

He dropped to the ground beside her. "It's a lovely evening
to delight in such beauty."

"It is beautiful at this hour with the shadows so long and
the sun kissing everything one last time before it goes."

"It was your beauty of which I spoke." He drew closer. "And
I could wish I were the sun if that is its prerogative."

Abbie smiled in spite of herself. "You're ever the silver-
tongued suitor, aren't you?"

"Only when it's true." Taking her hand in his, he brought
it to his lips. "Have you considered my words from the other
day?"

"I've thought some."

"My intention was to give you more time, but my will is not
what it once was, and my heart led me here, perhaps prema-
turely."

"Perhaps."

"Surely, Abbie, you can tell me if I have reason to hope."

Again she felt the stirring. "So much has happened, so
much changed."

"One thing that has never changed is my love for you. I
know it seems that I was false, but I swear I never intended it
that way."

"I know that, Monte."

"Shall I tell you why I married Sharlyn?"

"No. Keep it in silence as it's been. I believe you were bound
by the honor that is in you."

"Do I guess correctly that you have forgiven me?"

"I have."

He grabbed her hands to his chest. "You don't know what that means to me!"

Abbie smiled. "I only hope you've forgiven me as well."

"There's nothing to forgive."

"Oh yes, there is."

"Then I'm unaware of it."

She laughed. "I won't enlighten you. Suffice it to say there were thoughts in my mind that Father Dominic would give severe penance for. I felt not kindly toward you, as I know you were aware."

"Then I forgive you every one, and I'd gladly suffer the penance in your place if only . . . you'd give me one small indication that my efforts are not in vain."

"And what might suffice to convince you?" Abbie felt a quickening within.

Monte's fingers caressed her cheek, then cupped her face and lifted it to him. "Perhaps . . . a small demonstration of your affection. . . ."

"Such as?"

His lips drew close and lingered, anticipating the touch.

Abbie's heart sprang into a mighty dance as his mouth came home to hers. The dream that lay dormant, but not vanquished, quivered within.

"Oh, Abbie, will you suffer me to court you?"

"Monte . . ."

"Say yes, I beg you."

She felt the strength of his arms, the pounding of his chest. "I . . . suppose I could think on it." She couldn't stop the giggle that he quenched with a kiss, then crushed her so tightly she could only laugh harder. Cool, reserved Monte.

Overhead a crow scolded from the branches of the ponderosa, and he looked up. His smile pulled wickedly. "What do you say we see who can get to the top of this tree first?"

"Not on your life." Abbie sniffed. "I'm not going up unless you go first, and only if you promise not to tell Mama!"

Acknowledgments

Though it is impossible to name all those who encouraged, critiqued, and cheered this work, I would like to thank my family for their patience, my daughter, Jessie, for her unwavering belief, my husband, Jim, for his honest editing, and my three boys, Devin, Stephen, and Trevor, for understanding ". . . not now, I'm writing."

I would also like to thank my editor, Barb Lilland, whose hard work and excitement exceeds my own, and all the people at Bethany House Publishers who had faith in this work.

Most of all I thank the Blessed Savior, from whom all gifts come, the Holy Spirit whose working enables me, and God the Father, author of life.